SLEEPING AROUND

Also by Julie Highmore

Country Loving
Pure Fiction
Play It Again?

Sleeping Around

Julie Highmore

review

First published in 2005
by Review

An imprint of Headline Book Publishing

1

Cataloguing in Publication Data is available from the British Library

ISBN 0 7553 2116 2

Typeset in AGaramond by
Palimpsest Book Production Limited,
Polmont, Stirlingshire

Printed and bound in Great Britain by Clays Ltd, St Ives plc

HEADLINE BOOK PUBLISHING
A division of Hodder Headline
338 Euston Road
London NW1 3BH

www.reviewbooks.co.uk
www.hodderheadline.com

For Carol

Thanks to Sophie, Eliane and Justin,
and to Helena, Katherine, Nicola,
Joanna, Charlotte, Claire, Justinia,
Debbie and the wonderful Flora

FRIDAY

The man in the woolly hat was unloading his mud-coloured car. From her window, Jo watched him take out a rucksack, then a pair of hiking boots and a small suitcase. After contemplating the boots for a while, he chucked them back in. Jo pushed her glasses up her nose and saw that he was probably in his thirties – although hard to tell under the hat – and that his car wasn't mud-coloured, just covered in mud.

She let the lace curtain fall back in place and returned to her on-screen copy-editing. It was chapter three of Sergei's thesis, written in an interesting form of English and on the gripping topic of Russian Transport Law. So far as Jo could tell, Sergei's work contained neither original thought nor any attempt at an argument, but she guessed such things were waived when mega overseas students' fees were involved. Her eyes wandered back to the window.

She really couldn't see much through the lace, and wondered, as pretty as it was, if she should take it down and have a better view of the street. The idea was that it hid her monitor from passing burglars, but apparently they didn't bother with PCs any more. Too heavy. When number 7 was broken into, they just took the DVD player and Pippa's underwear.

With the tip of a finger, Jo eased the curtain to one side again and saw the newcomer's breath freeze as he locked his passenger door. The coldest March for decades, they were saying, which was why Lucy and Dom had shot off to their place in France, and why this person had come to house-cat-and-fish-sit for them.

She tried to remember his name. It was Mark or Marius, or something. Lucy and Dom hadn't been very forthcoming when Jo tried grilling them; appearing, in fact, to know nothing about him. Which was odd, considering how nosy Lucy was. 'We found him on the Internet,' she'd said. 'He gave us a glowing reference and we said yes. Who needs his life story?' Lucy and Dom were very trusting sorts.

After lugging his things up the path, the housesitter put his rucksack down and fumbled under a large and very obvious stone for the key. He then straightened up, turned, and with a broad smile beneath his snug-fitting hat gave Jo a wave before letting himself into the house.

'Oops,' she said, dropping the curtain and staring at it for a while. But then she shrugged, decided he was just being friendly, and set about chopping one of Sergei's interminable sentences into three.

Just before seven, she stopped work to focus on the lodgers' dinner. Would they notice if it was fish again? She was beginning to run out of ideas. Keiko, who weighed less than a small leaf, was the only person in the world still on the Atkins Diet while young Ernst refused to eat British beef, or even lamb – scrapie, apparently – and found vegetarian meals an enigma.

Having shut down the computer, Jo risked a peep over the road from her lamp-lit room. Back went the lace curtain again, very slowly, to reveal Lucy and Dom's house in total darkness. Mark or Marius must have gone out.

Marcus had woken a few minutes earlier to pitch-black, aware that he was in his coat and hat but with no idea of where he was. In his dream he'd been on the M6, but this didn't feel like the motorway. You wouldn't be horizontal on the M6. Not unless you'd been thrown from your car. Anyway, he was definitely stretched out on something soft and, what's more, it was pretty quiet. Just the sound of an engine running. But in the vicinity of his thighs? He stretched out a hand and encountered fur – lots of it – and the noise got louder. Cat, he thought, feeling whiskers. Cat . . . fish . . . house . . . Oxford . . . Oh, yeah.

After a noisy yawn that made the animal flee, Marcus eased himself up off the sofa and worked his way, arms waving before him, to where he thought the window might be. On hitting heavy hanging material, he tugged it first left, then right, before streetlamps and the last bit of daylight revealed the person opposite still looking his way from behind her net curtain. Oh, well. He guessed every street had one. When the phone gave a shrill ring on the far side of the room, he jumped out of his skin, then wandered into the darkness and found it.

'Hello?' he croaked, while the cat did a figure of eight around his ankles.

'Oh, good evening,' sang a familiar voice in soft Scottish tones. 'Would it be at all possible to speak to Mr Marcus Currie? If it's not too much trouble?'

Marcus cleared his throat. 'Yeah, it's me, Mum. I'll be the only housesitter here, so no need to ask for me.'

'Marcus, you don't sound yourself,' she said. 'Is your throat sore? It's not a dusty germ-filled place, I hope?'

'Um . . . no, I don't think so.' He peered into the darkness. 'I just fell asleep, that's all. As soon as I arrived.'

'I do worry about you, son.'

'There's no need, Mum. I am thirty-nine.'

'Not till next week. Listen, I'll put some vapour rub in with your prezzie, but don't overdo it, will you? Sheena McWhirter swears she got addicted. So, have you contacted her yet?'

'Sheena McWhirter?'

His mother tutted. 'No, *her*.'

Marcus was now keen to get off the phone. He really didn't want to discuss Hannah, plus the cat had begun chewing his shoe leather. 'Not yet,' he said. 'I'll call her later this evening.'

'Good idea, love. You're not sounding yourself at the moment.'

'So you said. Listen, I've got a ravenous moggy here I should feed.'

'Oh, OK. I'll ring again soon. Is there someone I can leave a message with if you're not in?'

Marcus sighed. She never listened, his mother. 'Just the machine, Mum. Anyway, take care of yourself, won't you? And get those brothers of mine to pull their weight in the restaurant.'

'That'll be the day,' she said. Andrew and Fraser's hearts had never been entirely in the family business. But then Marcus couldn't say his had, either. He'd just been better at hiding it.

After putting the phone down, he made his way through to the kitchen, gradually lighting up the house as he went. 'Dry food only,' said the note – one of many – 'and change water daily. NO CANNED FOOD! (Creates problems for Maidstone.)'

Marcus scratched at his hat and wondered where a large town in Kent came into it, before pouring out a bowl of food for the short-haired tabby and putting the kettle on. It was then that he took a good look around and realised what a terrific place he'd got himself. They'd even stocked the fridge and food cupboards for him. The prospect of three weeks in such surroundings for no financial outlay filled Marcus with sudden and unreserved glee. He tried not to think that might be the Scot in him and helped himself to a biscuit.

Mug in hand, he went and inspected the rest of the house, saying, 'Veeerrry nice,' in each room. The décor was sleek, chic and beautifully finished. Modern, but never at odds with the original features of the house: fireplaces, shiny brass door furniture, curly architraves. What topped it all, literally, was the attic, where Marcus stepped into a vast wooden-floored, white-walled, dormer-windowed area with lots of electrical equipment and several plasma screens. Some sort of office, it seemed.

What on earth did these people do to afford all this stuff? A large three-storey period house – OK, Victorian – full of expensive items in a prime location, *and* they had a house in France they could take off to at the drop of a hat. They'd sounded young on the phone and looked young in all the photos of the tall blond couple scattered around. He sipped at his coffee and shook his head. Wealthy parents, maybe.

As he began a tour of the room, Marcus heard the distant ding-dong of a bell. He trotted down two flights and found a woman on the doorstep, shivering in a thin polo-neck jumper. She was slim and of medium height, and in the streetlight her long, straight and very shiny hair was Titian red, as were her jeans. She had that alabaster skin of certain redheads – either that or hypothermia was setting in. She was definitely pretty. If asked how old she was, Marcus would have put her between twenty and forty, because he was hopeless at telling ages.

'Hi,' he was about to say as she charged over the threshold and threw herself against a radiator.

'Jesus,' she said, teeth chattering, arms wrapped around herself, then, 'Oh, Christ,' as she bounced back off the radiator. 'Didn't they tell you how to put the heating on?'

Who was this woman?

'Marcus,' he said, extending a hand.

'Oh, yeah. S-sorry, I'm J-Jo.' She untucked a hand and shook his. 'I'm a n-neighbour.'

'Jojo?'

She shook her head. 'J-Jo.'

He still wasn't sure. 'Would you like my coat?' he asked. He started taking it off and she didn't protest. 'Here.' He wrapped it around her quaking shoulders and she slipped her arms in. 'Come on through. I'll put the gas rings on. You must have come quite a way to be this frozen.'

'Only from over the road. I just feel the c-c-cold a lot. It's a thin-skin thing.'

When they got to the kitchen, he lit up all six Smeg rings and offered Jojo his hat. She nodded and thanked him, but when he pulled it off she gave a start.

'Oh,' she said, her cheeks now rosying up nicely, 'I thought you might have, er, dark hair, for some reason. And, you know, kind of thick and wavy . . . or something.' She looked a bit stunned.

Marcus raked fingers through his fair, some might say mousy, baby-fine locks in an attempt to bulk them up a bit. 'Can I get you anything?' he asked, aware of a curt edge to his voice. What was wrong with his hair, anyway? At least he still had some, unlike his brothers. 'Tea? Coffee?'

'No, thanks, I'm in the middle of cooking dinner. That's why I'm here, actually.'

'Oh?'

'I wondered if you'd like to join us. Me and my lodgers. Two foreign students. It's just fish.'

'Fish sounds good,' he said, putting the hair business to one side and smiling nicely at her. 'Yes, I'd love to come.'

'Great. I'm at number fifteen. Directly opposite.'

Marcus stared. It was the curtain twitcher. 'When shall I—'

'Eightish?'

'OK,' he said, and before he knew it she was flying back across the street in his coat and hat, shouting something about someone called Atkins.

Marcus closed the door with a frown and went back to look through Lucy and Dom's notes again. No, nothing about a care-in-the-community neighbour. Just one saying, 'Watch out for Pippa (No. 7) who will almost certainly ask you to remove large spider from bedroom whilst husband Ray is on car-factory night shift.'

Marcus shuddered at the words 'large' and 'spider'. Chances were he'd be calling Pippa in.

'At my home in Germany we are eating much veal but not so many fishes,' announced Ernst.

Keiko nodded and nodded and gave a quiet, 'Aaahhh,' then nodded some more and took a tiny sip of water.

Marcus nodded too but didn't say anything. Jo hoped he wasn't bored.

'Can I top up your coffee?' she asked.

'Thanks,' he said with a face-transforming smile. Not that he wasn't just as lovely at ease: blue eyes and that nice kind of dirty-blond hair. What a shock she'd had when he'd taken off the hat that had been hiding half his face. So good-looking, he'd taken her breath away. She'd blurted out something stupid about his hair, she remembered now. He seemed like a nice person too: talking football with Ernst; asking Keiko all about her family.

Jo filled his cup, but not Ernst's, and began clearing away the dessert dishes. 'Well,' she said, looking hopefully from student to student as she piled things up, 'I expect you two have lots of homework to do. Keiko?'

Keiko dabbed delicately at her mouth with some kitchen roll. She always wore red lipstick, even at breakfast. 'Yes,' she said. 'This weekend I must write essay about dinner party for me and favourite six guests. Who I invite if I can choose anybody. Even famous persons. Even if dead.'

Marcus said, 'That sounds interesting. Who are you going to invite?'

'Ah.' Keiko held up her dainty left hand and pointed at its thumb. 'First, my best friend, Hiroko.'

'Uh-huh.'

'Second, my second-best friend, Nyoko.'

'Right . . . You can invite *anyone*, you say?'

'Yes. Anybody. Even if dead.' She moved along to the middle finger. 'Number three is my teacher at language school, Adam.'

'Ha!' exclaimed Ernst. 'Every girl in my class is wanting to have a baby from Adam.'

Jo laughed. She'd heard so much about this Adam, she was now keen to meet him herself. And maybe have his baby.

Keiko giggled. 'He is very handsome and very kind. Number four and five is my parents.'

Jo tried not to laugh, while Marcus said, 'Hang on a minute,' lurching forward and fixing his gaze on her lucky lodger. 'What about, oh, I don't know . . . Elvis Presley? No, not him, but Jimi Hendrix, say. Or Joan of Arc? I'm sure your parents make great dinner-party guests but I think this is meant to be a special occasion. Don't you want someone hugely talented there? Or a hero or idol of some sort?'

'Yes,' said Keiko, moving on to the pinkie of her other hand. 'So, number six. One very famous, very special guest. But dead. Princess Diana.'

'Good choice,' said Jo, smiling Marcus's way as he slumped back in his chair. 'What about you, Ernst?'

'Me, I have to learn pub vocabulary, then go at nine thirty to meet our teacher Jeremy and the other students in the Eagle and Child. Jeremy wants us to practise our contractions.'

'Sounds like an ante-natal class,' said Marcus, pulling a face.

'For example, "What'll you have?" not "What will you have?".'

'Oh, right.'

'Very useful,' said Jo, clearing more items off the table. 'Well, no need to help,' she told her lodgers. 'Maybe you should get cracking on your homework.' The two of them stared at her, so she explained 'get cracking' and Keiko wrote it down in her notebook, before they went off to their respective rooms.

'Fancy a drink?' Jo asked Marcus.

'Mm?' he said, looking at her but somehow miles away. Perhaps he was still working on Keiko's guest list. 'Sorry, I should have brought a bottle.'

'Don't worry. I never serve alcohol with dinner, anyway. Wouldn't make any money if I did that.'

He leaned towards her. 'The profit margin on Keiko must be huge,' he said, lowering his voice. His eyes were a fabulous shade of blue. Deep blue. And the whites of his eyes were very white. Co-op store colours, she decided, while trying to think of a nicer comparison. A summer sky with cotton-wool clouds, a Hockney painting . . . 'I mean, what did she eat?' he continued. 'A forkful of salmon and a glass of tap water?'

'Yeah, well she makes up for it with long showers. Fifty

minutes this morning. Poor Ernst had to pee in the frozen garden.' Jo tore herself away and found a bottle of vodka left over from her Christmas party. 'We could start with a short?'

Her guest looked at his watch – a gesture guaranteed to ruin an evening – and said, 'I should really make a phone call before it gets too—'

'Call from here, if you like.'

'Ah, no. Thanks, anyway. It's a bit, you know . . .'

'Personal?'

'Yes.'

'Right,' said Jo, feeling oddly disappointed that this relative stranger had a significant other. After all, was he really her type? On the whole, she tended to go for darker men, plus how keen was she on that checked shirt? 'You could always go home, then come back,' she suggested.

She watched his eyes swivel around before he said, 'Oh, sod it, I'll call her tomorrow.' He grinned. 'Why ruin her evening?'

'So how come you don't have much of an accent?' she asked him.

They'd moved down to the floor cushions in front of the illegal log fire she'd thrown together. Her fires tended to be a bit hit and miss, but this one was behaving itself, still alight after an hour. They'd talked about politics and war, and she'd filled him in on the neighbours and the neighbourhood, but so far they hadn't touched on anything personal. They were sitting facing each other. His legs were crossed at the ankle, not far from her knees, and she looked approvingly at his nice shoes: dark brown, soft leather. A man's shoes had always been a gauge for Jo. No amount of good looks and charm could make up for shiny, buckled slip-ons.

'I think I lost a lot of it at university,' he said, as Jo reached for the bottle of wine – their second – and filled the glasses. 'I went to Sussex. Mind you, it comes flooding back when I'm at home. You should hear me.'

'I'm the same when I go back to Wales. I mean Way-yells.'

He smiled then went quiet for a while. 'So,' he said finally, looking up from his drink. 'What do you do behind your curtain all day, Jojo?'

She was on the verge of telling him she was just plain Jo, but a fierce knock on the door prevented her.

'I am going off now,' announced Ernst. His head appeared in a fur-edged hood, making him look nine rather than nineteen.

'OK,' said Jo. 'You'd better hurry, though. It's gone ten. Know all your pub vocabulary?'

'No, I have been sleeping. I know only "Same again?", "What'll you have?" and "My turn to get them in". These are the three Jeremy wants us mostly to practise on him.'

Marcus laughed. 'Sounds like a clever bloke.'

'Well, have a nice time,' said Jo.

'And you also,' replied Ernst. His eyes bounced from her to Marcus and back again, before he winked and disappeared.

Jo cringed and grabbed the poker, then spent some time stabbing at the fire.

'What's that log ever done to you?' Marcus asked.

'Mm? Oh.' She put the poker down and composed herself, as much as was possible after a vodka and two-and-a-half – or was it three-and-a-half? – glasses of wine. Large ones. 'I copy-edit,' she said, remembering his question. 'And I proofread. Mostly academic stuff. Dissertations, theses. It pays the bills, but it doesn't pay the mortgage arrears, the overdraft or the maxed-out credit cards. Hence the lodgers.' She was telling him too much, she knew, but she was feeling loose and her tongue was quite drunk. Or maybe the other way round.

11

For a while she watched the mirror beyond Marcus's head do a strange little dance – jigging and swaying – before she lowered her gaze to his. He was definitely giving her a funny look. A bit like the looks her Italian boy, Gianni, used to give her before he pounced on her that evening and she'd had to explain that landladies weren't supposed to sleep with their students. That if she started doing that, the school would stop sending people to her and she'd end up in Queen Street with only a blanket and a dog on a piece of rope. Gianni had said he understood and then apologised. He was just missing his mother, he'd explained alarmingly.

'You know, Jojo,' Marcus was saying, 'your hair's a fabulous colour. And so shiny.'

She blinked, taken aback at the turn in the conversation. Should she tell him it was hennaed? And what about the Jojo thing? 'Thanks,' she said, topping up their glasses again. 'And you?' she asked, deciding to keep to safe ground. 'What do you do?' She placed the bottle over by the wall, out of harm's way, and when she leaned back, Marcus was beside her, sharing her floor cushion, his arm resting on the seat of the sofa behind her. Actually, she thought, it was rather a nice shirt. And so very soft.

'Too boring to talk about,' he said. 'You know, I'm feeling what my mother would call "a wee bit merry".'

'Mm, me too.'

Something was trailing along her shoulder towards her neck. Marcus, now at very close range, looked at her with his one eye. Then with four. She blinked and he had two again. 'I'd love to kiss you,' he said.

'Would you?' she asked.

'Yes,' he said, and he did.

When he'd finished, Jo reached for her glass and gulped fairly furiously, then put it down, empty. What an unexpected evening this was turning out to be.

'I don't suppose I could stay here tonight?' Marcus asked.

She knew she should be shocked and wary, but Lucy and Dom had checked him out, sort of. And besides, her hand was in his lovely shirt now.

He stroked her hennaed hair. 'My house is so cold compared to yours. What do you say?'

'Erm . . . I don't know. Yes, I suppose so. But . . .'

'What?'

'Well, what about Maidstone?'

'Oh, no,' he said, now nuzzling her neck. 'Too far.'

SATURDAY

Robin woke to the sound – clomp, clomp, clomp – and then the feel – warm, slightly damp – of Freddie. It was dark, so he couldn't actually see him. As the little boy snuggled up under the duvet, Robin turned to the illuminated alarm and saw it wasn't yet six. Being the weekend, it was officially Hannah's turn to deal with Freddie, but she was dead to the world on the far side of their king-size bed, recharging herself after five days of abuse, more abuse and futile attempts to teach French at a bottom-of-the-league secondary school.

'Don't fidget, Fred,' whispered Robin. 'Just lie very still. That's it. Close your eyes . . . not too tight. And go back to sleep. That's what Daddy's going to do. Lovely, lovely sleeeep. Mmmm . . .'

'I spilled my water,' said Freddie. 'On my jim-jams.'

'Never mind. They'll soon dry off.'

'Daddy?'

'Sshhh, Freddie. Not so loud. What?'

'Why is water wet?'

Robin's heart sank. 'Well . . .' he began, still whispering, 'let me see . . .' Freddie's questions were always of this nature. Basically, impossible for Robin to answer. Never, 'Daddy, what's the connection between America's post-1945 international economic interests and its global political/military agenda?' In his forty-six years, Robin hadn't once wondered why water was wet. He doubted that Hannah, in her thirty-seven, had given it much thought either. Had they somehow freakily produced a little scientist, or had that paternity test been wrong, after all? 'It's because . . .' he said. 'Hey, want some breakfast?'

'Yeah, yeah, yeah!'

'Sshhh.'

'What would you like?' whispered Robin, lifting himself and his son up off the bed, as seamlessly as his back would allow. 'Yikes,' he said, straightening up. A recent rough and tumble with Freddie had left him, temporarily he hoped, with nasty back pain. He couldn't remember parenthood being so painful the first time round, but then he had been a lithe twenty-something when Theo was born. 'Creamy porridge again?' he asked.

'Yeah, yeah, yeah!'

'Sshhh.'

'Daddy?'

'Mm?' Robin felt around with an extended foot for his slippers. He came across one but not the other so gave up and, without turning on any lights, carried his son down the stairs. 'What, Freddie?'

'Why is the dark a black colour? I want it to be red. Why can't it be red, Daddy?'

Robin thought he might be able to have a stab at this one, but not till he'd had a coffee.

* * *

Marcus woke to total darkness, aware of a thumping headache and the aroma of old joss sticks, but with no idea of where he was. A faint engine noise filled his ears, bringing to mind the cat, so he felt around for fur, first on top of what felt like a duvet, then beneath it. What he came across, though, was flesh: soft . . . round . . . human . . . almost certainly female. He jerked his hand away and lay for a while, staring at where the ceiling should be, while beside him the owner of the flesh purred loudly, or maybe snored quietly. Somewhere between the two. Jojo, he reminded himself. Neighbour. Very friendly. One whose hospitality, in fact, stretched to unusual lengths.

Oh Christ, he thought. Big mistake. He really wasn't in the habit of bedding people he hardly knew. Not these days, anyway. Was he coerced? And how come they'd got through so much alcohol? Did she have a drink problem? But more importantly, where was the bathroom? As his eyes began to adjust, Marcus could make out a fireplace, a cupboard or wardrobe and, thank God, a door. After gently peeling the duvet away from his body, he eased himself up and tiptoed across the room, hoping, since he was quite naked, that Jojo's students didn't rise too early on Saturdays. Outside, he found the bathroom door ajar and hurried in, gathering from the total silence in the house that no one else was up.

Back in the bedroom, down on hands and knees, he groped around for his clothes. How rude would it be to go home? He could leave Jojo a note saying he'd had to feed the cat and didn't want to wake her. Yes, that was what he'd do. She was still snoring – rather endearingly – and Marcus guessed she'd be out of it for a while. He dressed in the bathroom and crept down the stairs. It was only at the bottom, when he was slipping his shoes on, that he heard the radio.

'Good morning,' sang a cheery voice in the distance.

Marcus looked down the hallway and saw a perfectly groomed Japanese girl holding a teapot aloft. 'Would you like?' she asked, while he tried to remember her name.

'Um . . . yeah, why not?' He needed to find pen and paper, anyway. 'Thanks.'

Someone was playing old sixties numbers on the radio, Jojo's student was grilling bacon and whisking eggs, and Marcus was gradually sliding an airmail envelope towards him to read the name of the addressee. Keiko, that was it. He pushed the letter back across the table just as she came forward and dolloped the contents of the saucepan on his plate.

'Aren't you having any, Keiko?' he asked.

'Yes,' she said, scraping the last teaspoonful on to her own plate.

Marcus then received two rashers of bacon and helped himself to the toast done especially for him. 'Do you always make your own breakfast?'

'Only sometimes. Mostly when Bram stays here for night with Jo.'

'Bram?'

'Yes.'

'No, I mean, who *is* Bram?'

'Ah. He is part-time Dutch boyfriend.'

'Oh, right.' Marcus tried to work out if Jojo having a bloke was good or bad news. 'Why is he only part-time?'

Keiko swallowed a milligram of egg. 'He is sometimes away long time with job.'

'Oh? What does he do?'

'He is . . .' She put her fork down and picked up a note-book with Marge Simpson on the front, then thumbed through it. 'Ah, yes. Eco-warrior.'

'Really?' Marcus pictured a crusty with nose rings and a mohican. Jojo was still an unknown quantity; who knew what sort she went for?

While he worked his way through breakfast, he took a look around to get some clues as to who she was. Everything was pretty tidy and clean and nicely painted. The house, he realised, was quite a bit smaller than his – he was thinking of it as *his* already – much narrower, definitely. Which explained why number 15 was opposite number 8, the houses on his side of the street all being larger. Jojo's kitchen was obviously part of an extension, with French windows overlooking a cheerful little walled garden, full of red and yellow tulips. Her modern table and chairs all matched and an old Welsh dresser had its shelves prettily lined with crockery and knick-knacks. Whatever else Jo was – seductress extraordinaire, lush – she wasn't sloppy around the house. The only messy thing in the room was a cork board covered in postcards. Many from Bram, no doubt. *Having a lovely time chained to Alaskan test-drill equipment. Weather nippy!*

Marcus asked, 'So is she Jo or Jojo?'

'Jo.'

'Oh.'

'But really Josephine.'

'Nice.' Marcus chewed on. 'Good eggs,' he told Keiko, and she thanked him for the compliment, then thanked him again. Once he'd finished and knocked back his tea, he borrowed a pencil, scribbled a note for 'Jo' on the back of an envelope and propped it against the toaster. He thanked Keiko for breakfast and, after a good hunt for them, left without his coat and hat.

'Hi, it's Marcus,' he said, holding his breath. Before phoning, he'd got the central heating going, soaked in a cast-iron bath that could take four more people, and fed the cat in a fresh bowl with 'Maidstone' written on it, so clearing up one puzzle.

'Oh,' Hannah said, rather flatly he felt. 'Hello.'

'How's things?'

'Fine.'

'And Freddie?'

'He's fine too.'

'Good,' said Marcus, raising his voice above the background noise. It sounded as though they were having building work done.

'And you?' she asked. 'I heard parts of Scotland are snowed in. Unusual for late March, I thought.'

'Actually, I'm not in Scotland.'

'No? Fred, don't do that to the cupboard, sweetie.'

Since when had he become Fred? 'I'm in Oxford,' he told her.

'Give the nail to Mummy, there's a good boy. And the hammer.'

Had she heard him? 'House-sitting in Jubilee Street.'

'Thank you, darling.'

'For three weeks.'

A silence followed and Marcus wasn't sure if she'd wandered off. 'Are you telling me,' she said, a small wobble in her voice, 'that you're two streets away?'

''Fraid so.'

'But how come? And why?'

'Well, the "how come" is I searched on the Internet for a house-sit in the Oxford area and found one. And the "why" is because I'd like to see Freddie.' And you, he wanted to add.

'Jesus,' she said. Then after a pause: 'What number?'

'Sorry?'

'Jubilee Street.'

'Oh, eight.'

'*What?*' she practically shrieked. 'Lucy and *Dom's?*'

19

'You *know* them?' he practically shrieked back.

'Yes, very well. I met them through Robin's friend, Jo. She lives op—'

'I know,' he said, wondering if he could have got off to a worse start. There he'd been, thinking he could quietly slip into Oxford for a few weeks and spend time with the little boy he'd thought was his son for two and a half years. Instead, he was in the house of some good friends of Hannah's, having shagged another one. Well, maybe he had. It was all a bit foggy.

'That's great,' she said unconvincingly. 'You must come round, but not just yet. Robin's gone back to bed. He was up early doing some carpentry with Fred and his new tools.'

'Right.' Hannah was still short in the sensitivity department, then. Didn't she remember how Marcus loved those early-morning sessions with Freddie? They'd watch *Teletubbies* videos and work their way through picture books, Freddie chewing messily on his Marmite soldiers. But how quickly they grow and change. Now Freddie and his real father were knocking up coffee tables at dawn. Well, Marcus thought, deciding not to be churlish, how nice that he had a proper DIY daddy.

Hannah tutted. 'Of course, Robin doesn't know a chisel from a wing nut. Look, I'll need to prepare Freddie rather than have you turn up out of the blue. It's been rather a shock for *me*, so . . .'

'That's OK. I'll come round later. I'm still settling myself in here. What do these people do, by the way?'

'Lucy and Dom? They're both graphic designers, doing brochures and marketing and that kind of thing, sometimes for quite big firms. They set up a business about five years ago with a couple of geeky guys who do all the website and software stuff. Anyway, it seems to have really taken off.'

'So I see.'

'It's a nice house, isn't it? Mind you, they deserve it. They're total workaholics, but every now and then they go off on a bit of a retreat.'

'Right.' That explained the mobile phones left up in the office. 'So how's your job going?' he asked.

'Oh, Christ, it's exhausting. I travel twenty miles to work each day, only to be given grief by these hormonal kids who don't want to speak French and wouldn't go to France if you paid them.' She attempted a laugh. 'It's hell.'

Marcus wondered if it was really that bad. He'd never known Hannah have a job she didn't moan about. 'Sounds awful.'

'Yes.'

'So, when shall I come round?'

'I don't know. Fourish? Fred sometimes still naps early afternoon. You know, I can't believe you're in Lucy and Dom's house. That's so weird. They said they were going away soon and might get a sitter. Sometimes I feed Maidstone, but he gets lonely if they're away more than a few days.'

'Right.' How tight Hannah was with them. 'Anyway,' he said, 'I'll see you around four.'

'Look forward to it.'

'Me too,' said Marcus, hanging up, then flopping against the wall, heart thumping. That could have gone worse.

I think I can recall . . .

Mary had a little lamb, its fleece . . . Marcus, just round the corner. Oh God. Everywhere that Mary went . . .

I think I can recall . . .

Dear Adrian . . . no, I'm not going to address this to my therapist. After all, I talk to him for a full fifty minutes every week. And what's more, he addresses almost nothing to me. No, I'll address it to myself. Or to whoever comes across it in the future and manages to break open the lock — not Freddie, I hope.

Anyway, I think I can recall the exact moment I knew for sure. It was when I collected the photos of Freddie's second birthday party. I went through them in the street and saw that one of me, Marcus and Freddie, just as Fred was blowing out his two candles. Fred with his thick dark curly hair. And those lips. Very full, rosy lips. Robin's lips. There were signs, even then, of a burgeoning nose. One that might one day be the size of Robin's. Plus the heavy-lidded brown eyes. Robin's best feature — still sparkling in his mid-forties. Marcus's eyes are blue, mine hazel. Yes, it was then. That photo. I stood staring at it outside the chemist's — Freddie looking so unlike either of us, a stranger would think he was adopted.

Ooch, he's so like his Great-uncle Robert, Marcus's mother would often comment, reassuring everyone — except me, of course — as Freddie entered his terrible-two period. Eyes like polished chestnuts, she'd say. Just like Robert's.

I knew I'd have to tell Marcus one day, but it never seemed to be the right day or the right moment to completely shatter his world. Our world.

Apples, butter, bleach, jam. Silver foil, sausages

But then, after months of guilt-ridden agonising on my part, Marcus asked me if Freddie was his. We were halfway up Lochnagar at the time — Marcus's second attempt at it and my first. I don't think so, I told him, and he went up the mountain and I went down and nothing was ever the same again. Prince Charles may love Lochnagar, but it's my least favourite place in the world — aside from the godawful school I work in, of course.

Four o'clock? I definitely can't wait that long.

* * *

Jo couldn't believe she'd slept till gone twelve. There were other things she couldn't believe she'd done either, like screwing a complete stranger.

'Shit,' she said, stepping into the shower. 'Shit, shit, shit.' And what's more it was someone she'd hardly be able to avoid for the next three weeks. Not unless she just stayed in the house. No, that was impossible. God, she was hungover. Not used to drinking, that was the problem.

But then she realised that staying home *was* feasible. The supermarkets could deliver everything the three of them needed, and she'd post her clients' work back to them instead of meeting up in a café to discuss the changes she'd made. Of course, she'd miss that human contact. It stopped her turning into another Len round the corner, who made exquisite leather goods in his basement all day but had completely lost the art of conversation.

Jo dried herself and dressed gingerly, every movement making her feel queasy, then, with a towel wrapped around her head, went down to the kitchen and found Ernst reading a newspaper behind the congealed remains of a fry-up.

'Good afternoon!' he bellowed, and Jo's palms flew to her ears. He lowered his paper and grinned at her as she tried hard not to look at his plate. 'I think maybe you are . . . let me remember . . . pissed as a newt?'

She shook her head – ouch – and switched the kettle on. 'That was last night, Ernst. Now I have a terrible hangover. You know "hangover"?'

'Ah, yes. This we were also discussing with Jeremy in the Eagle and Child.' He folded the newspaper, very neatly, and placed it on the table. 'One moment,' he said, getting up and heading for the door. 'I will find you a . . . oh, what is the word?'

'Mm?'

He stopped and turned back. 'Do you have scissors?'

'Er, yeah.' She took some from a drawer and handed them over.

'One moment,' he said again and disappeared, not upstairs but through the front door, which he left open.

When it became too cold for comfort, Jo slid herself sideways along the hall wall so that Marcus wouldn't see her from his living room. Then, with a foot, she hooked the door towards her, put it on the latch and shut it with a sigh. This would be no way to live for three weeks.

Just as she was taking her first reviving sip of tea, Ernst charged back in and said, 'Here!' holding out a closed fist. 'It is the hairs of a cat.'

'Sorry?'

'Our teacher has taught us that in Britain the very best thing for hanging over is the hairs of a dog. But in Jubilee Street I think there are no dogs, and, besides, what can be the difference?' He put the scissors down and tipped a clump of cat fur, looking horribly like Maidstone's, into her palm. 'Don't worry, Marcus gave me permission.'

'What,' she began, very afraid to ask, 'did you tell him?'

'That you are needing some animal hairs for medicine. But I didn't tell him you were hanging—'

'*Hungover*, Ernst.'

'Ah yes, hungover. Because I am a gentleman.' He beamed at her and bowed from the waist.

'Thanks, but actually I wish you had explained what you were doing.' She looked down at the little mound of Maidstone. 'And he said?'

'Nothing. Just "Hello" and then one nod when I asked permission, and then maybe a kind of strange face, and then "Bye".'

Jo took all this in. She wasn't planning on seeing any more of Marcus, so did it really matter? He'd gone off without saying goodbye or leaving her a note or anything, which was rather *un*gentlemanly. 'Ernst,' she said, 'that was very thoughtful of you, thank you. But I think you took your teacher too literally. Now why don't you sit down and I'll explain "hair of the dog" properly. Yeah?'

When she'd finished and Ernst was looking suitably embarrassed, he jumped up and dashed across the kitchen. 'In that case you must have some wine.'

'Oh no, I couldn't poss—'

'But you must,' he persisted. He placed a disgusting-smelling half-glass of red in her hand, and the bottle on the table. 'Hair of the dog, yes?'

Jo was on the verge of retching when the doorbell sounded.

'I will go,' announced Ernst, and he did, returning seconds later with Marcus in tow.

'Hi,' said Marcus. He was looking remarkably well, considering. Remarkably attractive too. How silly of her to think she needed to hide from him. She wanted to unwrap her head but wasn't sure what horrors lay beneath the towel. She did, however, casually remove her glasses.

Marcus cleared his throat. 'I was just wondering if . . .' His voice trailed off as he took in the scene, then his eyes darted to the wall clock and back. 'If I could, um, have my coat? And hat? It's just that I have to go out later.'

With all the dignity she could muster, Jo put the wine glass down and said, 'Of course. Sorry.' She'd get in touch with the school on Monday and ask for Ernst to be repatriated. 'I think they're in the middle room.'

After he left, hurriedly, Jo decided it probably wasn't going to be her day, so took a deep breath, knocked back the hair of the dog, dried her own hair and returned to bed. She took Ernst's tabloid with her, and although tales of celebrity humiliation and degradation helped a bit, she couldn't help thinking she should let Marcus know, somehow, that she wasn't the trollop of Jubilee Street – up for it with any Tom, Dick or housesitter that came along. It was so unfair, she felt, when the whole world knew it was Pippa who held that crown.

As he was scooping a dead fish out of the tank, Marcus heard the doorbell and hoped it wasn't Ernst again, sent by his landlady for bits of fingernail or eye of goldfish. How he'd managed to get involved with an alcoholic white witch within hours of arriving, he'd never know. He dropped the fish in a plastic bag, praying it wasn't going to be the first of many corpses, and was still carrying it when he opened the front door and found Hannah and Freddie there.

'Hello,' Hannah said, nose pink with the cold, face half wrapped in a blue scarf that matched her eyes and complemented her long grey coat. Marcus looked down at an equally well-turned-out Freddie, then back at Hannah, and found himself shocked; not just by their sudden appearance on his doorstep or by how big Freddie had become, but by something in Hannah's eyes. A sadness or hollowness, or something.

'Hi,' he managed. 'What a nice surprise. Hello, Freddie.'

'Hello,' said the little boy, staring at him blankly.

The thing Marcus had been dreading – Freddie having completely forgotten him – seemed to be happening. He did so want to bend down, pick the little boy up and give him a kiss, but instead he pointed at the large blue box in Freddie's gloved hand and said, 'What's that you're carrying?'

'My tools.'

'Oh, yes?'

Hannah said, 'He takes them everywhere. Anyway, we were just round the corner at the swings, so I thought—'

'Yeah, yeah. Come in. Great.'

'Thanks,' she said, and they stepped into the hallway. 'Gosh, it's lovely and warm in here.'

'Where's Lucy?' asked Freddie, looking confused.

That was it, decided Marcus. Freddie hadn't forgotten him; he was just having a problem with context. 'Lucy's gone away for a while, so's Dom.'

'Marcus is looking after the house for them,' said Hannah. She was staring at the bag dripping water in Marcus's hand.

'Dead fish,' he explained.

'Going to see the fish,' said Freddie, waddling off in his big outdoor kit, box still in hand.

When Hannah was taking her coat off and hanging it on the newel post, Marcus noticed that her brown hair was different somehow. Lighter? A touch longer? Nice, anyway. She might also have lost some weight. Not that there was much to lose. 'A wee slip of a thing' his mother used to call her, before she started calling her stronger things. Hannah was in a long skirt with a deep pink jumper that exactly matched her lipstick. Round her neck was an attractive silver necklace, and on her feet were expensive-looking black boots with a bit of a heel. He could smell that D & G perfume she liked so. What an effort she'd made for a walk to the swings.

She turned and smiled, and his insides did a spin. 'Some housesitter you are,' she said, nodding at the bag.

'You're looking very well,' she told him over Lucy and Dom's banquet-length kitchen table.

The boozy night had, he thought, left him looking unwell, but he thanked her anyway.

'Although a bit tired?' she added.

'It was a long drive down yesterday.'

'Must have been,' she said, one hand fiddling with a cork coaster, the other stirring her coffee. 'All on your own. I expect you made lots of stops?' Marcus nodded, then Hannah dropped the coaster and looked directly at him. 'How's your mother?' she asked.

'Fine. As energetic as ever.'

'I'm guessing she didn't send me her regards?'

'Mm? Oh, yeah. Yes, she did.'

'Liar.'

He shrugged and they took simultaneous sips at their coffees. Marcus then gestured to where Freddie was trying to unscrew the leg of a wooden footstool, his little face contorted with effort and concentration. The thing was beginning to wobble. Either the screws were already loose or Freddie had remarkable strength for a three year old. 'I'm not sure he remembers me,' Marcus said.

'Oh, he does,' said Hannah. 'We've just been talking about you. It's only been six months, after all.'

'Nine.'

'OK, nine. But still . . .'

'A fifth of his life.'

'Well, when you put it like that. Anyway, he does remember you, and the restaurant. How's business, by the way?'

'Not bad. Quiet at the moment, of course. Pre-Easter. Mum's running the show with help from my brothers. They *did* say to say hi to you.'

'Yes?' she said, a catch in her voice. 'Well, that's something.' Marcus saw her eyes flicker, and before she could get emotional and maybe vindictive – one of her less attractive traits – he turned his attention to Freddie and asked if he'd like some juice.

'Yes!'

'Yes, *please*,' Marcus corrected him. 'Sorry,' he said to Hannah. Her eyes were definitely filling up. 'Force of habit.'

'That's OK, he needs to be told.'

Marcus got up and went to the fridge. 'Come and choose what you want, Freddie. I've got . . . let me see . . . cranberry juice, orange juice, apple—'

'Apple!'

'Please.'

'*Pleeeze*,' said Freddie with that cheeky, full-lipped grin of his.

'OK, let's—'

'I just miss you,' Hannah suddenly wailed, '*so* much.'

Marcus's hand rested momentarily on the apple juice carton while he took in what he was hearing. He pulled it from the fridge door, poured some into a mug for Freddie, made sure Freddie was holding it properly, then sat on the chair beside Hannah and drew her towards him. 'Me too,' he said. 'Oh, me too.'

'Yeah?'

'Why do you think I'm *here*?'

She shuddered in his arms and mumbled something into his shirt.

'Sorry?' he asked.

She lifted her head. 'I said, what a horrible mess.'

He kissed her forehead – the only dry part of her face – and squeezed her harder, while Freddie looked on over the top of his mug. 'I know.'

When the phone rang, Marcus decided to let the machine pick up. Since arriving he'd had lots of calls for Lucy and Dom and only two for himself, from his mother.

'You wouldn't believe how much I've missed you two,' he whispered. The good times, anyway. Hannah rubbed a damp

29

cheek against his, and when Freddie climbed on both their laps, the three of them went into a communal hug.

As he listened to Dom's pre-recorded message, Marcus felt close to blubbing too. He hadn't been expecting an emotional reunion. Just the opposite, knowing Hannah: forced and frosty, even. Jesus, what a nightmare all this was. A stupid situation they'd each brought about in their own ways: Hannah with her incomprehensible fling with Robin, and he by withdrawing emotionally when the truth came out about Freddie. Then Hannah, feeling frozen out by Marcus and his family, running to the safety of the newly divorced Robin. Marcus not following her and begging her to come back . . .

'What have I done?' Hannah was asking him.

'It wasn't just you, you know that. I was a total wanker for months.'

'*Lang*uage,' she said, managing a giggle.

'Oops, sorry. Cover your ears, Freddie.'

'Anyway,' Hannah said, 'you being a total W was understandable.' She looked up and settled her watery eyes on his. 'I still have such strong feelings for you, you know.'

Beep went the machine. 'Hi, Marcus,' they heard in their little human cluster, and Marcus froze. 'It's Jo. Listen, about last night, as they say. I, er, think it was a mistake, don't you? And it's certainly not the kind of thing I do, you know, often. I mean ever, really. I . . . um, look, if you want to talk about it some time, I'm here. Not that you probably do, only maybe I do . . . so . . . oh shit, this isn't coming out right.'

Click went the machine, and for a while no one moved. Not until the leg dropped off the footstool and made them all jump.

Robin woke from his nap to an empty house and a note telling him Hannah and Freddie had gone to the park. He made a pot of coffee and took a shower, then settled down in his office with *American Beauty: the benefits of US foreign policy for a fucked up world*, which wasn't quite the title he and young Bridget had settled on in their tutorial. Without thinking, he put a hyphen between the *fucked* and the *up*, then shook his head. What was he doing? He scored through the offending words and scribbled 'unstable?' as an alternative, then braced himself for a eulogy on the United States.

How often this happened. They'd arrive at university in Oxford – albeit not *the* Oxford University – intelligent and articulate but with a wonderful blankness about them, keen to absorb the informed and clearly *correct* views of their lecturers. Then, two years later, they'd go into rebellious mode: Thatcher prevented Britain becoming a Third World country run by the unions; Kissinger saved the planet from nasty old Communism, and so on.

Robin couldn't help thinking that he, Patricia, Bill and the others were going about things the wrong way, and had said as much in meetings. He himself had taken steps to temper his criticism of right-wing, imperialist actions and philosophies, but for a dyed-in-the-wool type such as Bill, that would have been on a par with rolling up at work in a mini-skirt.

Yes, Robin thought, flicking through pages fairly quickly, it was the usual stuff: 'Without US help these poorer countries wouldn't have made progress. Their impoverished inhabitants would still be living barbaric, archaic, superstition-filled lives, instead of watching satellite TV, phoning friends on mobiles and eating wholesome Western food . . .' Robin underlined 'wholesome' and wrote 'Debatable?' above it.

'Daddy!' he suddenly heard behind him, and with some relief put Bridget's work to one side.

'Hi, Freddie. Didn't know you were back. Let's get you out

of your spacesuit, shall we? Did you have a nice time? Where did you go?'

Freddie put his toolbox down and came over to him. 'We went to the swings, then we seed my uvver daddy and Mummy cried.'

'Oh, yes?' asked Robin, wondering if he'd misheard.

'My uvver daddy killed a fish.'

'Uh-huh? Now, pull your arm out. That's it.' Hannah had probably been recounting some past event to Freddie. Keeping memories of Marcus alive, or something. 'Now the other one, there's a good boy.'

'And then he kissed Mummy and made her stop crying.'

'Oh, good.' Robin wasn't surprised to hear Hannah had been crying over a fish Marcus had caught, since she was totally soppy about animals. He'd never been sure she felt the same way about humans, though. Particularly the ones she taught. 'OK, Freddie, all done.'

'But best of all was when the leg fell off the stool. Which I done.'

Robin put Bridget's part-dissertation back in the pile he'd have to wade through over the weekend, then turned to his son, who'd opened his toolbox in the middle of the study floor and was rummaging through and humming to himself. Robin smiled. Although he sometimes suspected Freddie had an obsessive nature, it was actually quite endearing in a three year old, and maybe not that unusual. He thought back to Theo at that age, listening to *Jack and the Beanstalk*, over and over, on his Fisher Price cassette player.

'What stool?' he asked, putting the tedious marking out of his head. But his question was drowned out by Freddie, nailing – for reasons known only to himself – one small strip of wood to another.

SUNDAY

Major cock-up, decided Marcus. He stretched himself out in the colossal bath, head back, ears underwater, and contemplated going home. If only he'd found a B and B instead of a house-sit, his first meeting with Hannah might not have ended with her spitting, 'This is some kind of revenge, is it?' – and his 'No, of course not!' being met with a slamming of the front door. How quickly she'd turned from loving and remorseful to dry-eyed and furious. But why would that surprise him? He'd just forgotten, that was all, how Hannah's mood could turn on the slightest of things.

Should he write her a note? Phoning could be scary. He might get Robin. Not that Robin was in any way scary, apparently. 'An absolute pussycat,' Hannah had once described him as, tactful as ever.

Marcus pinched his nose and went right under the water for a while, then surfaced for air. However much of a pussycat Robin was, Hannah didn't seem that contented. But then, for the length of their relationship, Marcus always felt he hadn't quite come up to scratch either. Contentment wasn't a state that came naturally to Hannah.

No, he wouldn't write a note. He'd just go round to their house. Today. Meet this Robin bloke at last. Be affable. Play at DIY with Freddie. Explain to Hannah, in a quiet corner somewhere, that there was nothing going on with Jo. That he suspected she had a screw or two loose, and had no idea what her crazy answerphone message was about. Yes, he'd do that. No point in giving up and going home now. Not with a bath this size to wallow in and all that food they'd left. Besides, he'd be letting Maidstone down.

The man who answered the door was like Freddie, but around six foot two. Same eyes, mouth and colouring. He was dressed in a denim shirt that had seen better days, and green corduroy trousers that had seen them even longer ago. He looked well into his forties and his hair was thick, dark, wavy and on the long side.

'Robin?' asked Marcus.

'Yes.'

'I'm—'

'Marcus?'

'Yes.'

'I've seen photos,' Robin said with a disturbingly pleasant smile. 'Hannah told me you were in town. I'm afraid they're out, but do come in.'

'Thanks,' said Marcus, feeling this was all wrong. Shouldn't he be bopping this bloke on the nose? 'Nice house.'

'Thanks. A bit untidy, I'm afraid. Having a toddler can be—'

'I know.'

'Yes, of course. Sorry.'

Marcus was led through to the living room, where Robin removed toys from the sofa, then offered it to Marcus. 'Can I get you anything?' he asked. 'Beer, coffee?'

'No, I'm OK. Thanks.' With no Hannah or Freddie there, Marcus didn't intend to stay long.

'They're at a birthday party,' said Robin. 'Only just left, unfortunately.'

'Ah. Bad timing.' Marcus sank back in the cushions and looked around the room. There were photos on every surface and some on the walls. Hannah and Freddie. Robin and Freddie. Freddie on his own. There were lots of those. One picture was of all three of them wearing party hats. Christmas? Hannah was grinning broadly and looking beautiful, but there were those lifeless eyes again. Some photos were of a dark-haired, good-looking boy at different ages. Robin's other son, most likely.

'Good one of you over there,' said Robin, pointing.

So there was. He had a very young Freddie – six months? – on his back in a kiddie carrier. He remembered it well. They'd been taking a walk round Loch Muick. It had been a great day out, ruined in the end by some casual remark he'd made about Hannah finding a job to help out until the restaurant got itself re-established. His uncle had let the place slide before his death and there'd been some costly refurbishing to do, then advertising and so on. She'd stormed ahead to the car and not spoken on the journey home.

'Are you sure you wouldn't like something?' Robin was asking. 'Lager?'

Would it be rude to refuse a second time? Marcus actually fancied a cup of tea, but did men do that together? 'Go on then,' he said, and while Robin was out of the room, he soaked up its cosy, slightly shambolic family atmosphere. Freddie must be happy here, he thought, even if his mother wasn't. Marcus's eyes scanned the CDs, spotting Hannah's favourites – Norah Jones, Dixie Chicks – slotted amongst what must have been

Robin's – Bach, Pink Floyd, John Coltrane, Dvorak, Bob the Builder – Freddie's, hopefully.

'I'm really sorry,' Robin was saying. He handed Marcus a glass of beer, then took a seat opposite with his own.

'What for?'

'You know.'

'Oh. Right.'

'I didn't know at the time. About you.'

'No?'

'No.'

'I see,' said Marcus. He tapped at his glass, then took a long swig, hoping they weren't about to embark on a character assassination of Hannah, but suspecting Robin might not have the nature for it anyway. They could talk about Freddie, he thought, but that could be dangerous territory too. The room was very quiet.

'Any idea how the rugby's going?' he asked eventually.

'No, I haven't,' Robin said a little too brightly. He quickly reached for the remote. 'Let's find out, shall we?'

MONDAY

'Dear Jo, Thank you for a lovely evening' said the note she found beneath the toaster at nine o'clock Monday morning when she was giving the worktops a clean. 'Sorry for dashing off like this but must feed cat! See you later today, I hope. Love, Marcus.'

Jo slumped on to a kitchen chair in her usual morning gear: pyjamas, man's checked woollen dressing gown, socks, trainers and a long striped scarf wound twice round her neck. She tried not to use the heating during the day, so switched it off the moment the students left and, after a general tidy-up, worked in her bag-lady outfit until lunch and a hot bath. When it got really cold, as it had today, she added a back-to-front baseball cap.

'Bugger,' she said quietly. How she wished she hadn't left him that message. So insulting compared to this one he'd left her. No wonder she hadn't heard back from him. She'd have to go and see him; explain about the cat fur, and the midday boozing and not finding his note. She'd have a quick shower, put her contacts in and nip across the road in time for elevenses.

Everything could be sorted out by lunchtime, and then, well, who knew what path fate might take them down? Perhaps he could come and house-sit for her next? The only difference being she wouldn't go anywhere.

When the postman's jolly 'ring, ring-ring' brought her out of her fantasy, Jo clopped down the hall in her unlaced trainers to take whatever large package had arrived for proofing, but then stopped dead. What if it was Marcus? She couldn't be seen like this! The postman was used to it, but anyone else would reel back in horror. After the brass knocker gave several urgent raps, Jo crept to her living room-cum-office bay window, hooked the lace curtain to one side and saw the postman filling out one of his I-tried-to-deliver notes. She dashed back to the hall, opened the door and apologised, grateful that he was a very big man in a very big postman's jacket and completely hid her from view.

'I just wanted to explain about the cat-hair thing,' she said. He was staring at the kitchen table and chewing a finger. 'Marcus?'

'Mm?'

'I said . . . Oh, never mind. Are you all right?'

'Do you know who I am?' he asked, raising his eyes to hers.

Now it was Jo's turn to stare while she considered his question. He was famous and she hadn't recognised him? Was he a notorious ex-con, or the Duke of somewhere? She shook her head.

'Hannah's husband,' he said.

Robin's new partner? Jo didn't know another Hannah. 'Freddie's mum?' she asked.

He nodded. 'I expect Hannah's told you about the whole her, me, Freddie and Robin business?'

No, she hadn't, and neither had Robin. Hannah and Freddie had just sort of appeared. Moved in with Robin after his marriage broke up. Freddie was clearly his son, but Jo had never asked any questions. Robin had been an acquaintance, bordering on friend, for years – she was once his student and he now passed work her way – but Hannah she'd first met properly when she, Jo, had thrown a party the previous summer. Hannah had formed quite a friendship with Lucy over the road, so Jo occasionally came across her, but they hadn't exactly become bosom buddies.

'A little,' she told Marcus, hoping he'd feel it OK to expand. Which he did.

'Crikey,' she said when he'd finished.

'And *then*,' he said, not quite finished, '*just* when Hannah and I were about to declare our undying love for each other, you piped up on the answerphone with your about-last-night message. Hannah left soon after that, twice as upset. She was still a bit frosty when I rang yesterday evening. I reassured her you and I weren't . . . By the way, did we actually . . . ?'

'I'm not sure, to be honest. I found a thingy, you know, still in its packet, which was kind of half ripped open. So I guess we didn't. *Hope* we didn't. Me getting pregnant would hardly help!'

'Might balance things, though?'

'True,' she said, grinning. 'But I'm too poor to have a child, sorry.'

Marcus laughed. 'Maybe Robin would take you in.'

'Actually, he's such a nice guy, he probably would. Oh, sorry. I don't suppose you want to hear that.'

'No, it's all right. I know he's a nice guy, that's what's making this all so difficult.' Marcus stared at the table again for a while before seeming to blink himself out of his gloom. 'God, how remiss of me,' he said with the trace of a smile. 'It's almost noon and I haven't offered you any alcohol. You must be gasping?'

*   *   *

Jo was back at work by two, sober and learning more than she'd ever need to know about limited liability insurance for foot passengers on Russian ferries. It didn't make sense, she kept thinking, about both Sergei's work and Hannah's behaviour. She tried to imagine what she might have done in that situation. Moved in with the real father even though she didn't love him? No, never. Jo had sensed something not quite right between Robin and Hannah at the party she'd thrown. Some couples gel – pass each other knowing little looks and eyebrow bobs in company, occasionally touch – while other couples . . . well, they were like Hannah and Robin. Almost formal. Perhaps they hadn't known each other that well when Hannah landed on his doorstep. Crazy. Still, it must have been tempting for Hannah. Nice man, nice house . . . No, Jo couldn't decide what she would have done in the circumstances, she just felt pleased she wasn't Hannah. As she checked through Sergei's table: 'Compensation Amounts Paying Compulsory by Insurers of River and Sea Companies of Ferry Boats for Foot Passengers Who are Losing One or More Limb in Accident' – a table that was shorter than its title – she decided she might, in fact, have stuck it out with Marcus and his family in Scotland; maybe had another baby with him. She also decided it might be worth taking a trip on an ill-fated Russian ferry, since the compensation figures looked astronomical. In roubles, anyway.

My parents were stunned by, rather than disapproving of, their daughter getting married in a Presbyterian kirk. Neither of them had ever been church-goers, so they doubtless assumed I'd do what they did – ten minutes in the registry office and an off-the-peg reception.

We all stayed in the castle-cum-hotel where the reception was to be held, and when Mum caught me throwing up in the morning and said that she too had been a bag of nerves on her wedding day, I told her I wasn't nervous, just pregnant. And while she stared at me before saying anything, I imagined the mixed feelings going through her head. Excitement at the prospect of a first grandchild, but distress at how far away it would be. Disappointment too, in that I'd only just finished my PGCE in Oxford and, after years and years of miserable office work, I could have started a real career teaching French.

That's fantastic, love, she said, suddenly hugging me. Marcus must be thrilled.

We're hoping to keep it a secret till after the wedding, I told her (it was a lie, Marcus didn't know). So don't say anything, I begged her. Not even to Dad.

Later, walking down the aisle in that ludicrous dress, amidst all the happy faces, then seeing my adoring and much-loved bridegroom waiting for me, I felt certain fate wouldn't be so cruel as to make the baby Robin's.

Little Jack Horner sat in the corner . . .

How fantastic Marcus looked on Saturday, and how very Marcus-like he still is. Funny, slightly diffident, caring (up to a point). I hadn't planned to sob like that, or had I? I've certainly played out the repentant, heart-broken, please-forgive-me scene in my head many times, but have never had it interrupted by a call from one of Marcus's girlfriends. No matter how much he assured me over the phone last night that nothing's happened between him and Jo, I can't help a sudden intense dislike of her.

Shit, ten to one already. Once more into 9F.

As Marcus was setting off for a late-afternoon stroll into town, he saw a woman steer her Ford Ka nose-first into a small parking space that any thinking person would have reversed into. Many a time he'd had to gag himself while his mother did this very same thing. It was always painful to witness: those endless forward and backward movements that were never going to resolve the situation.

Yes, back and forth the Ka went and, as excruciating as it was, Marcus felt transfixed. Sometimes, miraculously, these forward-parkers managed it. The woman, who looked somewhere in the thirty-to-fifty spectrum, made an embarrassed face at him when she saw he was watching. Once again she went forward a couple of inches, then reversed a couple of inches, but ended up where she'd started, more or less diagonal. Marcus politely looked away, flung his scarf over one shoulder and strode purposefully along the pavement, past the manoeuvring car.

'Excuse me?' a voice called out to him.

He turned and saw a flawless, faintly orange face protruding from the nearside window. 'You couldn't help me out here, could you? Always been hopeless at parking in small spaces.'

'Sure.'

The woman got out and walked the quarter-mile to the kerb. 'Sorry,' she said, throwing her hands up, and Marcus slid into the driver's seat.

'You trust me not to drive off with it, then?' he asked with a grin, before shutting the door and finding himself cocooned in perfume and listening to Mick Hucknall. After a few nifty moves, the car was as snug as a bug, right beside the kerb. 'There,' he said, getting out and handing the owner her keys, trying not to look cocky.

'Thanks ever so,' she said, slowly undoing the buttons of her suit jacket. She was dressed for the office but came across as more beautician than secretary: a heavy make-up job, shoulder-length very blonde hair and pointed shoes. 'I'm Pippa, by the way.' She gave his hand a lingering shake. 'You're house-sitting, aren't you?'

'Yes,' he said, when she finally let go. 'I'm Marcus. Marcus Currie.'

'Marcus. Great name.'

'Is it?'

'Mm, very strong. Listen, I'm at number seven,' she pointed at a house with a nasty glass porch, 'if you need anything.'

'Oh, right. Thank you.'

Her hand slipped into her shoulder bag and pulled something out. 'I don't know if you like massages?'

Marcus's mouth opened but was unable to form a response. What was it about Jubilee Street, he wondered. Oestrogen in the water? He took the card being proffered and saw that she was, in fact, a qualified masseuse with letters after her name; just a businesswoman promoting a professional service. 'Thanks,' he said, smiling. 'I've always found massages very therapeutic.'

'I'm at Top to Toe during the day,' she informed him with a twiddle of her hair. She was quite attractive, he realised, with a very full bottom lip that gave her an alluring pout. Her eyes were enormous, although that could have been the mascara. 'But am more than happy to do a bit of extra-curricular at night,' she added. Her voice was husky and peppered with South London vowels, and managed to make 'curricular' sound pretty exciting.

Marcus rubbed his chin and pretended to read the card again. Once more he was confused and, in addition, he suddenly remembered Lucy and Dom's note.

'I think I should warn you I'm an arachnophobe,' he said. It was all he could think of.

*   *   *

Jo had witnessed the whole thing, her lace curtains having come down, for good, two hours before.

'Pathetic,' she whispered after Marcus and Pippa parted. In a parallel-parking competition, Pippa would beat her husband, and everyone else's, hands down. What, she wondered, made a woman so desperate as to pull a stunt like that?

The answer to Jo's question then appeared. Ray. Overweight and underexercised, messy-haired and carelessly dressed. He plodded across the road with his usual duck-like gait, spat on the pavement and got into the white van that was a throwback from his failed cowboy-builder days. Ray would return from the car factory in the morning, just before Pippa left for the salon. It was a perfect arrangement for the couple, once child-hood sweethearts but now the Charles and Diana of Jubilee Street. They had a student daughter, Sasha, who still came home for all the holidays. Pippa said that, for the sake of convenience, she'd wait for Sasha to graduate before leaving her husband.

Although Pippa was incredibly energetic, Ray lay at the other end of the dynamism scale. Pippa said if they learned how to graft TV remotes on to men's hands, Ray would be first in the queue. When Jo called in, there was always a full ashtray and an empty plate or two in his vicinity, and a vacant pissed-off expression on his puffy unshaved face, as though whatever he was watching was truly annoying him. Jo had no idea how Pippa stood it, but still, that didn't give her permission to hit on the new housesitter. Not when two other women had a prior claim on him. Maybe a little chat was called for. She shut down her computer, grabbed a jacket and made her way to number 7.

'Well, I never,' said Pippa, who'd swept Ray's crumbs into a dustpan, plumped up his cushions and given the armchair a good spray of Haze while Jo had been talking. 'Poor old Marcus, eh?'

Jo had told her everything, but with only a hint of the Friday-night business at her house. 'Yes,' she said. 'Anyway, he still seems to be pretty hung up on Hannah, so, as cute as he is, I think it might be playing with fire if I got involved with him.' Was Pippa getting the message? 'Wouldn't be good for *his* psyche, either,' she added for good measure.

'Hard to know.' Pippa flicked off her shoes and fell from Jo's height to around five-two, then dropped into a chair and propped her feet on Ray's pouf. 'Golly, I'm exhausted,' she sighed. 'Two of my staff are off with flu. You know, it really takes it out of you doing nine waxings, four nail extensions and five massages in a day.'

'I can imagine,' said Jo. The extent of her daytime exertion was lifting the kettle. She did, however, do an awful lot of it.

'Not to mention all the paperwork, the phone calls . . .'

Pippa's eyelids were beginning to droop, which was a little unnerving for Jo, who'd never seen her neighbour the least bit weary before. She wondered about asking her to dinner, but Pippa had an incredibly healthy diet which, when combined with Ernst and Keiko's restrictions, would leave them nothing but their placemats to eat. Was Pippa asleep now? Her eyes were closed. Maybe she'd caught the flu too, which might explain why she couldn't park earlier.

Jo got up and quietly refilled her cup from the teapot. It was a flowery affair, as were the cups and saucers, the carpet, the curtains and three-piece suite. All a bit sickly really. Borderline tacky. Jo had often found Pippa an odd, possibly evolving, char-acter: one foot in *Woman's Weekly* and the other in alfalfa and Qigong.

'That's better!' Pippa announced, eyes popping open scarily. 'Nothing like a power nap to revive you.'

'No?' said Jo, who regularly fell asleep over her work but always felt worse for it.

'So . . .' Pippa headed for the teapot, 'you say it's been nine months since Hannah left him?'

'Yep.'

'And he's still holding a candle for her, in spite of everything?'

'So it seems.'

'Hmm.' As she leaned against the dining table, Pippa tapped at her cup with a manicured nail, looking pensive. 'Would a massage help?'

'I'm fine, thanks.'

'I meant Marcus.'

'Actually,' Jo said, 'I had another idea. He let slip it was his birthday this Friday, and I thought maybe we could have a bit of a bash for him. You, me, Hannah, Freddie, my students.' The idea had, in fact, only just entered her head.

'And Robin?'

'If he wants to come.'

'Well, you can definitely count me in.'

'Great.' Jo was now quite warming to the idea. She'd get Keiko to make sushi and do some nice flower arrangements, and Ernst could go round saying, 'What'll you have?'

'You know, I think I'll give Marcus a home-treatment voucher,' said Pippa, running a chunky dried grass through her cupped hand, over and over. 'As a birthday present.'

Jo looked on suspiciously. One could never be really sure *quite* what went on in Pippa's home-treatment room.

'Then he can come when he pleases,' added Pippa worrying.

To market to market to buy a fat pig . . . tea, porridge, shampoo. I read recently that the seven-year itch now kicks in after two and a half years, people's boredom thresholds having dropped considerably. Could that explain how I fell into bed with Robin so easily? Marcus and I had been together almost three years when I applied to do teacher training in Oxford and he decided to help run his late uncle's restaurant near Braemar and we had our temporary parting of the ways.

I'm not sure we'd grown bored with one another, though, just the life we were leading. Marcus, having eventually got himself a law degree, was doing his Articles with some stuffy solicitors in Wimbledon and hating every day, and I was working for a temping agency in Central London, bouncing from one dreary bitchy office to another, dreaming of more money, more job satisfaction. Anyway, we knew we had to part for a while in order to have a nicer future, but found we missed each other dreadfully and, during a weekend together in Durham, decided we'd get married.

I wanted something quick and private and secular, but Marcus – a product of his upbringing – talked me into doing the whole church thing, just as soon as my one-year course was over. I'm not sure I can ever forgive him for that. Not now, looking back. Me, head to toe in white. All that pretentious Scottish castle stuff. It just made what happened three years later much worse somehow.

The lead-up to the wedding was a happy time. I felt loved, secure. I did well in my teaching placements and couldn't wait to join Marcus in Braemar and be married and have a job. Then, at a party at some postgrad-friend-of-a-friend's house, a softly spoken, good-looking man with dark brown eyes said he'd noticed me the other day in the university bookshop, buying Foucault. Are you doing French? he asked.

It turned out this nice bloke, Robin, was a history lecturer. He was quite self-deprecating – which I liked then, but obviously can't stand now – and was also interesting and amusing, and I found myself flattered by his attention. Recently separated from his wife, he told me. I didn't mention Marcus. We talked about French colonialism which, to be honest, made a refreshing change from wedding plans. OK, I said when, as the party broke up, he asked if he could have my phone number. It's funny how you can go along making lots of right decisions and then suddenly begin a whole string of wrong ones.

I think it's the sex I miss mostly with Marcus. Robin's adept, in a perfunctory way, but I have caught myself planning lessons in my head. I stopped faking months ago. He and his ex-wife had amazing sexual chemistry, he told me once when he'd had a few too many drinks. I can't say it bothered me.

TUESDAY

Keiko was practising 'Happy Birthday' on the piano in the middle room; always fine until she got to the third 'BIRTHday', when she faltered and hit two or three wrong chords before finding the correct one. She still had a few days to perfect it, if Jo didn't throttle her in the interim.

'Dinner's ready,' Jo called out. She'd done a kind of Chinese pork thing with noodles and exotic vegetables, from which she was now fishing bits of pork to put on Keiko's plate. 'It's going cold!' she added before Keiko had one more run-through.

'Oh, that is plenty,' said Keiko, appearing at the door. 'Thank you.'

'Are you sure?'

'I am on At-kin Diet.'

'Yes, I know. But I thought the idea was that you could eat as much as you wanted of certain things. Like meat? Here, have a little more.'

'But . . .'

'It's OK,' Jo told her, thinking Dr Atkins should have kept the word 'diet' out of his regime, so as not to confuse. 'Honestly.'

The rumble on the stairs told her Ernst was on his way, so when the doorbell rang, she let him get it, and was somewhat shocked when Hannah followed him into the kitchen.

'Hey,' Jo said, 'what a nice surprise.'

Hannah stopped in her tracks. 'Oh. You're just about to have dinner.'

'No, no, don't worry.' Jo introduced everyone, then said, 'Let's go through to the front room, shall we? Leave Ernst and Keiko to it.'

'Aren't you eating?'

'No, not hungry,' Jo lied. 'Glass of wine?' she offered, suddenly in need of a prop. Hannah had surely come to confront her.

'OK. Thanks.'

While Jo poured out the Chenin Blanc, Ernst shot her looks that might have said, 'How nicely a glass of chilled white wine would go with this splendid Chinese dish,' but she couldn't be sure.

'I shouldn't be drinking, really,' said Hannah. She had her feet tucked beside her in the big armchair while she watched Jo light a fire. 'Got preparation to do this evening. Honestly, it's relentless.'

Jo had run out of logs and was using smokeless coal. The fire was taking ages to get going but at least it was legal. 'Poor you,' she said to Hannah, 'hating your job so.' As much as Jo would rather not share her house with others, she had to admit it was better than real work.

'Yes, poor me. Although some of the brats are *almost* human.' She tittered and tucked her immaculately cut hair behind a perfect little ear. 'Anyway, I just wanted to come and have a chat.'

Jo pulled a horrified face that Hannah couldn't see. Had

Marcus confessed they'd spent an entire night together? 'Of course,' she said, turning with a smile. 'Are you OK?'

'No, to be honest.'

'Ah.'

'I know you and Marcus have become very friendly.'

'Nothing's happened between us,' Jo said, a bit too defensively. 'Not my type,' she added with a laugh, then wondered if that was a bit rude.

'No, I know nothing's happened. Not really. Marcus told me that you got him drunk and things turned a bit silly.'

Jo managed to stay composed. 'Oh, yes?'

'Mm. He also said you've got a boyfriend. Have I met him?'

Jo shook her head. If Hannah had met Bram, she'd have remembered. 'He's away a lot.'

'Ah. Well, I just wondered if Marcus has said anything about, you know, *me*. Him and me? Sometimes I can't make out what's going on in his head.'

Jo breathed out at last and hoisted herself from the floor to the sofa. 'Only that he's absolutely potty about you.'

Hannah grinned. 'And has he mentioned being involved with anyone? You know, back in Scotland? Or someone he's keen on?'

'Nope.'

'Or has anyone got their eye on him?'

Jo chose to discount half of Jubilee Street. 'Not as far as I know.'

'Well, that's good. I'd hate to make some huge decision, only to find there's a bloody woman in Marcus's life.'

'No,' said Jo. 'I don't suppose you would, but what about . . .'

'What?'

'Well, Robin.'

'Ah yes, Robin. Look, I know he's your friend and all that,

51

but to be honest, Jo, we're chalk and cheese. I messed up big time there. Anyway, he'd be all right. He could have Freddie for a while in the holidays, I suppose. If he insists. I mean, Robin did without Fred for his first two and a half years.'

Jo looked on stunned, trying to work out if Hannah was just a bit self-absorbed, or totally. 'Listen,' she said, 'I think I'll go and check on Ernst and—'

'Oh, don't worry, I'll be off now.' Hannah drained her glass, slipped her feet back into her elegant boots, stood up and kind of swirled herself back into her classy long coat. Jo felt she'd give anything to be that graceful.

'Excuse me, Jo,' they suddenly heard Ernst say, his face poking round the door. 'But I have finished my first course, as well as Keiko's. And I'm not sure, but maybe yours too.'

Jo, made even more peckish by the glass of wine, gave a disappointed, 'Oh.'

'It was very good. Better than Shanghai House takeaway.'

'Thanks,' said Jo. Quite a compliment.

After seeing Hannah out, Jo made her way to the kitchen and found Ernst helping himself to Ben and Jerry's, and Keiko helping herself to the washing up. She stood watching them for a while and a kind of maternal affection welled up in her, quite unexpectedly. This was what it must be like to have teenage children, she thought. Only not quite, because these two were helpful and polite and didn't say, '*Shit*, there's someone I know,' and dive down in the car when she took them out. How bad Jo felt at having done that to her parents so many times.

'Have you got homework tonight?' she asked.

Keiko shook her head and smiled. 'No. So, very luckily, I can practise more with "Happy Birthday".'

'Great,' said Jo, wondering where she could go. Marcus's?

*   *   *

'Come in. I'm just packing,' he said.

'What? Where are you going?'

'To the Cotswolds, tomorrow and Thursday. To do a bit of walking.'

'Ah. God, I'd love to do that.'

'Would you?'

'Mm, I adore going on long country rambles, but do you know how difficult it is for a woman to walk somewhere remote on her own?'

'I can imagine you might feel vulnerable. Well, why don't you come then?'

Jo's heart gave a leap. She wasn't sure if it was Marcus or the idea of a ramble. 'Yeah?'

'I was going to ask you to feed Maidstone but I suppose I can leave him masses of that dried stuff.'

'And I'm sure my students could look after themselves for one evening. I'll leave them money for a pizza or something.'

'It'd be nice to have the company. Got suitable footwear?'

'Yep,' said Jo, trying to picture where they might stay. A low-beamed inn with a log fire and a stag's head on the wall. There'd be a big old bed with huge pillows and a tapestry spread . . .

'Good,' he said. 'Nothing worse than walking with someone moaning about their feet all the time.'

'Don't worry. I'm quite hardy, as long as I'm wrapped up.'

'Oh, right, the thin-skin thing.'

'Listen, are you sure about this?'

'Absolutely. Are you?'

'Absolutely.'

Robin was trying to read a dense first novel that had received critical acclaim as well as Hannah's strong recommendation. He was about a quarter of the way into it and, so far, the book had involved unbelievable and unlikeable characters with ridiculous names, and not a whiff of a plot.

Hannah, sitting opposite, looked up from her writing. How she loved to scribble away in that new diary of hers, stopping occasionally to chew on her pen, deep in thought. The journal, or whatever, was always carefully locked after use, and the key secreted away somewhere Robin would never know. Still, as long as it worked. Adrian had suggested it as part of the therapy, apparently. Hannah was no doubt unleashing all sorts of bottled-up childhood anxieties on to those pages. Getting it out of her system. She looked up at him, perhaps sensing his eyes on her.

'Enjoying it?' she asked, nodding towards the hefty novel.

'Very much.'

'Terrific characters, aren't they?'

'Mm, terrific.'

'Don't you find Figgy Flybright totally fascinating?'

'Ah-ha,' he laughed. 'Yes.'

She went back to her writing and Robin frowned at his book, flicking it over to read the synopsis on the back. Who? He speed-read the blurb, but there was no mention of a Figgy Flybright. Oh well, with a bit of luck he or she would pop up later and turn this into his all-time favourite novel.

Robin had always had a problem with fiction. Even as a child he'd preferred books on the Second World War to Desperate Dan. Later, when all his friends were into *Portnoy's Complaint*, Robin would be devouring Pepys. And what, he'd often wondered, was the point of Dickens, when you had Booth's fascinating survey of life and labour in nineteenth-century London?

He turned a page – God, it was tedious – then looked up. 'Was that Freddie?' he asked Hannah.

She stopped writing and tilted her head to listen. 'I didn't hear anything, but I'll go, shall I?'

Robin snapped his book shut, not particularly caring that he'd lose his place. 'No, no, you stay put.'

Of course Freddie was dead to the world, all cherubic and adorable. Robin sat beside the bed for a while, just staring at his little miracle. What could he be dreaming about, he wondered. Having his very own shed?

Just write whatever comes into your head, Adrian said towards the end of our second session. Address it to me, or yourself, or to no one in particular. Try and do it every day. If you can't think of anything to say or if it becomes too difficult, too painful, just scribble a nursery rhyme or shopping list or some-thing – anything to keep the writing going. But obviously we want it to be cathartic, so don't just be writing nursery rhymes. And do try not to avoid painful subjects or episodes.

Undoubtedly, the most painful episode of all was leaving, last June. Marcus went out for the day without saying where – he didn't take the car, so for a walk, presumably – and my parents came and collected us. We're going to stay with Granny and Granddad for a while, I told Freddie, and he got all excited at the prospect, standing on the sofa to watch for them through the window for a full hour before the two of them arrived, a lot later than planned, exhausted and bitterly disap-pointed in their daughter, but stoically trying not to show it. Sometimes I wish they wouldn't be so bloody British about everything.

Marcus's timing couldn't have been worse. Thinking we'd be well on our way, he returned just as the last of the toys – Fred's pedal car – was being squeezed into the boot. The look on his face said it all, and I almost told Dad to take everything out again, we'd be staying. But then Freddie and Marcus were having one last cuddle and tears were filling Marcus's eyes, and mine and my mother's, and it was just . . . awful. Jack and Jill went up the hill . . . Jack fell down. Poor Jack. Poor me. I had to leave, didn't I? No one was speaking to me, least of all Marcus. But he never actually asked me to go. They all froze me out, though, the bastards. Soap powder, pan scourers, maple syrup. Maple syrup – would Freddie like that?

I think he must have gone back to sleep. Can't hear anything. I can tell Robin isn't into Divine and Conquered, *and is reading it, or pretending to, just to please me. When I tested him with a character I'd made up just now, he rather gave the game away. He's trying to be nice, but has no idea how infuriating I find that. What I once thought of as Robin's sensitivity, I now see as a kind of cowardice. He's back and picking up the novel again – my cue to yawn and say I think I'll turn in. If he offers to make us both a nice hot milky drink, I swear I'll scream.*

WEDNESDAY

As they headed west, Marcus wasn't exactly panicking, just fairly apprehensive about the venture. Jo, however, was chatty and excited as she pored over maps and walking guides, and it occurred to him that maybe she didn't get out of town much, what with the lodgers.

It was only for two days, he told himself. And, if they didn't hit it off for some reason, it would be just forty-odd miles back to Oxford. But no, that wasn't it. He was feeling bad about Hannah, that was the problem. Disloyal. Even though he'd called her earlier on her mobile and told her all about it. 'I'm sure Jo will be a great walking companion,' Hannah had said breezily. 'Have fun, won't you? Listen, got to go to class now. See you Friday.'

Fortunately, the further they got from Oxford, the more Marcus found himself relaxing and looking forward to a hike. They certainly couldn't have asked for better walking weather. It was all of a sudden bright and quite warm, as though someone – God? – had cleared his throat and politely informed the forgetful old sun that the first day of spring had come and gone.

The back of the car had been loaded with holdalls and ruck-sacks and, somewhat puzzlingly to Marcus, two carrier bags of food. 'I eat a lot when I walk,' Jo explained. 'Fuel.' Marcus had nodded and hoped he wouldn't gallantly volunteer to carry it.

'Anyway, listen,' she was saying now, head still bowed, 'I've found this brilliant-sounding circular walk. It's number twenty-four in my book, which means it's quite long, as they start with the shorter ones and—'

'How long?'

'Um . . . fourteen point five miles.'

'What!' No wonder she'd brought so many provisions.

'Too long?' she asked.

'I'll say.'

'OK, there's this other one that's ten point—'

'Down a bit.'

Jo reversed through the pages a way, then looked over at him and laughed. 'I thought you were a tough, energetic and adven-turous Scot?'

'Well,' he said, taking the turning he'd planned all along, towards the B and B and the six-mile walk he'd planned all along. 'You'd be right on one count.'

'Scot?'

'Yep.'

The landlady assumed they'd be sharing a room, but Marcus explained they'd need two singles. He was very apologetic, having booked only himself in over the phone.

'Are you sure?' Jo whispered in his ear. 'Wouldn't it be cheaper to share? Twin beds, of course.'

'It's the same price,' he whispered back. 'And, anyway, you snore.'

'I do not!'

'You're lucky the schools haven't broken up for Easter yet,' the landlady was saying. They were following her upstairs for an inspection. 'We're fully booked from the end of next week.'

Marcus didn't quite get the connection, as they weren't exactly in family-holiday country, so could only assume lots of child-less teachers headed Weston-on-the-Wold way.

'But I can certainly give you two tonight,' she added, opening a door with 'Lilac Room' on it, to a single room with a single bed and a single wardrobe, but not a single bit of space to manoeuvre. She'd obviously gone to an enormous amount of trouble with the décor, though, scouring the land for as many ruched things in different shades of lilac as she could find.

'Very nice,' said Jo. 'Why don't you take this one, Marcus?'

'Well, let's just see—'

'And here we have the Pink Room,' the woman said, step-ping across the landing and pushing open a second door.

Marcus popped his head in and saw that the Pink Room was, if anything, smaller and slightly frillier than the first, and that it lived up to its name admirably. He swung round and zoomed back to the first room before Jo had a chance to, and had his clothes strewn all over the lilac eiderdown by the time she entered.

'Oh, let's not bother unpacking now,' she said. She sat on the edge of the bed and began lacing up boots that looked as though they might have covered the whole of Nepal. How he'd got the impression Jo was a bit of a sloth, he wasn't sure. 'I'll just see if the landlady will fill my flask,' she added. 'See you downstairs in five?'

'Er . . .' he said, and she'd gone.

The lunch break has shrunk to fifty minutes. We grab food, have a coffee, tea, smoke, or whatever, and are back in the classroom before you can say, 'It used to be an hour and a half when I was a schoolgirl!' I remember sometimes opting for 'home dinners' and would amble back to my house, share a leisurely meal with Mum, and still have time back at school for skipping.

Today I'm not hungry, so have just got a coffee in a corner of the staffroom, trying not to feel extremely pissed off by Marcus going away with Jo. It's platonic, I'm sure. And, anyway, who am I to object? Marcus, after all, is the one with all the Brownie points. Depressing that I can't possibly catch up with him. Going back to Marcus would gain me points, but in taking Freddie from Robin, I'd lose even more. Hopeless. And so unfair. Adrian told me to focus on the positive, but didn't get round to pointing out what that might be.

I suppose she's quite pretty, Jo, in a kind of gangling, pseudo-hippy way. Mid-thirties? Hard to tell, since everyone looks so young these days. But what a conniving cow, not even mentioning this Cotswold trip yesterday evening. Is the whole world duplicitous? You have to wonder.

Mustn't think about Marcus moving in with her when his house-sit is up. Bath cleaner, bread, Marmite, ginger biscuits, juice. Things we do need, in fact – must make separate list before that effing bell goes.

'So are you sure everything's all right?' Jo shouted at Ernst on her mobile. She wasn't sure she needed to shout, but something about Ernst made her do that. She could hear Keiko on the piano in the background, still not quite managing that chord. She thought she heard the doorbell too.

'Everything is fine,' Ernst told her. 'Danielle, hi! Mimi, hi! Go on through. Come in, come in, Ahmed. Good to see you.'

'Ernst?' called out Jo. She was in her very pink room, stretched out on the bed after their walk and fairly surprised to find her phone had a signal.

'Cool, you have brought beers. Not such a good Muslim, ha ha.'

Jo heard the door slam. 'Ernst?'

'Sorry, Jo. Yes. Just go to the kitchen, Ahmed. Everyone else is in there.'

'What do you mean, "everyone else"?' asked Jo, when her phone suddenly died on her. 'Ernst?'

'I'm sure they'll behave themselves,' Marcus reassured her over their dinner. It was the usual simple menu of a modest country pub: *Roasted Quail with Juniper Berries, Grilled Shark Teriyaki.* Jo had gone for the *Armenian Pumpkin Stew* and wasn't regretting it, but Marcus seemed to be struggling with his *Chipirones en su Tinta*, which, if he'd only asked, he would have discovered to be squid in their own ink.

'I know, I know,' she said. 'They're all adults, of sorts. And I'm sure Keiko would scrub the place clean till dawn if necessary.' She took a swig of rip-off wine and watched Marcus's lemon-sucking expression. 'Look, we could swap meals, if you like?'

'Could we?'

She hadn't been expecting that response, but nevertheless handed over her plate and took his. She wouldn't have done that for just anybody, but they'd had such a lovely walk together. Well, not quite together, as his pace had often been slower than hers. Every now and then they'd level-pegged and chatted for a while. Yes, it *had* been nice. Too nice. And on top of that, this evening, amid flickering candles and the glow of firelight, he was looking so very shaggable.

'Thanks,' he said with that smile.

Jo was forcing herself not to be flirty with him, though. His response to her twin-bed suggestion had let her know the score in no uncertain terms, and she respected him for it. No way was she now going to stir up trouble and humiliate herself in the process. 'What kind of food do you serve in your restaurant?' she asked.

'It depends on who the chef is. They come and go. I don't get involved in that side of things. I just do the admin – ordering, marketing, the accounts. Anyway, we're doing Italian at the moment.'

'Don't customers get a bit confused? I mean, if you go back to a restaurant, it's because you liked what they offered, isn't it?'

'Well, the tourists don't care and the locals tell us they like the surprise element. Hey, this pumpkin stew's great.'

'Isn't it,' she said, quite wanting it back.

'It's not something I plan to do for the rest of my life,' he went on, 'helping run a restaurant. Tell the truth, I've pretty much had enough of it. That's part of the reason I'm taking this break. To have a think about what to do. Unfortunately, I'll have to go back, at least for a while. It's all hands to the deck in summer, right through to the Highland Games. We get a lot of royal watchers.'

'Balmoral?'

'Mm. And then there are all the walkers and climbers.'

'And where do you live?'

'Above the restaurant, which is a little way out of Braemar. It was my late uncle's restaurant. Well, more of a café when he had it. My mother inherited the lot when he died, but it was all a bit run down. We did the flat up, Hannah and I, when we were first married. She was pregnant and we made a great little nursery for Freddie. I think if they'd stayed we'd have had to move to something bigger eventually but, you know, it's fine for just me. All on my own.'

Marcus was sounding very matter-of-fact, but had stopped eating, Jo noticed, and was tapping the edge of his plate with his knife. She put a hand over his to stop him. 'I'm sure she loves you a lot.'

'Yeah, well, maybe.'

Jo uncovered his hand and picked up her wine. 'You know, Marcus, these things have a way of sorting themselves out.'

He raised a quizzical eyebrow at her.

'Yeah, yeah,' she said. 'I hate people who say things like that too. OK then, you've got yourselves into a horrible unsolvable situation, and it's going to make you miserable for the rest of your lives, so you may as well come to terms with it.'

Marcus looked down, stabbed at his food with his fork, then held up a piece of mouth-watering pumpkin between them. 'Actually,' he said, 'I'd prefer a platitude, if that's all right with you?'

She gave him a quick peck on the cheek outside his room, and said, 'Night. See you at breakfast,' before disappearing through her door.

'Good night,' he called out, surprised. He'd assumed they'd share the bottle of wine he'd packed, drinking it from the teacups provided in each room; carry on chatting till quite late. He hadn't imagined hitting the sack at – he checked his watch – 9.50.

Jo reappeared with a washbag and said, 'Bagsy first in the bathroom!'

'Yeah, go ahead,' he told her, still wondering what to do for the next couple of hours. He unlocked his door, thought better of switching the light on, and groped in his bag for the book he'd brought with him. He then locked up again and headed back to the pub they'd just left.

As he walked down the village's ancient main street, past tiny stone cottages and huge stone cottages, all of them weighted with history, Marcus wondered at the wisdom of picking *The Sexual Life of Catherine M* off Lucy and Dom's bookshelf. Incongruous, somehow. Plus, sad enough to be in a lonely corner of the pub with a solitary beer, but maybe entering perv territory to be reading erotica as well. He'd hide the cover, he told himself. Or, better still, get into conversation with someone.

When he approached the White Hart, he pushed Catherine deep into his jacket pocket and tried to recall if he'd ever heard anyone over ten say 'bagsy'.

'I *will* not go to his room on a pretext,' Jo affirmed one more time. 'Too degrading. And, besides, there's Hannah. Mind you, she's got Robin. No, no, I will *not* play second fiddle. Definitely not.'

She slapped another thick layer of face cream on as a kind of insurance, and carried on reading her whodunit. She thought it was probably Jason, the deceased's half-brother, who stood to inherit the Wiltshire estate and had a flimsy alibi. But then she always went for the red herring in these things.

After a while, she glanced at her travel alarm clock. It was 11.15 and her eyes were growing heavy, which was good. When she went back to the book, the words started swerving around and she gave up, closed it, switched off the light, clasped her hands and said a 'thank you' to God for keeping things simple between herself and Marcus. 'However,' she went on in a slow, deep-breathing whisper, 'if you have any of that potion, like, you know the one in *A Midsummer Night's Dream* – the stuff that makes people fall in love with the first person, or donkey, they see when they wake up – well, perhaps you'd see fit to use some on Mar . . .'

The next thing she heard was a tap, tap, tap at her door, and her heart thumped wildly from the shock of it. 'Sshhh!' she said, swinging herself out of bed.

His mother, Moira, drove me mad with her fussiness, and was always telling me things I was perfectly well aware of, thank you. Obviously, Freddie's cot should go against the inner wall of the nursery, away from the slightly draughty window. Yes, it was wise to take a first aid kit out in the car, when we were so far from a hospital.

She'd come round and tidy our kitchen cupboards, which left me gobsmacked the first time and fuming after that. But only once did I march her to the door with a 'Look, maybe some other time?' Mind you, I have to admit she had quite a knack for grouping things handily – for example, everything you could possibly want to make gravy or sauces on one shelf, pasta, rice and pulses on another. Herbs and spices would be graded from most used at the front to only used at Christmas at the back. When she stopped visiting the flat altogether – as they all did – I almost missed the interfering biddy sorting things out.

I shouldn't be up this late, not with work tomorrow, but am being tortured – despite taking two of Dr Maxwell's chill pills – by images of Marcus and bitch Jo making other-worldly love in an Elizabethan four-poster with flimsy curtains.

FRIDAY

Robin was in Jo's middle room, listening to Freddie rampaging over the piano keys. 'Very good,' he said, which encouraged Freddie to bash away more wildly and at greater volume. Robin got up and shut the door. He wasn't that keen on joining in the celebrations, anyway. Although he felt it was nice for Freddie and Hannah to still be part of Marcus's life, he couldn't help wishing the chap had had his birthday at a more convenient time. Two weeks ago would have been good.

He sat back down in a half-upholstered armchair, avoiding the pins, and carried on perusing the interesting things Jo kept in her middle room. Aside from the upright walnut piano, there was a tailor's dummy, an easel, a knitting machine and a collection of things for brewing beer in. On the windowsill were seed trays, and on top of the piano sat *Calligraphy Made Easy, Volume I*. Either Jo frenetically spent her leisure time making music, jumpers and lager, or she took up and dropped an awful lot of hobbies. On closer inspection, most things had a fairly unused look about them.

Freddie's discordant playing was beginning to grate, so Robin hoisted himself from the chair and went and sat beside him on the piano stool. 'OK, Fred, that's enough,' he said. 'Fred!' The little boy stopped at the unusual sound of his father's raised voice. 'Right,' continued Robin. 'Now, how would you like to learn "Baa, Baa, Black Sheep"?'

Freddie pulled a face. 'Can you learn me how to do "Wheels on the Bus"?'

'Sorry, Fred. Don't know that one.'

'It's like this,' Freddie said, and began singing it.

'Yes, I know the song, Fred, but let's play "Baa, Baa, Black Sheep", eh? It's nice and easy and you can play it with one finger. Like this. Watch. You put your finger on that key first. It's called Middle C.'

'But I want you to learn me "Wheels on the Bus". *Pleeze*, Daddy. It's my best.'

'*Teach* me, Freddie. Not learn me. Look, I'm sorry, but I only know "Baa, Baa, Black Sheep".'

'Mummy played me "Wheels on the Bus" when we went to Granny and Granddad's.'

'Yes, but Mummy's got her grade eight piano. Daddy hasn't. Daddy's good at other things. OK, let's have a go at "Baa, Baa, Black Sheep", shall we? Finger on Middle C. Finger, not thumb, Fred. No, just one finger.'

'Oh, I'm sorry,' said Jo's Japanese student at the door. 'Excuse me. But it is time for cake and "Happy Birthday" tune on piano.'

'Yes, of course,' said Robin, whisking his son off the stool as people wandered into the room carrying glasses, followed by Jo with a large cake ablaze with candles. Quite a lot, Robin was pleased to see.

Marcus was looking forward to a break from the women, if only for the time it took them to sing 'Happy Birthday'. Hannah had been surprisingly attentive and tactile, considering Robin was there, and the Pippa woman had stood behind him and massaged his shoulders for an entire, rather one-sided conversation on detox diets. As for Jo, well, she was being pleasant but a little distant. Maybe because Hannah was there, but more likely on account of the incident in the Pink Room the other night after he'd consumed way too much *Catherine M* in a corner of the pub. She'd responded to his taps at her door, let him in with a 'Shhh, you'll wake everyone else up too,' and led him the two steps to her bed in the darkness, where they'd fallen in a clinch and hungrily sought out each other's lips. But when Marcus found his cheeks, nose, chin and everything else swimming around in a sea of something unpleasantly warm and sticky, he'd pulled back with a 'Yeeuchh'.

'Oh, shoot, my face cream,' she'd said sleepily, before heaving herself up and over him and leaving the room.

When she returned, cream wiped off, they'd had a laugh about it before chastely kissing each other good night again. No mention was made of the incident the following day during their gruelling nine-miler.

But now she'd unexpectedly come over and was clinging on to him as they all sang 'Happy Birthday'. She seemed tense, he noticed; her nails digging uncomfortably into his arm until the song finished, when she let go, rushed over to Keiko at the piano and gave her an inexplicable hug.

Everyone then grouped around the cake and Marcus managed to blow his candles out in one long puff, while the multi-tasking Keiko took photos. When someone put a knife in his hand he plunged it into the cake and, as he did so, his spare arm was hooked by Hannah.

'Did you make a wish?' she asked quietly.

'Oh yes,' he said, turning and giving her a tender look. He'd forgotten to, in fact, but was doing it now. Hannah and Freddie coming back to him, with Robin happily turning into a convivial visiting-uncle figure . . . maybe.

'Here, Marcus,' said Pippa, eyes wide, mouth somewhere between a smile and a pout. 'Happy Birthday.'

He put the knife down and took an envelope from her, expecting just a card but also finding inside a voucher for one massage at 7 Jubilee Street. His heart sank. 'Hey, that's great!' he said. He let her kiss his cheek, then added, 'You shouldn't have.'

'Come along any time,' she told him, kissing the other cheek. He felt the full force of her chest against his, before his attention was taken up by Keiko handing him a string of origami birds.

'I have made them especially for you,' she said with a giggle, a cocked head and a twinkle in her eye. Was she coming on to him too? He'd always been baffled by Japanese girls. Keen to bag a Western husband or just incredibly sweet?

'Thank you,' he said, while she snapped him – once, twice, three times – holding up the string of birds. 'How clever of you.'

Marcus was beginning to feel a bit overwhelmed, and after Pippa and Keiko wandered off, longed to go and join the fat bloke watching a gardening programme in the front room. When Jo came over he asked who the man was.

'Ray,' she said. 'Pippa's husband.'

'No!'

'Hard to believe, isn't it? She calls him her current husband, so watch out.'

Marcus slipped Pippa's voucher deep into his shirt pocket. If it went through a 60-degree wash cycle, she might refuse to accept it.

*   *   *

Seven people, a child and a couch potato did not a party make, decided Jo. It was all rather quiet and strained which, given the relationship tangles, wasn't surprising. If only she hadn't shot off to the Cotswolds for two days, she might have got round to inviting a few extra friends and neighbours. A bit insulting to go knocking on Conrad's door at this late stage, or to phone Jez and Alice. 'Hi, I don't suppose you'd like to come to a party? . . . Well, actually it's going on now. We're a bit short, you see.' Jo had an idea, though. She manoeuvred Ernst into the hall and had a word, and within seconds he was chatting away on his mobile.

'I know, Ahmed,' he chuckled. 'I am very lucky with my landlady. OK. Tell the others and bring more beers, yeah?'

'Thanks, Ernst,' Jo said, before rejoining the very quiet group in the middle room. 'Hey, does anyone play the piano?' she called out, then pretended not to see Keiko raise a tentative hand.

'Hannah's very good,' said Marcus. 'Aren't you?'

'Oh, no, I'd be far too rusty.'

'Nonsense,' chipped in Robin.

'Play "Wheels on the Bus", Mummy?' shouted Freddie.

Jo crossed to the piano stool and opened it up. 'I've got a Beatles songbook, somewhere.' She rummaged through her untouched-for-years sheet music and took it out. 'Here.'

'Oh, all right,' said Hannah with a shrug. She came over to Jo, gave her the meanest of looks – another one – snatched the book and sat on the stool. 'But first "Wheels on the Bus" for Freddie.'

Freddie jumped on the spot with excitement and then, when the song began, everyone followed his lead with the words and the actions. It was great fun, and quite long, Jo was pleased to discover. After the wheels had gone round and the horn had beeped and the wipers had swished and the bell had dinged, and so on, all eight people in the room applauded. It was only when the noise died down and Hannah was flicking through the Beatles songbook, that they heard the very loud and agitated voices coming through the wall. Jo's heart raced, before she recognised the distinctive sound of *EastEnders*.

'Oh, for Christ's sake . . .' said Pippa, storming from the room.

After six of Ernst's classmates rolled up, the event went in a whole different direction. The Beatles songs had gone down well but had, at the same time, clearly hit the nail on the head, pressed buttons, and in the case of 'Yesterday', turned on the waterworks for Hannah.

Now, at ten past ten, after Ray had long since slouched home, they were all dancing to an ancient mixed tape of Jo's in a dimly lit kitchen. Even Robin, Jo was pleased to see. Marcus had an attractive Spanish girl gyrating in front of him, Pippa and Hannah dancing on either side of him and Freddie on his shoulders, and seemed to be having a pretty good birthday. Jo herself was dancing with Ahmed, who moved like a dream, but didn't stop her craving a slow dance with Marcus.

When, all of a sudden, Eric Clapton was singing about how wonderful she looked tonight, Jo excused herself and crossed the kitchen. But by the time she got to Marcus, he and several competing women had formed a sort of linked-arm dance. It looked somewhere between 'Auld Lang Syne' and a rugby scrum and didn't seem to be working that well, so when Robin hoisted Freddie from Marcus's shoulders and left the kitchen, Jo followed them into the middle room.

'I think I should get this little chap to bed,' Robin said. 'No, Fred. No more piano playing. Let's find your coat. And where did you leave your toolbox?'

'I put it by the front door,' said Jo, picking Freddie's coat out of a pile. 'I'm really pleased you came, you know, Robin. I wasn't sure . . .'

He gave her a warm smile. 'No, neither was I. But, it's been fun. I managed to chat with Marcus for a while, which was good.'

'Yes, I saw.'

'He called in the other day, but it was a bit awkward. Nice chap, though.'

'Yes.'

'Anyway, we talked about Scotland. My son's at Edinburgh. And a bit about sport.' Robin ran a sleeve up a tired-looking Freddie's arm. 'But not about why he's suddenly hanging out in Oxford. Nothing personal. Typical men, eh?'

Jo laughed. 'Yes.'

He eased Freddie's other arm into the coat and looked up at her from where he was kneeling. 'I don't suppose you know, do you?'

'What?'

'Why he's here?'

Jo, suddenly wishing she'd joined Marcus's entourage, said, 'I think he just wanted to see Freddie.'

'That's what Hannah says, but she's behaving weirdly.'

She certainly was. Hannah had elbowed Jo in the ribs during the cake-cutting, pretending it was an accident. 'Oops, sorry,' she'd said. 'Thought you were the curtain in that outfit.' Jo's stripy top did indeed resemble her stripy curtains, but anyway, what kind of a person went around jabbing at curtains? One who suspected the curtains of sleeping with her bloke, presumably.

'Is she?' Jo said to Robin. He was pulling Freddie's hood up and fastening a popper. Although keen to know more, she found herself slowly backing towards the door. Where were the guests wanting directions to the bathroom when you needed them? 'Well,' she said when she got to it, 'thank you so much for coming to the party, Freddie.' She held out a hand to him. 'I expect you'd like to say goodbye to Marcus?'

'Yes, let's,' said Robin enthusiastically. He probably wanted to break up the love-in as much as she did.

After he'd kissed Freddie's cheek and shaken Robin's hand, Marcus turned back to his fellow dancers. Why he'd been uncomfortable with all the female attention earlier, he didn't know. It was great. Of course, he couldn't be sure they weren't just being nice because it was his birthday. But, whatever, it was a great ego-boost, and to have a semi-dressed, black-haired young Spanish beauty cavorting before you was something to be appreciated. He was, in fact, having a ball. When had he last been touched so often and by so many people? Playing rugby seventeen years ago? Of course that was all blokes and these were all birds. A whole flock. All to himself! He stopped and swigged at his lager bottle, then looked around briefly for Jo. Still seeing Robin out, perhaps. It was a bit odd that Hannah hadn't left with him. But then maybe it wasn't, Marcus thought, throwing himself back into the dance he'd cultivated aged sixteen and stuck with ever since.

When someone put reggae on there was a big cheer and even shy Keiko, who'd spent most of the evening finding things to wash up, came and danced with him. She *was* very sweet, he decided. Hannah, beside her, looked gorgeous, and Pippa was being vampish, regularly running her hands over her buttocks in lap-dancer mode. Not that he'd ever seen a lap dancer. In fact, Marcus was beginning to think he'd been leading far too sheltered a life. Could Oxford provide a new and exciting milieu for him? He slipped an arm around

Hannah's waist and was making sexy eye contact with the Spanish girl when someone all of a sudden yelled, 'Bram!' over the music.

It was Jo, now on the far side of the kitchen. She dropped what she was doing and, with the biggest smile, hurried towards Marcus. Well, towards the door behind him.

'Oh my God, it's Bram!' cried Pippa, as Marcus spun round and caught sight of a very tall black guy – coffee-coloured, maybe – with a head of small tight dreads. Pippa handed Marcus her glass and was off. Within seconds, Jo was up in the man's arms, legs wrapped around his waist, and Pippa was planting a kiss on his cheek.

Marcus stood still and blinked, finding it hard to adjust to the sudden change in atmosphere. Only a minute ago he'd been in the midst of the sensual and highly charged, but now the music had gone down and someone had switched on a stark overhead light. Possibly Bram. Marcus heard Keiko sighing beside him. 'Aahh, Bram. Very handsome.'

'You think so?' he asked, but then saw that even the Spanish girl had stopped her dance marathon and was staring at the latest guest with *mucho gusto*.

'Hey, everyone,' Jo was saying as she untangled herself from her man, 'this is Bram.'

Bram beamed a very white smile and waved. 'Hello, everyone,' he said in a voice much too deep and resonant for Marcus's liking.

'Hello, Bram!' shouted all the foreign students.

Marcus then turned to Hannah on the other side of him and found that she too was glued to the newcomer, with an expression similar to the Spanish girl's. 'Wow,' she was saying as she groped, without looking, for her glass of wine on the worktop.

*   *   *

With Freddie tucked up and fast asleep, Robin settled in an armchair with *Divine and Conquered* and something of a heavy heart. Not so much heavy, perhaps, as unsettled. He turned over a page he hadn't really read and thought back to the relative stability he'd been enjoying just a week ago: his little family unit pottering along nicely. It was all so easy compared to his first attempt at living with someone. None of the high drama of his marriage to Judith. No affairs (Judith's), plates hurtling his way, or week-long sulks (Judith's again). He'd loved his wife with a passion he could never feel for Hannah, but how much better *not* to feel too much in the way of possessiveness or jealousy with one's partner. So much more relaxing.

Obviously, there was a physical attraction between himself and Hannah – a little more on his side, perhaps – and, despite their differing political stances, they could engage for hours in affable discussions about the state of the world. Conversations dotted with, 'Mm, yes, I see what you mean . . .' or, 'Good point!' They'd never rowed, as far as he could recall. Although Hannah would return from school some days and rant in a surprisingly foul-mouthed way, Robin had never personally felt the force of her venom. Whenever he'd caught the odd dismissive look from her that might have been interpreted as *God, you're a pillock*, or *Christ, you bore me, Robin*, he tended to put it down to Hannah's work-related fatigue and despair, and tried even harder to make her home life run as smoothly and pleasantly as possible.

A couple of days back he'd suggested she find another job, or maybe stay home with Freddie for a while. They could scrape by on his salary, even taking into account his having to support Theo at university. Also, he'd pointed out, if she wasn't teaching they might not have to fork out for the shrink she was seeing and those pills she took. He'd received one of her dismissive looks then, he recalled. 'You think teaching's the biggest problem?' she'd sighed before opening up her diary and going incommunicado on him again.

Anyway, their life together was relatively tranquil, and that was what he liked most about it. *Had* liked about it.

It was Freddie he was passionate about now, of course. With an emotional chasm and several hundred miles between Marcus and Hannah, Robin had felt relatively secure as he'd grown to know his son. Grown to love his son too, and wonder in his development and try to teach him things, such as – before they'd set off for the party today – basic time-telling. Freddie hadn't quite been able to distinguish the little from the big hand on Robin's Tissot, but it had been fun.

Now Marcus – still officially Hannah's husband – was a matter of yards away and dancing with her. Yes, it was all too unsettling. Where would he stand if she decided to go back to him? What access rights would he be given? What would be the chances that he could keep Freddie? Zero, probably, judging from those desperate disaffected fathers who'd mounted cranes and thrown condoms at the PM.

Robin turned another unread page and glanced at his watch again. The little hand was on the twelve and the big hand on the two. Funny. Most Friday nights saw Hannah wrung out and in bed before both hands reached the ten.

MONDAY

In the village of Laroche-les-Bois it was raining cold rain for the fifth day in a row, and Bertrand was still having trouble getting hold of the floor tiles Lucy and Dom wanted to run through the whole of downstairs. He'd be sure to find them in Montpellier, he'd assured them, and off he'd gone in his battered Peugeot. That had been early yesterday and there'd been no sign of him since. In Bertrand's absence the electricity had conked out again, owing to his recent wiring job, and there was still a sheet of plastic where the back door should have been, owing to his mismeasuring the first time and having to reorder. Lucy and Dom wanted to go home. Desperately.

'Any luck?' Lucy asked when Dom returned from using Madame Bouziges's phone, three houses along.

He shook his head. 'Still the machine. I'm beginning to wonder if we actually have a housesitter.'

'What an awful thought,' Lucy said, picturing Maidstone all skeletal and scratching limply at neighbours' doors.

'I'll go back and try Jo. What's her number?'

Lucy wrote it down for him and he disappeared again, leaving her in the semi-darkness of the house they'd had such great plans for until the wonderful, skilful, super-efficient young Claude had decided he'd rather be an air-traffic controller than a builder and went off to Clermont-Ferrand to train, leaving Bertrand in charge. All Claude's work looked good and worked well because he was painstaking and thorough in everything he did – just the kind of person you'd want guiding your plane in, in fact. But, with Bertrand having made zero progress since their last stay, at Christmas, Lucy and Dom were keen to pay him off and look for another local builder with a good reputation. Unfortunately, they couldn't find one and, added to that, there were feelings to be considered. Bertrand was the widowed Madame Bouziges's father-in-law, and Madame Bouziges, Claude's aunt and a total gem, had been promised the job of cleaner/keeper of keys when Lucy and Dom started letting the house to holidaymakers.

Some hope, thought Lucy, tugging a jumper of Dom's on over her own and staring gloomily at the cold and cavernous living/dining area with its fabulous beams and wonderfully rustic walls. One day it would be terrific. But when? They'd told all their friends about this amazing place they'd bought and now there was a waiting list of people wanting to stay there. 'Just needs a bit more work,' Lucy would say, but always held back on telling them just how much work, in case they lost interest and wandered off. They had to start getting rent for it soon as they were mortgaged to the hilt on both their houses. Their only hope was that Claude would fail some vital air-traffic controlling test and come hurrying home.

Lucy placed another log on the open fire – the one thing that had been keeping their spirits up – and settled back into her armchair with a torch and a deeply annoying book about some Brits who'd moved to southern Italy and found nirvana.

'Success!' shouted Dom, entering from the back of the house, then padding in socks over the concrete floor to kneel and warm his hands by the fire. 'Jo said she'll ask Marcus to give us a ring. Apparently, he's turned the volume down on the answerphone because all the calls were for us.'

'God, that's a relief,' said Lucy. She wondered how many calls were work-related. Although they'd come to France on a telephone- and computer-free retreat, she couldn't help yearning to get back to their business. Not to mention electricity.

'Anyway,' said Dom, plonking his bottom on the concrete, 'you'll never guess who our housesitter's turned out to be.'

'Who?'

'OK, who do we know who often mentions a Marcus?'

'Well, only Han—'

'*Monsieur Rrrrobson?*' cried Madame Bouziges from the region of the plastic sheet door. '*Le téléphone!*'

'Ah,' said Dom, getting up again and hopping back over the uneven concrete. 'Here goes.'

'Good luck!' Lucy called out.

'So let me get this right,' said Marcus, eyeing Jo's closed bedroom curtains through his living-room window. 'Are you saying you're coming back this week if you can get your flights changed and that it might be best if I vacated, as you do some of your work from home?' He squinted hard. Had those curtains moved? Maybe a tad?

Dom said, 'Um, yes, I suppose that sums it up.'

'Right.' Jo's downstairs curtains had also been closed for over two days, but Marcus knew the entire household hadn't been slain or asphyxiated because he'd seen Ernst and Keiko come and go. All weekend he'd wanted to thank Jo for the party – he'd even bought flowers – but decided to wait till she'd flung open those curtains, and maybe a sash window or two. He didn't want to feel he was intruding.

'And obviously,' went on Dom, 'we feel bad about doing this to you.'

'Uh-huh?'

'And that's why we'd like to offer you the use of this house, in France.'

'I'm sorry?'

'Here in Laroche-les-Bois.'

'Do you mean for a week and a half? The rest of the time I'd have been house-sitting in Oxford?'

'No, no,' chortled Dom. 'As long as you like. To be honest, Marcus, you'd be doing us a favour. We've got some last-minute repairs going on here, so it'd be good to have someone keep an eye on things. How's your French?'

'Well, I did it for six years at school.'

'Pretty ropey then?'

'Yeah. The thing is, I wanted to spend time in Oxford, not Latouche-the-whatever. Where is it, anyway?'

'The Auvergne. We're about an hour and a half north of Nîmes. In the mountains. Beautiful spot.'

Marcus thought of Freddie. He couldn't just shoot off now, not having really spent any time with him yet.

Unless . . .

'How big is this place?' he asked.

'Five bedrooms. We like to say it sleeps twelve. Well, it will.'

'Sounds spacious. And is there a garden?' Freddie would need somewhere to play.

'Big garden, yep. It's, um, in the process of being landscaped.'

Marcus spotted Jo's bedroom curtains being parted and his eyes widened. There in the window stood Bram – either naked or near naked – hands now clasped behind his head as he flexed and stretched various upper-body muscles, like a man who'd been horizontal for a long time. 'Sounds good.'

'So do you think you might be interested? We'd have to let Madame Bouziges know. She has the keys. Does a bit of cleaning.'

'Let me think about it,' said Marcus, as Bram hoisted a window and stuck his head out. Jo then emerged from the front door and looked up. They blew each other kisses and she bounced – yes, she was definitely bouncing – down Jubilee Street, swinging a straw shopping bag. 'And maybe check out flights. Can I call you back later?'

'Sure. Not too late, though. Madame Bouziges tends to retire early.'

'OK.'

Marcus hung up and was halfway across the room when he stopped in his tracks, turned, and looked back at the phone. He could almost feel the exclamation mark above his head as the contents and implications of the conversation suddenly sank in: Lucy and Dom returning . . . vacate house . . . south of France . . .

It sounded tempting but he wasn't sure he wanted to be there on his own. How he'd love to take Freddie with him, but then Hannah would have to come. Would that be possible? The Easter holidays were close. Hannah wouldn't be teaching . . . He checked his watch – it was probably her lunchtime – and found the mobile number she'd given him after the party. He dialled but was put straight through to voicemail, so left a call-me message.

'Adrian, it's Hannah. Just ringing in my lunch break, hoping you'd be there. Oh well. Listen, can I come and see you after school today, or maybe tomorrow? Text me or something and

81

let me know? There have been developments since I saw you last week. You know how I was all wound up about Marcus and Jo sloping off to the Cotswolds? Well, nothing happened, according to Marcus, and anyway, it seems this mysterious bloke of hers does exist after all. Turned up on Friday, thank God, right in the middle of Marcus's birthday party. You'd think bloody Jude Law or someone had walked in from the reception he got. Nice-looking, though. After all the kerfuffle, I found Marcus slumped in front of the TV, knocking back some ghastly Schnapps-type drink one of the guests had brought along. Well, to cut a long story short, we went back to his place and cuddled on the sofa. It was a beautifully relaxing and peaceful platonic union, and I could have stayed like that, curled up all night, but then Marcus suddenly felt sick and had to go to the bathroom. I found him asleep, spreadeagled diagonally across the bed, so I covered him up and kissed him good night. He mumbled, "Night night, Jojo," which, as you can imagine, pissed me off. I haven't heard from him since. No apology or anything. Perhaps he doesn't remember, but all the same . . .

'Do you know, I feel better for airing all this, even if it is to your voicemail. So . . . well, maybe I don't need to come and see you till Wednesday, now I've got it off my chest. But listen, Adrian, I'd prefer it if you didn't charge me again. You know, for having to listen to my message? I did feel that was rather mean of you last time.'

Jo was aware of a spring in her step as she went round the covered market. Spring was also in the air and, best of all, in Bram's vital organ. How many times had they made love in three days? A lot, as usual. But then there were his long absences to make up for.

She turned into the olive shop. It was Monday and she should have been working, but she'd catch up after he left on Wednesday. Off on a secret mission. It was all terribly romantic. Jo often wondered if she'd feel the same way about Bram if he worked in Dixons.

'Could I have some of the chilli ones?' she asked, pointing at a bowl through the glass counter. 'A large tub?'

For two years now they'd had this strange but exciting, semi-attached relationship. Mostly, he'd turn up out of the blue – she liked that – then disappear again, sometimes after only a night or two. His absences ranged from a week to, once, four months. It made it difficult to plan things to do together, which was a bit of a bore. Once, amazingly, he'd come to Wales with her to visit her parents, although most of the time they were there he'd rambled in nearby Snowdonia. The longest they'd spent in each other's company was three weeks. Not that this didn't suit Jo, in a way. Usually, by the time he was due to leave her place, the fact that he didn't always get her humour and liked to win every argument was beginning to tarnish Bram's prodigal-boyfriend appeal. Mostly, it was his certainty that got to Jo. He was clever and knowledgeable and stuck rigidly to his beliefs, so entering into an argument with Bram wasn't something she did lightly. But when, for example, he said people like her parents, who drove to the end of the road to post a letter, should be taken to court, well . . . she could hardly not go on the defensive. Her parents lived on a steep hill, after all.

When Bram wasn't being intense, though, he could be great company. He was informative and had lots of tales of daring to tell. That was what Jo liked most about him. Well, apart from the obvious.

'And a tubful of those with the peppers,' she told the assistant, pointing again. Bram loved olives.

She left the market and meandered around town, treating

herself to a new pair of jeans, then bumping into a friend who told her she was looking really well. They went for a coffee and Jo told her *why* she was looking so well.

'How come I've never met this guy of yours in two years?' Jo was asked, and she laughed and said she'd barely met him herself. 'Don't you long to have someone around all the time?' said the friend. 'Isn't there anyone local you could go for?'

'Not really,' Jo replied, her head filling with Marcus. She hadn't seen him for three days and suddenly found herself wondering how he was. Had he and Hannah got together after the party? Her stomach tensed slightly at the thought of that and she promptly excused herself and caught a bus home, where she showed Bram all the food she'd bought and said she might invite Marcus for dinner.

'Didn't you just throw a party for him?' he asked in the Dutch accent that made him sound vaguely American. 'Shouldn't he be inviting us over?'

'Marcus may run a restaurant but I'm pretty sure he never cooks. You know, like I never write a thesis and Richard Branson never mends a train.'

Bram came over and cuddled her from behind. 'You don't fancy him, do you?' he asked. 'He's very pretty, mind you. I could almost go for him myself.'

'Yeah, I'm sure,' laughed Jo, feeling him grow larger in the small of her back.

Robin's in his study and I'm at the kitchen table feeling tense and considering a trip to the supermarket. Freddie's watching TV. Washing-up liquid, milk, grapefruit. Sometimes mindless shopping helps. My first reaction to Marcus's suggestion was that he'd lost it. Freddie and I to come to France for the Easter holidays? Have you gone barking? I said.

But now I've had the slow, rush-hour drive home to think about it . . . well, Robin, after all, is planning a few days in Edinburgh with Theo, who would come to Oxford if he didn't have to work full time during the holidays to keep up his student lifestyle: iPod, clubbing, meals out and a wardrobe ten times the size of mine and Robin's put together. Theo, named after his Greek maternal grandfather, looks like Robin – a little less angular, maybe – but with all the same colouring. How Freddie might turn out, I expect.

I could just boldly march into the study now and say, Robin, I'm thinking of taking Freddie to France for a week or so. With Marcus. How would you feel about it? We need light-bulbs as well. It's funny how they all tend to blow around the same time. No, actually it makes perfect sense.

Might postpone the Robin encounter until I've aired things in my session tomorrow. Not that Adrian will offer any advice. After the initial How have you been feeling? he rarely says a word. Money for old rope, if you ask me – and all that profes-sional prestige with it. Would love to see Adrian in a class-room with 9F, trying to get them to conjugate 'to be' for the umpteenth time, while they're chewing banned gum, sending banned text messages and asking with monotonous regularity whether he got shagged last night.

'No, thanks,' Marcus told Keiko when she waved the bowl at him again. 'I couldn't possibly manage another. I'll have olives coming out my ears soon.'

Keiko replaced the bowl and from the depths of her lap produced Marge Simpson and a retractable pencil. 'I am sorry. Could you repeat and explain? Olives out of ears? Is it idiom?'

'Um . . .' he said, but then Jo came to the rescue with a neat explanation and Keiko stopped staring at his ears, and Marcus, perversely, reached over for another olive. 'These are *really* good,' he told Jo.

'Aren't they?' She was dividing up a lasagne with a spatula. Marcus guessed the inch-square segment was for Keiko. 'Pass your plate, Marcus?'

'Sure.' He handed it to Keiko, who passed it to Ernst, who held it while a huge slab of steaming lasagne was slipped on.

'There's salad and bread to go with it,' Jo told him.

'Thanks. This all looks great.'

'I hear you never cook,' said Bram, turning Marcus's way. Being a large man, Bram had one long side of the table to himself. Keiko and Ernst shared the other, and Jo was at the head of the table facing Marcus, which pleased him as she was looking particularly radiant.

'I didn't say that,' Jo snapped at Bram.

'It's true, though,' said Marcus, sensing a little tension in the air. 'Well, hardly ever.'

'My father has never cooked one meal in his life inside his house,' said Ernst. 'But always he is the barbecue chef.'

Jo laughed. 'My dad's the same.'

'In Japan,' said Keiko quietly, 'women cook everything.' She took her tiny portion from Jo with a 'Thank you,' put it down and began fishing out the pasta.

'No, Keiko,' said Bram fairly forcefully. 'You don't mean women cook *everything*. That means women cook, you know, like the cat, the sofa, their mother-in-law. You mean women do all the cooking.'

Keiko covered her mouth and said, 'Ohhh,' behind her hand. 'My English is very bad.'

'No, it's not,' said Jo. She seemed to be smiling at Keiko and scowling at Bram at the same time. 'You're going great guns. One more term at the school and you'll be like a native speaker!'

Keiko giggled and thanked her. She carried on fishing out small strips of pasta, then stopped. Up from her lap came Marge and the pencil again. 'Please, could you explain why I have "great gun"?'

Jo did so with her usual patience, while Bram took his – quite a bit smaller than Marcus's – serving of lasagne from her.

Marcus warmed to Bram more as the meal went on; not a pedant after all, just a fairly straightforward, keen-on-facts, literal type of guy. He seemed to have an endless stream of interesting but fairly humourless saving-the-world stories and an opinion on everything. At one point Bram and Ernst discussed, in a quite heated manner, the subject of fining people for not recycling. Marcus got the impression Bram entered into such an argument on a daily basis, as he was pretty persuasive. In the end, he even had Ernst agreeing with the idea of cameras beside litter bins to catch those daring to throw away anything but the odd apple core.

'In Germany,' Ernst said, 'it would not surprise me for such a thing to happen.'

Bram gave an approving nod. 'Germany has definitely led the way when it comes to recycling. Along with Austria, New Zealand—'

'More lasagne, Marcus?' called Jo from the far end of the table. She looked great. She wasn't wearing her glasses, making her lovely brown eyes look half as big again. Her black top had a flattering neckline, and she wore a really pretty choker made of leather strips and beads; a present from Bram's travels, perhaps. The room was slowly growing darker, one or two candles were flickering and, all in all, the light was having a very flattering effect on her.

'Please,' he said, handing his plate to Keiko to pass on.

'I must admit recycling schemes have improved a lot here,' continued Bram. 'But, you know, you English still have a long way to go to catch up with more enlightened countries.'

Marcus realised he was getting a bit fed up with the topic now. 'Actually,' he told Bram with a curt smile, 'I'm Scottish.'

'And I'm Welsh,' said Jo, passing the heaped plate back. 'Is that enough, Marcus?'

'Plenty. I'll be stuffed if I eat all that.'

When Marge Simpson and the pencil appeared again, Marcus was quick off the mark. 'It means very, very full,' he told Keiko, patting his tummy.

'Aahh.'

'You know,' said Jo almost dreamily, staring at the bowl of olives, spatula dangling in the air, 'I can't think of anyone at the party last week who was totally English.'

'Robin?' asked Marcus.

'His grandfather was Greek, mother half-Greek.'

'Ah yeah. Forgot.' Freddie was part Greek and, on Hannah's side, a quarter Welsh. Obviously, he had no Scot at all in him. 'But surely Pippa's English?' Marcus asked.

'Brought up in London, yes, but her mother's Irish. Oh, I suppose Hannah might be—'

'Welsh mother. So, no.'

'Hannah's Welsh too?' said Jo. She looked vaguely annoyed.

'This is an explanation,' said Ernst while he chewed, 'for why the party was such good fun.'

'True,' they all agreed, laughing, and someone said, 'Down with the boring English!' and they clinked their glasses and went back to their food.

'Oh,' said Jo after a while, 'I've just thought of an English person at the party.'

Marcus looked up. 'Who was that?'

'Pippa's husband, Ray.'

'Are you sure?'

'Oh, yes. An Oxfordshire family through and through.'

He laughed. 'I meant are you sure he was at the party?'

Jo couldn't make out if it was the candlelight, the white wine or having too much sex over the past few days that was giving her these fantasies. Dark, almost glistening Bram was contrasting beautifully with Marcus and his Brideshead looks. Deep brown eyes/bright blue eyes. Big pale-chocolate biceps bulging from tight black T-shirt/slim golden-haired forearms below rolled-up sleeves. Raven chunky dreadlocks/soft blond flyaway hair. Ernst was saying something to her, but all Jo could think about was lying in bed between both men.

'Sorry, Ernst,' she said. 'I didn't quite catch that. Something about a member?'

'No. I said I re*member* the first time I was visiting England and it was raining for the whole week. It was a student exchange when I was twelve years old. My family I stayed with said they were sorry but that it rains a lot in Manchester. When I left to catch my plane I had a cold and the mother, her name was Mrs Ashby, she gave threesome Beechams Powders.'

'Threesome?'

'Jo, I think maybe you are not listening. Mrs Ashby gave me some Beechams Powders. They were very disgusting but maybe magical. When my parents met me I had no cold. I told them I'm never wanting to go to England again, but that we must find Beechams Powders in Germany!'

'And did you?' she asked, her eyes fixed on Bram's earring. Why the earrings? And why those coloured braided whatnots on both wrists? What she'd once thought was a part-hippy, part-African-roots aspect of Bram was now looking a shade immature. She noticed his head was gradually moving towards Marcus's, and while Ernst talked German pharmacies in her ear, she tried hard to hear what was being discussed animatedly at the far end of the table. When Ernst paused for breath she said loudly, 'Could you pass the white wine, Bram?'

Both beautiful faces looked her way and, once again, she saw herself sandwiched between the two men. Which one would she most want to be facing? She swallowed hard and took the bottle being handed her. 'What are you two deep in conversation about?' she asked with a big smile.

'Gaia,' said Bram.

'Ah.' Jo had never quite got the Gaia theory, which sees Earth as a living being; an organism that will inevitably reach the end of its life one day. Hopefully, not before her three-in-a-bed event.

'It's an interesting proposition,' said Marcus, bobbing his eyebrows at her over the top of his glass. Had he been reading her mind, or was he talking about Gaia?

'Excuse me,' said Keiko, who'd been awfully quiet. She raised her pencil in the air and turned to Jo. 'But what is meaning of threesome?'

Jo decided to pick nonchalantly at the salad on her plate. 'It just means, oh, three people, well, doing something together.' The other end of the table was eerily silent. Were they still looking her way?

'Ahh. So, when me and my friends Hiroko and Nyoko go to downtown Tokyo for shopping, we are doing threesome?'

Marcus said, 'Let me know next time you do that, Keiko. I'd like to come and watch.'

'It's not an expression we use much,' Jo said hurriedly. 'Honestly, I wouldn't even bother writing it down.'

'No?'

'No.'

There followed a bit of a silence when everyone went back to eating and drinking, until Marcus said, 'I haven't told you my big news, Jo.'

'Oh?' She didn't like the sound of this. Was that her alarm clock going off upstairs or something inside her head? 'What news?'

'Dom called. He and Lucy are coming home on Friday. Cutting their holiday short. They, er, want their house back.'

'What!'

He nodded.

'But . . .' said Jo.

'They have, however, offered me their house in France. For as long as I want it, apparently.'

'But . . .'

'I think I might go for it. Although I'd feel a bit bad as it's going to be busy in Braemar. Easter always is. Anyway—'

'On your own?' asked Jo, finding her tongue again. *Please say yes.*

Marcus shrugged. 'I don't know yet.'

Jo glued a smile to her face and said, 'Sounds great,' as her head moved on to a quite different fantasy. She, Bram and Marcus were in a hot-air balloon and rapidly losing height over treacherous terrain. Someone was going to have to go overboard to lighten the load. The men were saying she should decide.

'I was hoping Hannah and Freddie might join me,' Marcus said. 'But it looks like that might be tricky. You know . . . Robin.'

'Right.'

Bram reached for an olive and said, 'Which part of France?'

'Sort of the Auvergne, Cévennes area. Do you know it?'

'I know *of* it. Not such a good recycling record down there. Better in the north of France.'

91

'Well, it's pretty mountainous where I'm going, so perhaps they can be forgiven.'

'There's never an excuse,' replied Bram, wagging a finger at no one in particular, or maybe the whole of humanity, 'for squandering the world's resources.'

Jo sighed and her eyes went from Marcus to Bram, to Marcus again. Back in the basket, above the Alps or wherever, Bram's ankles were now firmly clasped in her hands and, with the sudden strength of an ox, she was heaving him over the side.

'Excuse me,' she said, standing up. 'Back in a tick, then we'll have dessert.'

On the way to the bathroom, she crept into her front room to check that her passport was still valid. On her way back she checked it again.

That settles it, thought Marcus, on arriving home and listening to Hannah's whispered message. She'd spoken to Robin and he'd flipped, apparently, so no way could she and Freddie come to France with him.

He flopped on the sofa and Maidstone immediately jumped up and demanded food. Others might have seen all the purring and rubbing and pummelling as a friendly greeting, but Marcus knew better. Maidstone showed zero affection when he wasn't hungry, just buggered off out to do cat stuff until his next feed.

'In a minute,' Marcus said. 'Let me just have an existential moment, would you?'

Maidstone carried on pawing at his chest with his sharp claws, while Marcus contemplated his own place and purpose in the world and how he alone must be responsible for his actions. Ignoring the fact that Maidstone was actually hurting him, he then moved on to Jeremy Bentham's 'Greatest Happiness Principle', and how he, Marcus, ought not jeopardise Hannah, Robin and Freddie's welfare for the sake of his own selfish yearnings. What sort of a cad would do that? But then, what sort of a cad would impregnate a woman on the verge of getting married to someone else? Mind you, Robin claimed not to have known.

As the ethics of it all began to get blurry round the edges and it felt as though Maidstone might be drawing blood, Marcus gave up on his ruminations. There'd be plenty of time for that, all alone in France. It briefly flashed through his mind that he could invite Jo and her bloke to Laroche-la-thingy, if Lucy and Dom didn't mind. But would Bram be easy company? Doubtful. Jo on her own might be another matter. He conjured up the image of her over dinner, all soft round the edges in the candle-light. Lovely. But partnered. Like all the women he fancied.

When, ten minutes later, well-fed Maidstone shot through the catflap for the night, Marcus decided to turn in. He tidied up a bit, switched off lights and made his way up to the large bedroom he was going to be reluctant to give up, what with its TV, stereo and ensuite bathroom. As he closed the curtains he spotted Jo, also at her bedroom window, just standing there with the light behind her. Looking his way? It seemed so. Now he felt a bit awkward. Should he continue drawing the curtains, or acknowledge he'd seen her? He decided to wave. She waved back. They both closed their curtains.

WEDNESDAY

'Bye!' Jo called out to Bram. 'Bye! Have a good trip!'

He disappeared round the corner, on his way to the bus he always insisted on taking to the railway station if he had the time. She'd often go with him but today was feigning a headache. She stepped back into the hall and began counting. 'One, potato, two, potato . . .' When she got to twenty, she grabbed her keys and strode across the road.

'Hey,' Marcus said, looking pleased to see her.

'Hey,' she said back, and he let her in.

'How's it going?'

'Fine. When are you off?'

'Friday.'

Invite me to go with you. 'Looking forward to it?'

'Don't know, to be honest.'

'I'm sure it'll be great.'

'Yeah, yeah.' He led her through to the living room where she plonked herself on a sofa. He came and joined her as she hoped he would. 'And if it's not . . .' he said, 'you know, if it gets a bit lonely . . .'

'Yes?'

'Well, I can always go back to Scotland.'

Invite me to Scotland. 'Be a shame not to make the most of it, though.'

'True. Although I'm still hoping Hannah and Freddie will be able to come.'

'Oh?'

'Mm. She's going to sound Robin out once again this evening, so keep your fingers crossed.'

'Will do.'

'Where's Bram?' asked Marcus.

'Gone.'

'Already? I didn't get to say goodbye.'

'No,' said Jo. If she told him Bram was still at the bus stop, he'd be bound to leave the sofa. And she didn't want that. 'On his way to . . . wherever,' she said with an apologetic shrug.

'That's a shame.'

'Mm.'

Not for the first time, Marcus checked his watch. Then checked it again. 'She said she'd ring,' he told Jo. 'And let me know.'

'Ah.'

'I'm not very hopeful.'

'No.'

'You know, if Hannah and Freddie can't come, I was wondering if maybe you—'

The phone rang and he sprang across the room and grabbed it. 'Uh-huh,' he said after a while. 'Oh. Well, only to be expected . . . Mm? . . . Listen, try not to be too upset, Hannah.'

Jo got up and went to the loo, just to be out of the way for a while. On returning to the living room, she expected to find Marcus holding a miserable head in his hands, but he didn't look particularly miserable at all. In fact, he seemed quite chipper and was even humming. 'They can't come,' he said.

'Shame,' said Jo, placing herself back on the sofa. 'What were you about to say before Hannah called?'

'Um . . .'

'You said if Hannah and Freddie can't— *Christ*, what was that?'

They'd both jumped at the sudden rapping on the window. Jo turned and there was Bram mouthing something. 'What?' she said, while Marcus hurried from the room. Jo followed.

'I just missed a bus,' panted Bram on the doorstep. 'Now I'm worried I'll miss my train too. You couldn't give us a lift, could you, Jo?'

Get a taxi, I'm busy! 'Yeah, I sup—'

'I'll take you,' said Marcus, picking up keys and unhooking a jacket. 'Got nothing else to do.'

While Bram nattered away beside him, Marcus tried to understand why he was feeling relieved. Borderline happy, even. He felt sorry for Hannah, who was distraught, by the sound of it, but he couldn't feel sorry for himself. Just pleased, in the end, that they weren't going to go upsetting Robin, causing unnecessary friction. Of course, a little 'family' holiday would have been nice, but had it been a selfish request on his part? Surely not, after all he'd gone through. Or maybe it had been. Hard to know who deserved what in such a weird situation.

'She's a wonderful woman – Jo,' Bram was saying.

'Yes.'

'Bright. Fun.'

'Yes.'

Another explanation might be that his feelings for Hannah had become . . . what? Murkier? Less clear, anyway. How easy it was to build someone up in their absence, only to be horribly reminded of their flaws as soon as you were with them again. She could be very bossy; he'd forgotten that. And her mood could change in the blink of an eye. On the plus side, she was gorgeous to look at. And clever. Well, in some ways she was. Running to Robin hadn't perhaps been the cleverest of moves.

'I'm very lucky to have her,' said Bram.

'Yes, you are.'

'But why she doesn't get herself a proper boyfriend beats me.'

Marcus turned to Bram. 'She could just like the lack of commitment?'

Bram shook his head. 'I don't think so. If the right person came along and wanted happy ever after, she'd jump at it. I'm sure she would.'

'Oh?'

'And he'd be one lucky guy, I tell you.'

'Well, here we are,' said Marcus, slowing down and wondering where to park. 'Shall I just pull in by the entrance and you can jump out?'

'Cheers,' said Bram. 'I owe you one!' He got out, hauled his bag from the back seat and ran into the station, leaving Marcus with the notion that it might also be Bram's departure that was lifting his spirits.

SATURDAY

At Freddie's request, Robin was being a trampoline. Like the one at nursery, Freddie said as he bounced on his father's spine, that Mrs Jessup let them go on if they did good colouring-in. 'But we have to promise to do little jumps,' he puffed, 'like this, and this and this.'

'Aarrgh,' went Robin again and again, and Freddie laughed because he knew his dad was only pretending it hurt. Robin was, in fact, pretending to pretend it hurt. But a bit of a sore back for a few more days didn't seem much in the scheme of things, so he carried on pretending to pretend until Freddie bounced off him and whacked his head on the coffee table, cried for a bit, then went back to his woodwork.

Fairly glad the game was over, Robin lay recovering, trying to think of something fun for the two of them, or even the three of them, to do. It was the first day of Hannah and Freddie's Easter holidays and Robin was experiencing a certain lightness of heart. Marcus had left Oxford. Had left the country, even. Things were back to normal.

Almost.

When Hannah stopped being watery-eyed and monosyllabic, then things would be back to normal. Had she really expected him to agree to her taking Fred on holiday with Marcus? What was to say they'd ever come back, he'd asked, and she'd said not to be ridiculous, of course they would. What kind of a person did he think she was?

Robin had been quietly furious and more than a little shocked that she should suggest such a thing. It seemed out of character, but then Hannah had been very out of character over the past week or so. Definitely more miserable and short-tempered, very weepy, snapping at both himself and Freddie for no apparent reason. Anyway, this had been their first major confrontation, even though neither of them had exactly shouted and ranted, what with Freddie still being up. All the emotions of previous marital discord came flooding back to Robin and had left him shaken and drained for a full two days – between Monday evening when Hannah had first made her crazy request, and last night when Marcus popped round to say goodbye. Hannah had been teary afterwards, taking herself off to bed at 9.30.

Robin sat up and rubbed at his middle back. 'What are you making now, Fred?' he asked.

'A clock. So you can learn me the time on it.'

'*Teach* me, Freddie, not learn me.'

'I made a big hand, look.'

'Oh, yes.' The hand was actually bigger than the clock itself but perhaps Freddie could take a saw, or whatever was needed, to it. Robin picked it up. Aha, balsa wood. In that case, he thought, a sharp kitchen knife should do the trick. But when he got up and tried sneaking out of the room with it, Freddie protested and waved a nail at him.

'I need it *now*, Daddy, to hammer it on.'

Robin knew better than to stem the flow of his son's creative genius, so gave him the very *big* big hand and said, 'How would you like to go and see Theo?'

Freddie hammered while he thought about it, then stopped, but still held the nail in place. 'Do you mean Feo at nursery? Or do you mean Feo my bruvver?'

'Half-brother,' Robin said, then wished he hadn't. Too hard to explain. 'Theo, in Edinburgh. I know he'd love to see *you*.' A slight exaggeration, maybe.

'Alright. But can we go to the zoo again?'

'I expect so.' Even as he spoke, Robin knew he should have consulted Hannah first. Hadn't she said something about taking Freddie to see her parents while he was away visiting Theo? Damn.

When she came into the room, still in her dressing gown, Freddie stopped work and said, 'Daddy said we can go to the zoo!'

'Which zoo?' Hannah asked, frowning Robin's way.

'Er, Edinburgh. It was just an idea. I thought maybe you could both come with me? We could find a B and B.' He forced a laugh. 'Save me having to stay at Theo's place.'

The look Hannah gave him was a resigned and miserable one. 'But I told my parents Fred and I would—'

Robin smacked his brow. 'God, sorry. Forgot. Maybe next time then, Fred. Hey, it'll be fun staying with Granny and Granddad, won't it?' What was fun about an ornament-filled semi in a publess sprawling village twelve miles from Leicester was beyond Robin, but his son seemed to think it was Heaven on Earth. Maybe if Ruth and Vic didn't treat Robin with un-disguised contempt – understandably, some might say – he'd find it Heaven on Earth too. Robin had been cold-shouldered throughout his one overnight stay at the confusingly named 'Copse View' – it looked out on a dozen starter homes – and vowed not to repeat the experience. Most phone conversations between himself and Hannah's parents consisted of, 'Is Hannah there?' 'I'll just get her.'

'I want to go to the zoo,' Freddie was whining. 'Mummy, *pleeze* can we go to the zoo with Daddy?'

Hannah rolled her eyes and left the room, and Robin wondered if he ought to go after her.

'My best thing in the zoo is the grillas,' Freddie said. He placed a nail and a very short hand on his clock and began bashing.

'They were great, weren't they?'

'Will the grillas be there this time?'

'I expect so. Listen, Fred, perhaps we could go and see Theo and the zoo one weekend soon. After you've been to Granny and Granddad's. In the meantime,' he lowered his voice, 'it might be best not to mention it to Mummy again.'

Freddie stared up at him. ''Cos she might cry?'

'Yes,' said Robin, rubbing his wonderful little son's head. What a fantastically sensitive and caring little boy he was.

'Mummy cries even more than Millie at playgroup,' said Freddie. 'And Millie at playgroup cries even if you just do this.' He put his hammer down and pinched the skin near Robin's wrist, long and hard. It was a very thin pinch, the type that hurts a lot.

'Ouch!' Robin cried. 'Stop!' He pulled his arm away and examined the growing red mark. Christ. Was there another side to Freddie that only little girls saw? 'You absolutely *mustn't* pinch anyone like that *ever* again. OK?'

Freddie continued to hammer.

'OK?' repeated Robin.

'Ok*aay.*'

'Good boy.' Robin stood upright, rubbed at the pain and

wondered what to do with himself while Fred was happily occupied.

'But anyway,' said Freddie, 'now I don't pinch Henrietta or Lara any more, 'cos they always kicked me really hard.'

'Good for them.' This was terrible. Could three year olds be excluded? He'd have a word with Mrs Jessup.

On his way out of the room, Hannah passed him. 'When were you planning on going to Edinburgh?' she asked.

'The day after tomorrow.' He'd told her several times, he knew he had. 'Monday,' he added. Was she now considering joining him?

'Back when?'

'Well, it depends on Theo. And how long I can bear the lifestyle. Saturday, I expect.'

'Right,' she said, and headed for an armchair. She held her locked diary flat against her chest, which meant she too would be occupied for some time.

There was nothing for it, Robin decided, but to go and read Bridget's next chapter on US foreign policy, entitled 'Military Intelligence'. Would he write his usual 'Oxymoron?' wisecrack next to her heading? Maybe not.

'*Monsieur Kewrrriee!*' Marcus thought he heard outside his window. His eyes sprang open. Kewrriee? Curie? Currie? '*Monsieur Kewrriee!*' came the voice again. Marcus waited for a rap on the door, then remembered there wasn't one.

'Coming!' he called back, hauling himself from the bed. He opened the nearest window, pleased he hadn't closed the shutters as well, and stuck his head out.

'*Le téléphone!*' said Madame Bouziges, holding an invisible receiver to her ear in the back garden.

'Ah,' said Marcus. '*Un momento!* I mean . . .' God, this was far too early in the day to attempt French. He tugged on jeans, grabbed a jumper, found his shoes, stepped over a pile of floorboards on the landing, went past four empty bedrooms, down the stairs – careful with the missing one – then over the potholed concrete floor, under the dangling electric wires and through a plastic sheet. Madame Bouziges – trim, dark-haired, late forties and in chic red wellies – was charging homeward through the decidedly unlandscaped garden and Marcus hurried to catch up.

'Oh, hi, Mum,' he croaked once inside an interesting room: ancient beams with dried herbs hanging from them, sepia photos of ancestors on a dark and heavy sideboard, two small yapping dogs and a huge TV. 'How are you doing?'

'Ooch, are you all right?' she asked. 'You're sounding a bit poorly. It's not a dusty, germ-filled place you're staying in?'

Well, now she came to mention it . . . 'I'm fine,' he said. Had he been a bit hasty in giving his mother this contact number? He was sure he'd stressed it was for emergencies only. 'I need a *café au lait*, that's all. Just woken up.'

From the doorway, Madame Bouziges gave him a knowing nod and before Marcus's mother had finished telling him about the large party they'd had in the restaurant, all the way from South Africa, the dear woman was back with a bowl the size of a chamber pot, full of strong milky coffee. If he'd known her a little better he'd have kissed her.

'No, Mum,' he said as he took sips and felt the caffeine hit. 'I'm *not* thinking of making house-sitting a way of life.' If she could see his present house she'd know why. 'I'm just sort of doing these people a favour, keeping an eye on their useless builder.' Madame Bouziges's eyebrows shot up and Marcus, horrified, wondered if her lack of English had been a ruse. But then she took a gentle swipe at one of the terriers who'd jumped in an armchair and Marcus relaxed again.

'So long as you're keeping warm,' said his mother, who'd always put that as her number-one priority in life. Being a petite woman in Scottish climes, it was understandable.

'Well, it'll be a bit more comfortable when the electricity's on again.'

Marcus laughed but his mother didn't. She just tutted and told him what a worry he was, then said, 'Have you got your sweater with you? The one I sent you for your birthday?'

'Yes, I have,' Marcus could answer honestly. He'd packed it at the last minute, guessing he'd be able to wear it in the French wilderness with no fear of bumping into an acquaintance. And, who knew, maybe red-and-yellow tartan was the new black in Laroche-les-Bois. 'Anyway, it's a beautiful spot, so I'll be out walking a lot. Keeping warm. However, the lady who looks after the house says the weather forecast is good.'

At least he *thought* that was what she was telling him at a rate of knots when he arrived last night, knackered from the long winding uphill drive. It could equally have been, 'Five stamps for England, please,' he realised later, flicking through his phrase book in bed. Or, 'Open wide, I'm going to give you an injection.' The sentence he'd been searching for – 'What the fuck have I come to here?' – was nowhere to be found. Thank *God* Hannah and Freddie hadn't come, he'd just kept thinking, until sleep took over.

'OK, Mum,' he said, raising his voice to add authority. 'I'll speak to you soon. Not too soon, though, eh? We don't want to keep disturbing Madame— . . . Mm? . . . Oh, I dunno. My car's booked into the airport car park for a month but I might cut it short; come back to Braemar. Although you seem to be coping without me.'

'Vinko says to tell you there's no hurry.'

'Who?'

'The new chef.' She chuckled. 'Actually, I think he's rather enjoying your flat.'

'What! Since when are we giving the chefs my flat?' The caffeine was well and truly kicking in now, and all Marcus's senses were coming alive. Particularly his sense of outrage. 'What's wrong with the room out the back?'

'Oh, Vinko said that in Slovenia he was used to a little more comfort, so—'

'Are you saying we're doing Slovenian food now?'

'Aye. Going down a treat it is. Anyway, son, as I say, there's no need to rush back. But do let me know how you're keeping, and how the sweater washes up, won't you? No higher than thirty degrees. Short spin.'

'Yeah, OK. But first I'll need electricity, don't forget.'

'And a quick press with a tepid iron wouldn't do it any harm.'

'Right,' he sighed. Sometimes his mother's inability, or unwillingness, to listen was a worry, sometimes a blessing. Often he *thought* she'd heard something he'd said, only to discover, next time they spoke perhaps, that she hadn't absorbed it at all. But at least she was like that with everybody. At one point, Hannah had started referring to her as Granny Groundhog Day, until Freddie began using it in his grandmother's presence but leaving off the 'Day' bit, making it sound plain rude.

'Don't worry,' he said. 'I'll take good care of the jumper. Anyway, gotta go. Madame Bouziges needs to use the phone.'

Marcus thanked her for calling and hung up, then went to find Madame Bouziges. She was plucking something in the kitchen, and through a combination of his limited comprehension and a lot of gestures on her part, Marcus gathered that he was invited to partake of whatever was dangling from her hand, at eight that evening.

*   *   *

I should be over the moon – no teaching for two weeks – but am feeling shitty. Marcus has buggered off, having totally disrupted our lives and spent almost no time with Freddie. How thoughtless of Lucy and Dom to return like this. According to Lucy, they were happy to let Marcus stay on for the weekend, since they'd decided to shoot up to Dom's parents for some family event. But Marcus had already booked his flight by the time they offered. Sometimes I despair of those two. So up themselves.

Had I really thought Robin would be cool about me taking Fred to France? Go on your own, he said, if you feel you and Marcus have got things to resolve, but you're not taking Freddie. I've never seen Robin seethe as he did on first Monday, then Wednesday. He shook, and actually scared me a little, so I backed down – charmingly, I think – and said I understood and pecked him on the cheek. Just thought I'd ask, I said, then went and sobbed into the phone to Marcus. I keep catching sight of myself in mirrors and shop windows, crying. Unaware that I have been. Are you all right? people keep asking me at work. Fine, I say, then dash to the loos and there they are again, those red teary eyes.

It's all such a muddle, but also strangely clear – I don't love Robin, I do love Marcus. But maybe the gods are conspiring to keep me and M apart – keep me with Robin – keep things stable for Freddie.

Maybe the gods are conspiring to do my head in too, although Robin thinks it's the antidepressants that are fucking me up. Why not ask Dr Maxwell to review your prescription? he said. So I did. Yesterday afternoon. Maxwell took my blood pressure, checked my throat and ears for some reason, put his cold stethoscope on my bare back, gave me a clean bill of

*health and suggested I double the dose when I feel the need.
I didn't tell him I was already doing that. He's hopeless – close
to retirement and looks at his watch a lot, as though counting
the minutes till his sixty-fifth birthday.*

*One thing's for sure – I'd recover quickly, flush the pills
away and be my old self, if only I were with Marcus, as in
with Marcus. Shall I go and see him, anyway? If Fred and I
went for just a couple of days, Robin need never know – or
I just deal with the consequences when we get back.*

*Last night I went online and checked flights to Nîmes and
Montpellier, thinking they'd be fully booked as it's Easter. Not
the case, it seems. Potatoes, honey, newspaper, oh, fuck these
stupid shopping lists. Adrian's such a prick. Things to do:
warn my parents we might not be visiting; put on a better
front for Robin before he has me sectioned; go and feed
Maidstone.*

Keiko was being terrific, bringing her mugs of tea and saying,
'Don't worry, Jo. Bram will be back soon.'

Eventually, Jo said, 'It's not him I'm missing, Keiko.'

'No?' said her surprised lodger. She held out Ibuprofen and
Jo took them from her. 'Then are you sad because Ernst has
gone to see family?'

Jo sniffed and shook her head. 'Uh-uh. But I'll let you have
one more guess.'

Keiko put a finger on her red, red lips while she had a think,
then stared at Jo and said, 'Aaahh, it is Marcus?'

'Mm,' nodded Jo. 'Marcus. Listen, Keiko, you couldn't fetch
the Milk Tray, could you?' She decided she might as well make
the most of this. 'You know, the chocolates I wouldn't let myself
eat? They're in the recycling cupboard, hidden in a cardboard
box behind the bag of cans.'

Keiko headed back towards the kitchen. 'In Japan,' she said, 'girls eat many chocolate when boyfriend is unkind.'

Jo laughed. 'Yeah, it's the same here. Or even when they're not unkind.' She took a couple of painkillers, hoping they worked on heartache, and realised she *was* missing Ernst: his funny off-key wailing when plugged into his personal CD player; the way he ran not just up, but *down* the stairs two at a time, without even holding the handrail. How was that humanly possible? Ernst added a bit of young-male zing to the household, which was complemented by Keiko's sweetness and calmness. A nice easy couple of students, once you disregarded their dietary quirks. Unlike the two girls she'd had for a term before Christmas; close friends from the same Austrian town. Both had boyfriend-back-home problems they liked to share with her, mobiles that never stopped, a tendency to come home pissed at two a.m., and a daily stack of laundry for her to do. How she'd like to keep Keiko and Ernst for ever, but they'd be gone by July, when she'd be forced to have some of the younger summer-term students, many packed off by parents wanting a break.

She sighed and took the Milk Tray from Keiko. 'Thanks. Want one? Oh no, I forgot.'

While she worked her way through the chocolates, starting with her favourites and planning to end with praline, Keiko sat across the room examining a large book on her lap at very close quarters. 'What's that?' Jo asked.

'It is your map book of Europe.'

'Oh?'

'Middle and south of France pages.'

'Really?'

'To find where Marcus has gone.'

Jo put the chocolates down and joined Keiko on the sofa.

'Do you know the name of the place?' she asked.

Keiko produced a piece of paper. 'I ask Marcus for address to send photos of dinner to. Very good photos.' From the back of the atlas came a set of prints. 'Especially one of you in middle of Bram and Marcus.'

'Pardon?' said Jo, grabbing them. She went through the ten or so pictures and felt small pangs each time she came across Marcus, and something else altogether when she saw Bram: not much, in fact. What she couldn't get over was how good *she'd* been looking that evening. Irresistible, she'd say. How Marcus hadn't thrown caution to the wind and begged her to come to France was most puzzling. There was one hideous shot of her, though, taken when she was shovelling something in her mouth. Jo sneaked that beneath a buttock, plus a particularly dreamy one of Marcus, and handed the rest back to Keiko. 'You must send them to him. They're great.'

'Thank you.'

Jo helped Keiko check the address against the map, and eventually spotted the nearest town. 'Gosh, looks pretty remote,' she said. It looked pretty high too, if Jo was reading the contours correctly. What on earth was Marcus going to do there? He'd be able to roam in the hills, of course, but she knew from experience that he wasn't a fanatical walker. It was a great-looking house, though. She'd seen photos of the outside: an imposing stone building, covered in shutters. Really spacious, Lucy had said. Something like five bedrooms. So many bedrooms, thought Jo, that maybe you wouldn't even notice if you had a guest. Or two.

'Have you ever been to France?' she asked Keiko.

'Only once to Paris with my parents on whistle-shop tour of Europe. But not any more parts of France.'

'Do you mean whistle-stop?'

'No. Definitely whistle-shop. It was special shopping holiday for Japanese persons.'

'Ah. Well, do you think you'd like to see more of France?'

Keiko nodded and looked wistful. 'Yes. Very much.'

'This week?'

The thing Madame Bouziges had been plucking turned out to be a duck, now tender and tasty and accompanied by beans and assorted vegetables in a delicious cassoulet. Marcus thought about asking for the recipe for his restaurant in case they went French, but two things were stopping him. What were the chances of a French chef who *didn't* know how to make this national dish turning up in Braemar? And, even if Marcus made himself understood, would he grasp Madame Bouziges's reply? The past fifteen minutes had been spent delving into the depths of his brain for annoying little words he kept hearing, such as *donc, devant, depuis.*

'*C'est très bon,*' he said again and was rewarded with another dollop of cassoulet.

Marcus, Madame Bouziges and her father-in-law, Bertrand – a bulging and undulating man who'd clearly enjoyed many a cassoulet – had, in mostly one-word sentences on Marcus's part, covered the weather, the local towns and villages and the two family dogs. But now it had gone very quiet. After telling them the food was *très bon* again, Marcus wondered where they could go next, conversationally. He ruled out twentieth-century French feminist criticism and the films of Jean-Luc Godard and opted, instead, for making appreciative noises as he ate, just to fill the void.

It was a silence that seemed to go on interminably. He continued with the occasional 'Mmmm', and Bertrand's teeth clattered a bit, but that was all that could be heard. Surely he knew more French than 'Mmmm', Marcus kept thinking. All those years of study. Although he'd holidayed in France several times before, he'd been with the fluent Hannah and hadn't needed to say more than the odd *merci*.

However, he decided, this might be a golden opportunity to improve his language skills. Beginning now. In his head he started forming the French version of, 'Bertrand, are you thinking of pulling your finger out and getting my electricity back on?' – *Excusez-moi, Bertrand, mais quand—* when the dining-room door flew open and a shortish, muscular young man with dark hair, olive skin and a big smile burst in. Madame Bouziges exclaimed something, dabbed at her mouth with a napkin and accepted three kisses from him.

After receiving a wordy explanation as to whom Marcus was, the newcomer was then introduced as Claude. Marcus gave a slightly Del Boy, *'Bonsoir, bonsoir,'* as the two of them shook hands, then Claude sat down on the next chair and lifted the casserole lid to inspect.

'C'est très bon,' Marcus informed him.

Claude turned and nodded. 'Yes, it would be. My aunt is famous for her cassoulet, you know. Some consider it unsurpassable, although I personally think she overdoes the beans and underdoes the garlic.' He smiled at Madame Bouziges as he took a plate and a wine glass from her. 'Don't worry,' he murmured. 'She doesn't understand a word.'

Rather than fall off his chair with shock and gratitude at hearing English, Marcus said, 'Tastes perfect to me.'

Dinner went swimmingly after that, with Claude interpreting deftly and amusingly. He'd been an only child, Marcus learned, orphaned aged eight and brought up by his mother's sister and her husband. 'Tragically, we lost my uncle in a wild-boar shooting accident in Languedoc,' Claude added. 'Just last year. My aunt was inconsolable for months.' Marcus expressed his commiserations. He told Claude his own father had passed away too after a long illness. Then they moved themselves on to less painful matters. Claude was training to be an air-traffic controller, but was home on three weeks' leave and, to Marcus's joy, intended to make Lucy and Dom's house 'spick and span' before he went back.

'How come your English is better than mine?' Marcus asked as he passively enjoyed the post-prandial, continental-smelling cigarettes fugging up the room nicely.

'Years and years of classes,' explained Claude, taking another long drag. 'And many a misspent night reading English diction-aries.' He exhaled all over Marcus. 'When I do something, I like to do it well, you see. Plus, you have to have a good command of English in my chosen profession.'

'I'm sure you do. I mean, you don't want to be getting your "Left a bit"/"Right a bit"s mixed up, do you?'

Claude laughed. 'Not forgetting "Watch out behind you!"' He drew on his cigarette again. 'I take it you don't know any French?'

'What gave you that idea?'

'My aunt. She said you have slightly less vocabulary than Piaf.'

'Well, I'll take that as a compliment.'

'Piaf is one of her goats. Her favourite, as a matter of fact. She's sweet-natured and very productive but no, she doesn't have a great command of our language.' Claude smiled. 'I expect it's just a vernacular problem you're having. The vowel sounds are quite different around here.'

'Ah,' Marcus said, not totally convinced and reeling slightly from Madame Bouziges's comparison. She seemed too nice a lady to be comparing him with a goat. 'That could be it.'

Later, when Madame Bouziges produced grapes and a living, breathing and possibly thinking slab of Brie, Marcus said a self-conscious, '*Oui, merci,*' when offered some, but skipped the '*C'est trés bon*' as he ate.

MONDAY

For such a little person, Keiko certainly packed a big suitcase. It was 8.15 and a bit of a shock to Jo's system to be up, dressed and ready for a holiday so early on a Monday morning. 'You know it's only for a week,' she told her lodger, 'not the rest of our lives?'

Keiko giggled as she bumped her luggage down the last stair. It was mostly her language books, she explained, because she wanted to work hard and impress her teacher, Adam, next term. 'But also mountain clothes from sports shop and climbing boots. Very expensive boots. More than one hundred fifty pounds, but man in shop said essential.'

'I'm sure he did,' said Jo, wondering what kind of walking companion Keiko might make. Tough and speedy, or like Marcus?

Once Keiko had made it round the corner and along the hallway, Jo opened the front door to Pippa, who was calling in on her way to work for housecare instructions: plant watering, picking up emails and passing on anything really urgent via Madame Bouziges's phone. 'Feel free to stay here,' said Jo, 'if Ray's driving you nuts.'

Pippa beamed and clasped hands under her chin. 'Great! I'll bring my stuff over tonight.'

'Are you being serious?' Jo had meant it as a throwaway remark. Did she really want Pippa living in her house? What if she refurbished it as a nice surprise for her?

'Deadly.'

'Well, OK. But—'

'Sasha's home for the holidays. It'll be nice for her to have a bit of bonding time with her dad.'

Jo said, 'Oh, I see,' but didn't see at all. Surely it would be like trying to bond with a table leg? Harder, maybe. 'Let me explain the heating to you, then,' she insisted. 'You know, the timer, where the thermostat is . . .' Pippa was looking at her blankly, as though she'd never heard of such things. Someone who kept her house at constant Dubai temperatures probably hadn't. 'It's best to light a fire if it gets chilly,' Jo added, wishing it was August and not early April. 'Nice and cosy and saves on the bills.'

'I think taxi has arrived,' said Keiko, squinting through the frosted glass of the front door.

'Look, here are the keys,' Jo told Pippa. 'I'm sure you'll work everything out for yourself. And remember, if Bram rings, I've gone to stay with an old friend.'

'Yeah, yeah,' said Pippa, casually rearranging the hall table and looking awfully at home. 'Off you go.' She air-kissed Jo's cheeks, then Keiko's. 'And have a *fabulous* time.'

Keiko yanked at her suitcase. 'Thank you.'

'We'll try!' said Jo, grabbing her stuff.

Pippa held the front door open for them, then waved them off down the short path. 'Oh, and tell Marcus there's no expiry date on that voucher!' she called out.

Once inside the taxi and gliding down the Iffley Road towards town, Jo flopped back in the rear seat and pictured the surprised and hopefully thrilled look on Marcus's face when she and Keiko rolled up at around seven or eight o'clock that evening. She'd tried Lucy and Dom's door a couple of times over the weekend, to ask if it would be OK to go, but they'd obviously shot off somewhere on Saturday and still weren't back. She couldn't get them on their mobiles either, so had put a note through the letterbox an hour ago, hoping they'd be cool about it. They'd told her enough times she should go to their place in France when it was done, so Jo didn't feel she was taking liberties. Neither was she going to feel bad about Hannah after that elbow in the stomach.

Jo smiled to herself, thinking of Marcus. Just before leaving on Friday, he'd hugged and squeezed her and caressed her back, shoulders, upper arms – a grope, in fact – ending with a kiss slightly to the left of her lips and a stroke of her cheek with a finger. 'You are wonderful,' he said. 'I'm really going to miss you. If only you didn't have the lodgers to feed, you could—'

'Actually, Ernst has gone back to Germany for the holidays. And Keiko's more than—'

'But, who knows,' he said, burying his face in her hair, 'maybe solitude will be good for my soul.'

'Maybe . . .' Jo had replied, considering herself invited.

The one thing she was now hoping was that Lucy and Dom wouldn't get back soon and ignore her request not to call France and spoil the surprise.

On the other side of the taxi, Keiko was quietly humming to herself. How great this trip would be for her. The language school was always encouraging host families to take their students out and about. They probably meant ten-pin bowling rather than the south of France, but Jo couldn't see it would do her landlady rating any harm. Once again she checked she had everything: passport, detailed directions to Laroche-les-Bois gleaned from the Internet, emailed confirmation of flights and car hire and, finally, the beta-blockers she resorted to every time she had to endure air travel.

'Do you enjoy flying?' she asked Keiko.

Keiko shrugged and pulled a face. 'Usually I sleep. Japanese always fall asleep on travel. Sometimes even when we stand up on train or bus.'

'I've heard about that. One theory is that Japanese babies are carried by their mothers all the time, so that kind of rocking, rolling movement sends you off.'

'Aaahh,' nodded Keiko. 'Interesting. But my mother doesn't like rock and roll. She is big fan of Dolly Parton.'

'Right.'

Claude began work at 9.30, blasting Marcus from sleep with a series of short sharp drillings that resounded painfully through the walls, floors and everything else of the bare and ancient house. There followed some tapping and a good deal of cheerful whistling, and before Marcus had formed the entire thought that he'd rather like to be home in Scotland, a bulb lit up, not far above his head.

'Yes!' he said, punching the air.

He then lay for a while contemplating the coffee he could now make and the bath he'd be able to take, but also considering what he was going to do with his days in Laroche-les-Bois. From his first couple of forays down the hill and into the village centre the previous day, he'd discovered the only lively place – apart from the male-filled and fairly scary 'Sports Bar' he'd popped his head into – to be the church. More of an abbey really. It was a huge affair, which the board outside explained the history of, in great detail and no doubt interestingly. The abbey had a vast car park and people poured into the village to pray and sing there; then in the evening, returned to pray and sing again. Meanwhile, the shop across the square was totally shuttered up and looking as though it hadn't seen any business since Vichy days.

He'd have another stroll down later, Marcus decided. Maybe Sunday hadn't been the best time to check out where it was happening in a deeply Catholic community. He'd try the shop again and watch the boules. There were bound to be boules. If only he had a string vest and a suspicious stare, he could get to know the guys in the Sports Bar.

'Hold that, would you?' asked Claude.

Marcus put his coffee down and steadied the top end of the back door, laid on its side, while Claude planed the very bottom.

'So what is there to do around here?' Marcus asked. 'For fun.'

'It depends. Do you like water sports?'

'I've been known to fish.'

'Only the canoeing's terrific over in the gorges. You should come with us some time. Give it a go.'

'Great,' Marcus said as Claude blew sawdust in both their faces, then planed a bit more. After a while they tried the door in its frame and it seemed to fit, so Marcus continued holding it as Claude worked away at screws and hinges.

'Of course, it's unutterably dull for adolescents in the village,' Claude continued, 'and they sometimes get into trouble. Intemperance and so on. But most of them leave for the cities as soon as they can. Nice, Montpellier, Paris even. Some stay, though, and get married and procreate. The guys learn trades and repair the houses for the Germans and Dutch and British who buy up all the decrepit properties around here. It's not a bad life, and family is very important, you know. Big extended-family meals are *de rigueur*, especially at weekends.'

'Is that so?' Marcus was still pondering on 'intemperance' – bad temper or drunkenness? – when someone hooted loudly out in the road.

'It's the bread van,' explained Claude. 'You'd better hurry. She doesn't hang around for long.'

Marcus grabbed some change and went and bought himself two baguettes from a charming young woman who clearly had the fresh-bread market cornered in the area. When he returned, Claude was shaking his head at the door.

'It's still sticking a little,' he said. 'I think it's this small protuberance here, by the hinge.'

Marcus looked closely. 'I could always just give it a bit of a kick when I need to shut it.'

Claude tutted and began unscrewing things. 'No, no. I tend to be punctilious in my work, I'm afraid. Just my nature.'

The door came off again, Marcus held it again and Claude planed again. When it shut perfectly the second time it was screwed in, both men gave a little whoop and Claude took a fag break. 'The thing is,' he said, after they'd talked more about the exodus of young people from the area, 'I could do with a mate.'

'Oh?' said Marcus. 'Aren't there any nice women in Clermont-Ferrand?'

'No, I mean now. On this job. Perhaps I've used the wrong word. Um . . . an assistant?'

'Ah. Sorry. No, mate was the right word.'

'I don't suppose you'd be interested? Bertrand is of no use.' Claude grinned. 'My aunt always says he is as indolent as de Gaulle.'

Rude? wondered Marcus. No, that was *insolent*. Two days abroad and he was already losing his language. 'President or goat?' he asked Claude.

'Her least favourite goat. I'd pay you, of course, out of my remuneration from Lucy and Dom.'

'Well!' Marcus gave an embarrassed laugh and didn't quite know what to say. A builder's mate? It was an idea, actually. Give him something to do. Bit of exercise. There was one drawback, though. 'I have absolutely no skills,' he told Claude.

'Can you hold a ladder?'

'I guess so.'

'Carry stones and tiles?'

'Possibly.'

Claude lifted his coffee cup in the air. 'In that case, you're hired!'

Marcus lifted his too. 'Great!' he said, not certain he meant it but hoping he could help speed up the building process, just in case Hannah changed her mind. Or rather, Robin did. And, hey, he told himself, he might even improve his English if he hung out with Claude long enough.

Earlier, I gathered up Lucy and Dom's letters from their doormat, including a hand-delivered one, and tried not to get maudlin about Marcus no longer being in the house, as happened each time I fed Maidstone over the weekend. After all, I'll be seeing him tomorrow!

This evening we're booked on a flight to Montpellier, where we'll stay the night in a hotel and pick up a hire car in the morning. After rifling through drawers and papers in Lucy and Dom's attic office, then tapping into their Word files, I finally found the address of, and even directions to, their place in France.

Their two mobiles were charging up, side by side next to the computer, which explained why I hadn't been able to ring them yesterday. Actually, I was quite pleased not to get through, just in case they were a bit anti me joining Marcus. Lucy, I know, is particularly fond of Robin. The whole world's fond of Robin – apart from my parents and possibly his ex-wife. I left them a note telling them my plans and asking them to keep it under their hats as I wanted to surprise Marcus. And definitely not to tell Robin. All would be explained when I got back, I promised. I poured a second helping of dried food into Maidstone's bowl, then popped Lucy and Dom's key through Jo's letterbox, with a note asking her to feed the cat till they got back.

So, everything's sorted. Now what I have to do is talk Freddie out of taking his cumbersome toolbox to France. He'll never let it go into the hold with our cases, suspecting everyone of wanting to run off with his mini hand-drill. He's even begun tucking the box under his duvet at night. Cute or weird? I asked Adrian last week and he managed a few words. No doubt it's to do with loss, he said, making me feel fairly crappy for the rest of the session.

Just the thought of getting away from here and being with Marcus has lifted my spirits. So much so that I'm considering not taking this diary with me. Why would I need to sit in a corner and scribble my heart out if I'm with Marcus?

I have to say, Lucy and Dom's house looks stunning in the photos I found. So romantic. Has Lucy ever mentioned a pool? Freddie would love that, and it's bound to be warmer down there, even in April. Mustn't forget suncream.

Even with the beta-blocker it was white-knuckle time for Jo. The engines were making that 'Hold tight, we're about to explode!' roar, as the plane raced along the runway with the ridiculous idea that it could get off the ground if it only went fast enough. She turned to Keiko to utter a few last words, but found her companion already dead to the world – as opposed to dead, which they all would be soon. 'Please God, make me Japanese next time?' Jo said out loud, just to make sure He heard.

When the great overloaded hulk of a thing dragged itself into the air – the most dangerous time in any flight, apparently – and Jo had squeezed all the life out of her armrests, the white-haired man in the window seat to her left said, 'It's OK, don't worry,' in a French accent. 'I used to be joose like you.' He covered her hand reassuringly with his in a way an Englishman wouldn't dream of.

'Did you?'

'*Oui*. But then my wife was knocked from her *bicyclette* and killed by a madman in a Peugeot. And now I see ow safe flying is compared to our roads *en France*.'

'I'm so sorry,' she said, a bead of sweat trickling over one eye. He really wasn't helping, just confirming how fragile life was.

'But why?' the kindly man asked. 'You were not driving.'

'No. It's just what we say. It means I'm sorry to hear your story.'

'You would rather I did not tell you?'

Yes, actually. 'No, not at all.'

The man laughed and Jo realised he was joking. 'I am tugging your leg,' he said.

'Pulling.'

'Of course. Pulling. I think of tug of war.' He lifted his hand and replaced it in his lap but carried on reassuring her with his warm, twinkling eyes. 'You have far too many words to say the same thing.'

'I know. I help foreign people with their English and they can't believe how many ways there are of saying, oh . . . "look" for example. Peer, glance, glimpse, peep, stare, gawk, gawp, and more, all with a different meaning, sometimes just a subtle one. You know, we can't just "walk", we're ambling or rambling, or strolling or striding. Sauntering, tramping, shuffling, meandering.' Jo laughed. 'I could go on,' she said, and she did. All the way to Nîmes.

When everyone but Jo was preparing for landing – she'd been ready from the word go, belt buckled throughout – she couldn't quite believe how quickly and painlessly the journey had passed. Clearly, the thing to do on all future flights was to bore a neighbour rigid on the intricacies of English.

When the plane taxied to a halt beside the terminal, Keiko's eyes popped open, as though the hypnotist inside her head had counted down from ten and arrived at one, just as the engines shut down. 'Ah,' she said, leaning forward and peering, peeping or possibly peeking through their little window. 'We land in France. I am very happy!'

'Not as happy as I am,' said Jo, releasing herself at last and breaking her long-held record by, for once, not being the first to stand up.

On leaving the building to search for their car, Jo and Keiko were hit by a disappointing chilliness and slight drizzle. They stopped, groaned, opened their bags and took out coats – in Keiko's case, a brand new Scott-of-the-Antarctic affair – but then found their gleaming, plum-coloured, latest-model Renault and immediately cheered up.

As usual, it took a while to get the hang of driving from the wrong side of the car and on the wrong side of the road, but by the time they reached the dual carriageway Jo found it coming easily. How crazy and perverse of the Brits to drive on the left, she decided. Such an unnatural place to be. She checked the car's clock: 4.50. They'd have to stop somewhere and eat, as there wasn't much point in relying on Marcus for dinner, but even taking that into account they ought to be with him by eight at the latest.

'Are you OK to map read?' she asked Keiko, who was holding the large road atlas in front of her, staring hard at it.

'OK. First I find Nîmes, yes?'

'Yep. Got it?'

'Um . . . it is very hard.'

Jo glanced over again, then looked back at the road as cars overtook her at aircraft speed. 'Here,' she said, reaching across and turning the map 180 degrees. 'See if that helps.'

When Theo said they were going clubbing, Robin hadn't expected to be listening to Herman's Hermits, Procol Harum and, twice, Perry Como. It was fifties/sixties night, a favourite with students, apparently. Robin thought Edinburgh would be empty of undergraduates, but according to Theo almost everyone he knew had a job they couldn't leave in the holidays for fear of it being snapped up by some other student.

What serious and unrecognisable lives these young people lived. All for the sake – well, in Theo's case at least – of yet more CDs, when he already had a wall covered in the things. Robin thought back to the half-dozen played-to-death LPs that had seen him all the way through university. And how he'd eked his grant out by making one potato into an entire meal and drinking mostly shandy. Had Theo and his friends even heard of shandy? Robin sipped at his Backwards Blow Job – a cocktail Theo had talked him into – and watched, with some astonishment, as the mere children around him mouthed the words to 'Catch a Falling Star'.

'Can I get you another one of those?' Theo shouted in his ear, just as the DJ announced that the next track was for the

First Polo Team and everyone in their group broke into a cheer.

'You play *polo*?' Robin asked.

Theo said, 'Yeah,' although it bordered dangerously on a 'Yah'. He tapped his foot and bobbed his head in time to 'Puppet on a String' without any apparent embarrassment. 'Terrific fun and a bit of a chick magnet,' he added with a nudge that sent some of Robin's horrible drink on to the floor.

'I might have something different this time,' Robin said, and he turned to the list of cocktails. He'd heard of a Gin Sling, but what was a Pan-Galactic Gargle Blaster? Or an Anne Robinson? He worked his way down the menu, hoping to find Pot of Tea for One at the bottom. 'Actually,' he shouted, raising his almost empty glass. 'I think I'll be off soon.'

'You can't do that,' Theo shouted back. 'We've only just got going. Take advantage of not having Freddie with you. How is he, anyway? Still taking that fire engine everywhere?'

'It's his toolbox now,' Robin said, laughing but getting a sudden Freddie pang. He thanked God he'd booked himself into a B and B. As much as he enjoyed hanging out with Theo, he felt he'd learned all he needed to know about the price of clothes for one day, and wanted to hit the sack. It was now past ten o'clock and he was keen to get back to the amiable but very elderly landlady he felt sure would accidentally lock him out after eleven. He gave this excuse to his son.

'Oh right,' said Theo. He didn't look too disappointed that his dad wouldn't, after all, be grooving till dawn with him. 'But come and see me in the shop tomorrow, yeah? I can give you my staff discount on any of the clothes.'

'Great. Will do.'

Robin pretended to knock back the last of his drink then shouted goodbyes to Jasper, Joss, Jonty and others. After weaving his way through a sea of young bodies, he reached the exit just as 'Tears' came on and the whole place erupted – as indeed it would have done in Robin's day, should anyone have played a Ken Dodd record.

Out in the street, he checked his phone and listened to a message from Hannah in a call box, telling him she'd dropped her mobile and it no longer seemed to be working. Robin swore. It was his main lifeline to Hannah and Freddie when they stayed with her parents. Now, when he got desperate to talk to them – Fred in particular – he'd have to call Ruth and Vic's number. But, dammit, he didn't have it with him. And weren't they ex-directory owing to Vic having been a copper?

'Bugger,' he said, switching off his phone, then looking up at the castle, towering majestically over him. He'd always thought of Edinburgh as a very masculine city, rather like Oxford but more so. All that granite, no doubt. Cambridge was feminine, as was Lincoln. Durham was definitely masculine. He continued this train of thought as he strode towards his guesthouse – Warwick masculine, Chichester feminine – but when he found himself deciding Brighton and Bristol were androgynous, Robin began to wonder what the hell they put in those Backwards Blow Jobs.

'*Oh. My. God,*' said Lucy.

'What?' Dom called out. He was rushing around, drawing curtains, turning the thermostat up, pouring food into Maidstone's bowl.

'*Shit.*'

'What?' he said again, appearing in the hallway with wine in his hand. 'Huge phone bill?'

Lucy shook her head and reread the note. 'Hannah's taken Freddie to Laroche-les-Bois.'

'Oh, bloody hell. To our house, I take it?'

126

'Yep. Looks like they left some time today.'

'Christ. Has Robin gone with them?'

'It seems not.'

'We should phone. Apologise for there only being one bedroom in operation and no electricity or hot water.'

'No point in trying Hannah's mobile; she wouldn't have a signal. Madame Bouziges will be asleep, so we shouldn't phone there. And anyway, Hannah's asked us not to let Marcus know they're coming. Wants it to be a surprise.'

Dom snorted. 'I think Hannah will be the one getting the surprise. Jesus, all those bare wires and missing floors. Pretty dangerous for a kid.'

'Well,' said Lucy, 'there's nothing we can do about it. Not from here, and certainly not tonight.'

'True. Maybe we should try and get some cash to Marcus as soon as poss.'

'You mean the money your parents just lent us? I think I'm going to cry.'

'No choice,' sighed Dom. 'Anyway, fancy a glass of wine?'

'Yeah. May as well celebrate our last hours of freedom.'

'Actually, I'm quite looking forward to going back to the office. Seeing the boys.'

'Me too.'

Dom headed back to the kitchen. 'Red or white?' he called out.

Lucy began working her way through the stack of letters they hadn't bothered looking at on Friday. Bills, bank statements, junk, and one with just 'Lucy and Dom' written on it. 'Red,' she shouted back, ripping open the envelope, taking the single sheet of paper out and immediately checking the name on the bottom – 'Jo'.

At first she couldn't quite take it in. Then she did take it in, and thought maybe Jo and Hannah were playing some kind of practical joke on them. But it wasn't April the first and, really, how amusing a prank would it be? No, Lucy realised on a third reading, Jo too had gone to Laroche-les-Bois to stay in their uninhabitable house, and, what's more, had taken her Japanese student with her. She made no mention of Hannah.

When Dom came back with her glass of wine, she said, 'It just got worse,' handing him the note. '*Much* worse.'

TUESDAY

Marcus woke to a combination of sounds: a familiar purring-cum-snoring, a page being turned, then another, and someone clearing his or her throat. He felt far too knackered to open his eyes and tried to drift off again, only the person doing the throat clearing continued to make noises, so he couldn't. He opened one eye and saw a blurry Claude, with hands on hips and a startled expression.

'I wondered whose the car was,' Claude said. 'I'd no idea you were expecting two, er, guests. I'm so sorry. Do excuse me, I will leave you to it.'

Not a dream, Marcus realised as he slowly came round. He *was* lying between two bodies; all three of them fully dressed, by the feel of it. To his right he saw the back of Jo's head as she slumbered, and when he turned to his left, there was Keiko holding an English coursebook aloft. 'Present Perfect' was the heading on the page she had open and Marcus thought: no, not exactly perfect.

'Good morning,' whispered Keiko.

'Hi,' he said. 'Did you sleep well?'

'Yes, thank you. Although very short sleep.'

'Mm.'

They'd got to bed at around three, after much hemming and hawing about sleeping arrangements. Marcus had offered to curl up in the one proper armchair, so the women could have the double bed, but they seemed to think that a bit unfair. He said he'd be OK on the floor in one of the other upstairs rooms but then realised there wasn't any spare bedding to put either under or over himself.

They'd carried on discussing the matter and drinking wine until eventually Jo said, 'I think there is only one solution,' and they all trundled up to the one bed, in the one proper bedroom, and crawled under the one duvet.

While Marcus was attempting to slip back into sleep, the bread-van hooter honked loudly, making Keiko jump and then quietly gasp as Marcus hauled himself over her and hurried from the room to catch the impatient baker. There was nothing more miserable and rock-like than yesterday's baguette, he'd discovered.

He found some money then queued behind the van for a while and told an inquisitive Madame Bouziges that the new *voiture* in his drive belonged to his *amies*, who'd come to *rester à la maison pour une semaine*.

Feeling pleased with himself, Marcus then grew ambitious and tried to formulate, 'You wouldn't have a spare room you'd like to let to them?' when he found himself at the head of the queue, having to concentrate instead on loaves and euros and a short interaction on the prospects of a sunny day. As a concerned-looking Madame Bouziges, bread in hand, accompanied him up the path towards where Claude was tinkering quietly in the kitchen, Marcus hoped there wasn't going to be a confrontation of any sort.

But, after a short conversation, Claude said, 'My aunt has a spare mattress you can borrow, but stipulates that it must not be put directly on the hideously filthy floors upstairs. However, I have plastic sheeting, which will solve that problem.'

'Great. Maybe I can go and buy some duvets and pillows and things today.'

'Ha! My new assistant is taking time off already?'

'Is that OK?'

'Well,' said Claude, leaning towards him, 'that would depend. I mean, if you ever find having *two* beautiful lovers a little debilitating . . .'

Marcus grinned. 'Yeah, yeah, I'll let you know.'

Later, as he drove along the narrow winding roads on his way to civilisation and bedding shops, Marcus wondered what had motivated Jo's spur-of-the-moment journey. Was it the prospect of a cheap holiday for herself and her student? Did she just feel sorry for him, all on his own? Or was she more keen on him than she'd let on? She'd definitely been up for it on his first day in Oxford, and she hadn't spurned him the night he almost drowned in her face cream. But didn't Jo have every woman's fantasy as her boyfriend? Marcus was decidedly short of glistening coffee-coloured muscles and hadn't intercepted a single thing on the high seas. It didn't make sense.

As yet another vehicle to his rear waited for a blind bend to appear before overtaking him, Marcus sighed, not just at the daring of French drivers but at how irritating it was that women were so hard to read. It had been lovely to see Jo when she and Keiko arrived around ten last night – a fantastic surprise, in fact – but there'd been no polite way of asking, 'So why exactly are you here?'

* * *

'But I thought cords were making a comeback?' Robin said to Theo.

'Not ones with ink on them and bald patches on the knees and that elephant-bum look at the back. Honestly, Dad, you could fit another set of buttocks in there.'

Robin peered over his shoulder at the mirror. Theo was right. Did corduroy expand when spun twice a week for fifteen years, or had he simply lost weight? 'I see what you mean.'

'Here, try these,' Theo said, handing him a pair of black trousers in a synthetic material that Robin might have marched against at one time.

'Well, OK,' he said reluctantly, while his son whooshed a changing-room curtain back for him. 'But I'm happier sticking to cotton and wool, as you know.'

'These are eighty per cent cotton,' said Theo, closing the curtain.

Robin pulled a doubtful face and checked the label. So they were. He stripped off, and before he'd got the trousers done up, Theo was back with a kind of grey/black shirt and a light-coloured jacket that had something of the lounge lizard about it. 'Thanks,' Robin said, and proceeded to pour himself into the ridiculously stylish items, thanking heaven he wasn't in Oxford and likely to bump into a friend or, worse still, one of his students. He put his shoes back on and tried to get a good view of himself, but the cubicle was too small, so he coura-geously stepped out into the shop, where Theo and another male assistant both cried, 'Oh, yes!'

'Are you sure?'

'Absolutely,' said Theo.

'*Quelle transformation*,' said his camp colleague.

Robin found himself being spun round to face a full-length mirror, in which was the image of a hip middle-aged guy who'd

132

probably partied at many a Soho loft. It was a man who spotted and bought the work of up-and-coming artists and who hadn't dated anyone over thirty, ever. It definitely wasn't Robin, but he nevertheless slipped his hands into the trouser pockets to see what the effect would be. Pretty cool, actually, but how they'd mock him in the department if he pranced around looking like a lost graphic designer.

'I could arrange a great haircut for you with Crispin at Snip 'n' Tuck,' Theo was saying. 'Get rid of those ageing-hippy locks. What do you think?'

Robin wasn't sure what he thought. He was fond of his old look. He and it had been together a long time. And, what's more, he'd only had a haircut last week.

'I'm not sure,' he said, swinging his shoulders as he carried on checking himself out in the mirror. 'Hey, where are you going with my clothes?' he called out to Theo's retreating back.

'I'll bag them up for you, shall I? You could always drop them off at the Save the Children, next street on the right. How did you want to pay? Debit card, credit card?'

'Look, I'm not so sure it's *me*,' said Robin, as a thirtysome-thing couple were sifting through shirts on a nearby rail.

'What do you think of this blue?' the man asked his partner, but the woman was looking Robin's way and smiling quite beau-tifully at him. She gave his outfit an approving nod and Robin mouthed, 'Really?' and she nodded again and he decided he'd stick it all on the credit card.

Once Theo had removed all the labels, he put the transac-tion through the till and asked his father for £285.

'Bloody hell,' Robin said, wavering with his card. He lowered his voice. 'What happened to the discount you promised?'

'That's been taken off.' Theo raised an eyebrow. 'Style doesn't come cheap, you know.'

'Cheaply,' corrected Robin, trying to get at least one up on his son.

'I was told to ask for Crispin?' he said to a girl of around ten. All members of staff were ten years old and all were dressed in black but with lots of bare bits showing. There was no excess flesh on any of them.

'Do you have an appointment?' she asked, all wide-eyed and clear-skinned and silky-haired.

'No, but I think my son may have phoned him.'

'Just one moment,' the girl said, and she slinked across the room to a skinny boy who was tousling a woman's hair with a serious-looking dryer. The girl said something to him, the boy nodded, and the girl slinked back again. 'Crispin's going to squeeze you in,' she told Robin. 'He won't be long.'

'Great.'

'Would you like a coffee?'

'That would be nice.'

'Filter, cappuccino, latte, espresso, mocha?'

'Filter, please. Black.'

'Decaff?'

'No, thanks.'

'Fairtrade?'

'Why not.'

Robin took a seat and flicked through magazines aimed at the kind of men who wore the clothes he himself was wearing, only they'd be a good deal younger, he suspected. Sport, women, music, cars, women, gadgets, movies, fitness, women . . . The magazine posed lots of questions. 'Is this the sexiest woman on TV?' it asked of someone he didn't recognise, straddling a chair in the altogether. Robin's answer was, 'Almost certainly.' Next came, 'Is your shower gel letting you down?' Robin, a confirmed bar-of-soap man, moved on to what he thought was a sports article – 'Boxer comeback?' – but which turned out to be an underwear feature. Having discovered the joy of boxers only last year – Hannah had insisted – Robin was quite pleased to see they'd be around a bit longer.

'Do you want to come through?' he was suddenly being asked. 'Jade will shampoo you, then I'll bring you your coffee.'

Robin took one last look at the sexiest woman on TV, closed the magazine and prepared to be cruelly ejected from his floppy-fringed comfort zone. How had he let his son talk him into this? 'May as well go for the whole look,' Theo had said loudly enough for the lovely woman shopping with her chap to hear. Once again she'd nodded at him.

Robin got up and made for Jade by the washbasins. Just a tidy-up was what he'd insist on with Crispin. Bit of a trim, no more.

Jo pulled her arm out from under the duvet and swivelled her watch around. It was late. Past eleven. She rolled over to discover the rest of the bed was empty, and for a while luxuriated in being able to stretch in all directions after the sardine-can night. She heard a man and a woman speaking French somewhere nearby but couldn't catch what they were saying. There were bumping noises and rustling noises and what might have been the odd swear word.

She lay for a while thinking she ought to get up, but inspected the room instead. Unlike the rest of the house, it was very pleasant. It had a nice wooden floor and its wonderfully uneven walls had been painted white. There was an antique chest of drawers and an equally old-looking mirror, and on two of the walls hung primary-coloured bits of modern art. The bed itself had a frame of good, solid wood and had no doubt cost a fortune. Light filtered in through thin orangey-red curtains, giving the room a cosiness that was going to be hard to leave. But leave she must, for the sake of politeness. She reached for her glasses, got out of bed fully clothed, put her shoes on and approached the French voices.

'*Bonjour*,' said a dark-haired woman holding one end of an upright double mattress.

'*Bonjour*,' replied Jo. She stood still while the mattress bent itself round a door frame and the person at the other end came into view.

'Good morning,' puffed the man, who was younger than the woman but just as dark-haired and olive-skinned. He was a couple of inches shorter than Jo. 'Excuse us. We've just got to get this through . . . ah, success. I'm Claude, by the way. And this is my aunt, whom Dom and Lucy always call Madame Bouziges, so you may as well, too.'

'*Enchantée*,' Jo said to the woman. '*Je m'appelle Jo.*'

'Yes,' Claude said. 'We know.'

With the mattress settled on top of a large sheet of plastic, Jo went over and shook hands with first Claude, then Madame Bouziges, who told her Marcus had gone off to buy bedding and wouldn't be back for a couple of hours, so why didn't she and her friend join her for lunch? Jo said they'd be delighted, but that she'd like to have a shower first, and Madame Bouziges wandered off with a smile and a wave, apologising in advance that it would be a plain meal of bread, cheese and fruit.

'That's very kind of your aunt,' Jo said.

'I think she's just delighted to have someone here who understands her.'

'Oh? Marcus told me he spoke French quite well.'

Claude sniggered, then said, 'Look, I'm afraid the shower isn't yet connected, however the bath *is* functioning at last.'

'It wasn't when Lucy and Dom were here?'

'I believe not.'

'Blimey.'

'Tell me,' said Claude, pushing the door to, 'your friend, Keiko – does she have a paramour?'

'You mean bloke?'

'Yes.'

'Not so far as I know.'

'Excellent. Well, I must be getting back to work. When you've finished your ablutions I'll take you to my aunt's house.'

'Pardon?'

'After you've bathed, I'll—'

'Oh, right.'

The bath was surprisingly brand-new-looking and clean, and from where she lay up to her chin in bubbles, Jo was able to enjoy a spectacular view of the distant hills and forests, thanks to a hole in the wall where a first-floor outside door had been, and where a window would be. Apparently, the old cast-iron bath had exited the building that way.

It was a glorious day, much better than the previous one, and now that the bed situation was getting sorted, Jo was sure the holiday would work out well. Poor Marcus. So flummoxed last night. Although he'd appeared genuinely pleased to see them, he'd been embarrassed by the state of the place, and talked about finding them accommodation in the nearest town, fifteen kilometres away. Now what fun would that have been?

Jo could hear Claude talking as he sawed at something beneath the window – or hole – then Keiko giggling, then Claude talking again and sawing. All the while, the aroma of his Gauloise hung in the air, confirming for Jo, as no other smell could, that she was on a continental holiday.

After dressing in shorts and T-shirt and applying lots of sunblock, just in case Madame Bouziges liked to lunch in the garden, Jo headed for the stairs saying, '*Don't* forget the missing one,' over and over to herself. Last night, she and Marcus had had to lift small Keiko over the gap.

Thanks to a fairly generous credit transfer from Lucy and Dom, Marcus had not only gone to town, but he'd also gone to town. In the back of the car were the required sheets, pillows and duvets, as well as a hammock and a badminton net to set up in the garden, and table football for indoors. Did women like table football? Well, he'd find out. In addition, he'd bought a portable television with built-in DVD player, a stack of DVDs – all either French or dubbed in French – several French board games and half a dozen French novels. If his grasp of the language didn't improve after that lot, he'd be amazed.

Obviously, they wouldn't spend all their time playing games and watching films. If he put in a few hours each morning with Claude – something he felt he was pretty much committed to now – then he and the women could go out on trips, see the gorges and caves, that kind of thing. How brilliant that Jo and Keiko were here, he found himself thinking and, fairly guiltily, how good that Hannah and Freddie weren't. He'd more or less decided before leaving Oxford not to rock that particular boat any longer. Or put all his eggs in one basket. Messier still, of course, would be to rock the boat *with* the basket of eggs in it.

As he pulled up outside the house in Laroche-les-Bois, Marcus continued the maritime theme, telling himself that time and tide wait for no man and that there were plenty more fish in the sea besides Hannah. He took the boxed TV from the passenger seat and carried it past a strange car – a friend of Claude's? – and through to the living room, where he stopped and blinked several times at what he saw. Either Claude had shrunk to half his size in the past three hours, or Freddie was crossing the floor with an enormous hammer in his hand. Marcus blinked again and had the wherewithal not to drop the brand-new television on to the concrete beneath him.

'Freddie?' he said nervously, as though waiting for the spooky apparition to fade away.

'I'm going to be Claude's mate,' said the ghost. ''Cos his old one's buggered off.'

'No, no,' Claude called out from a far corner. 'I said "bunked" off, Freddie.' He looked over at Marcus. 'Isn't that the right expression?'

'Hello, Marcus,' came Hannah's voice from somewhere. He turned and she rushed towards him, then managed to hug both him and the TV. 'I couldn't not come,' she said.

Claude was giving him a kind of ooh-la-la, aren't-you-the-lucky-one smirk, but as Marcus kissed Hannah's cheek and said how great it was to see her, his head filled up with rocky boats and baskets of eggs.

Jo was learning all there was to know about Laroche-les-Bois. How the local mine had closed down – she hadn't quite caught what kind of mine – and how that had led to high unemployment and a general deterioration in the area. Homes needing so many repairs they were often simply abandoned, young people fleeing the moment they were old enough. When they'd all finished eating and Madame Bouziges and her father-in-law, Bertrand, stopped talking to light cigarettes, Jo translated for the excluded Keiko.

'Ah yes, Claude told me,' Keiko said. 'But he also said many foreign persons come to buy houses and have holiday, and so local economy is now . . . uh . . .' she delved into the bag at her feet for her notebook, opened it up and said, 'relatively buoyant.'

'Really?'

'And that many rural place who rely on farming and mining must expect, er, vi-cissi-tu-di-nous times.'

'Sorry?'

'I look up. It means changing fortune.'

'I know,' said Jo. Of course she knew.

Madame Bouziges had her eyebrows raised as though waiting for a translation, but Jo didn't feel she had the energy, so told her Keiko had enjoyed the lunch very much and said to thank her. Keiko, abandoning her diet, had launched into the bread with gusto and practically ignored the cheeses, pissing Jo off somewhat after the lengths she'd gone to over the months.

Madame Bouziges said they were both welcome, then asked, pointing at Keiko, if she was from a wealthy family.

'*Je ne sais pas,*' said Jo with a shrug, although she thought perhaps she was. Keiko was quite a shopper and two terms at the best language school in town would have set the family back a bob or two.

It was just that her nephew could do with a rich wife to help him through air-traffic school, Madame Bouziges went on. She and her father-in-law gave throaty laughs and Keiko began to look a bit uncomfortable.

'Madame Bouziges says the mining was a dangerous and filthy job,' Jo told her, suddenly keen to get back to the house. She liked Madame Bouziges and Bertrand very much, but she liked Marcus more. 'And that most people were glad to see the industry die out.'

'Ah.'

After profuse thanks and the promise to cook some Japanese food for Madame Bouziges if they could find the ingredients,

Jo and Keiko headed back, hoping Marcus had managed to find them some bedding. His car was in front of the house, parked behind another Jo didn't recognise. While passing, she stopped and peered through one of its windows and saw assorted comics and children's books strewn over the back seat. All of them English. At the far end of the seat sat a small blue box, open and spilling mini-sized tools. 'Keiko,' she said, steadying herself on her lodger, 'it might be time for chocolate again.'

Keiko opened up her bag and dug around. 'I have only energy tablets, which man in mountain clothes shop said hikers must carry all times.'

'They'll do.'

WEDNESDAY

It was Theo's day off and they'd done the castle and were on their way to an art gallery, when Robin, missing Freddie quite badly, said, 'How do you fancy going to the zoo?'

Theo gave a snort. 'I am twenty, you know, Dad.'

'Is that a no, then?'

'I vote we skip the modern art and go and meet up with Joss and Jonty at Va Va Voom. You'll love it. Cocktails to die for and the fittest women in town serving you. What do you say?' He looked anxiously at his watch in a way that indicated he'd prearranged the Va Va Voom thing and they were running late. But it wasn't yet one o'clock and the last thing Robin felt like was a drink with a rude name. On the other hand, he wasn't that bothered about the modern art either. He just wanted to be at the zoo, with a wide-eyed, loving-it-all Freddie. And he wanted to be there *now*, before Freddie grew old and cynical and took up polo.

'Tell you what,' said Robin, 'why don't you go and meet your friends and I'll nip round the gallery and catch up with you later? Text me to let me know where you are.'

'Yeah?' said Theo, taking small backward steps away from his father. 'Are you sure?'

'Quite sure. Plus, I need to buy a hat to cover this hair.' Robin laughed. 'Or rather, lack of it.' Young Crispin had obviously misheard 'Just a bit of a trim' as, 'Take it down to an inch and nice and spiky on top.'

'You look great,' Theo called out, now well on his way. 'Very De Niro!'

Oh sure, thought Robin, but he nevertheless wandered over to the nearest shop window to check himself out, hands in trouser pockets, stomach tucked in. Yes, in actual fact there was something of the younger Robert De Niro about him, although his colouring was more Pacino, perhaps. As the new look began to grow on him, Robin noticed someone waving at him from inside the shop. He stepped back, looked up, and saw that he was outside Snip 'n' Tuck, so waved back at the person in black – Crispin or Jade, he wasn't sure – and, suddenly getting his bearings, realised he was very close to Theo's clothes shop.

He took a jacket, two pairs of trousers, two shirts and a couple of nice ties to the young woman at the till, and she removed the big plastic tags and scanned the bar codes, all the while making pleasant conversation about the weather, the number of visitors in Edinburgh and how Oxford was one of her favourite cities. Robin had found nothing but the utmost courtesy and friendliness since his arrival in Scotland and told her so.

'Why thank you,' she said graciously, then asked him for five hundred and something pounds.

'Really?' Robin leaned forward and, behind a hand, whispered, 'My son Theo works here, and yesterday passed on his staff discount to me. I don't suppose . . .'

He stopped because the young woman's demeanour was changing. Her eyes narrowed, her lips pursed themselves, and she finally said, '*Did* he indeed? Well, I shall be having a word with him about that tomorrow.'

'Oh dear. Are you the manager?'

'Yes. As I said, that'll be £594.50 please.'

'Of course,' said Robin, handing over his card. 'Cheap at the price. And such excellent quality. As Theo is always saying.' He would have carried on but could see from her face that his attempts at damage limitation weren't working. His son would be out of a job tomorrow. Should he track him down and tell him, or just quietly slip out of town?

While the till made its processing noises, the woman said, 'It's just that I'm sure he gives all those poncy uni friends his discount, by pretending he's buying for himself.'

'Actually, I could verify that Theo does have a remarkably extensive wardrobe,' Robin told her. 'You know, if it ever went to court.'

She laughed and looked friendly again. Very friendly. 'Listen,' she said, 'if you fancy meeting up for a drink later, I could overlook what he did yesterday.'

Robin – truly stunned – took in the person before him. Mid-thirties at most. Pretty. Slim, but at the same time curvaceous. Dark hair held back in some kind of comb thing. Interesting grey eyes. It seemed to Robin that, for the sake of his son, he had no alternative but to accept her invitation.

Hooray. In spite of fly-in-the-ointment Jo – Jesus, what a shock to find her here – am feeling happy, happy, happy. This morning I found myself missing the daily writing habit, so managed to pick up this little notebook in the village shop. As I sit here on a bench in the middle of Laroche-les-Bois,

*under a fabulously clear April sky (praying Freddie isn't elec-
trocuting himself up at the house) I'm wondering – despite
current cheerfulness – which would be the best method of elim-
inating the opposition. Poison, strangulation, or a knife in the
middle of the night?*

*The trouble is, apart from the sneaky, duplicitous side of
Jo's character, I do almost like her. Even when she walked in
yesterday afternoon and found that Freddie and I had turned
up to spoil her party – her face was a giveaway – she came
and gave us both a hug and immediately went to talk to the
caretaker woman about getting more beds. Hard to push
someone like that down one of the steep inclines round here.*

*Well, she didn't actually succeed on the bed front, so Fred
and I slept with Marcus in the one decent room in the house
and Jo and Keiko shared a double mattress in a shell of a
room nearby. (Hannah 1 – Jo 0.) During cuddles – no more,
unfortunately – and whispers in the middle of the night,
Marcus assured me he and Jo weren't an item. That Jo had
turned up out of the blue, and that he wasn't sure why but
thought maybe she just fancied getting away and having a
cheap holiday.*

I wonder what it is that makes men so unperceptive?

*With Lucy and Dom's permission, Claude has gone off in
his big van to buy dining chairs and crockery and other stuff.
I suppose some of us could move out to make things easier,
but then there'd have to be pistols at dawn to sort out who
goes.*

*Jo and Keiko are walking in the hills – here's hoping they
get terminally lost – and Marcus is doing one or two little
jobs in Claude's absence – with Freddie's help. Or hindrance.
Maybe I should get back and check they're OK. It is glorious,
sitting here in the sun, but I do feel I've been examined enough*

*by those two guys outside the Sports Bar, silently drinking beer
and watching the minimal village activity. These are the things
I love about rural France — the almost standstill pace of life,
the lack of materialism . . . Heaven.*

It was a punishing walk. A good thing, Jo told herself. She
needed punishing for coming to France in the first place, when
there'd been, if she'd only stopped to think, a strong chance of
Hannah turning up. She also needed punishing for letting herself
get carried away on the Marcus front, and for bringing her
lodger to a place with a lot of tension in the atmosphere, not
to mention a missing bathroom wall and barely a place to sit.

Hopefully, Claude was sorting out the seating problem as she
and Keiko lost, then found, then lost again, the footpath that
was on Lucy and Dom's map but wasn't always on the ground.
Many of the hill paths were excruciatingly steep, and some
became fairly precipitous ledges that turned her knees to jelly.
It was hell. And it was hot. Far too hot for their altitude and
for April, *and* she'd foolishly worn a jumper.

She cupped hands around her mouth and yelled, 'Keiko!' to
the figure a long way ahead and growing smaller. 'Lunch!'

'OK!' Keiko shouted. She arrived back, in sleeveless T-shirt
and no perspiration, to where Jo had thrown herself and small
rucksack down and was now fishing around for water.

'I'm not usually like this on walks,' she told Keiko. 'Honestly.
Normally, I've got bags of energy and enthusiasm, but at the
moment I just want to go back and read a book in a very dark
place.'

'I think maybe you are tired. Last night, all the night, you
were like this.' Keiko did an imitation of someone flailing in
their sleep. She even shut her eyes.

'Was I?'

'Yes. Very much. Is it because Hannah has come to house?'

'*No.*'

'Claude and me think you and Marcus is perfect couple.'

'Oh, yeah?' chuckled Jo. 'When did you discuss this?'

'Today, before he went to buy marbles.'

'Actually, I think he went to buy furniture.'

'Yes, marbles. It is French word for furniture.'

'Of course. So, listen, what else did Claude say about Marcus and me?'

'That Hannah is very beautiful, but you have . . . uh.' She took a book out of her bag – a new notebook that didn't have Marge Simspon on the front – and turned to the first page. 'Ah yes, *joie de vivre*, and also handsome *derrière*.'

Jo laughed. 'Are you sure he said handsome?' It made her bottom sound a bit too substantial.

Keiko nodded.

'Not sexy or alluring?'

'No.'

Oh well, handsome was probably better than nothing. 'So he thinks Hannah is beautiful?'

'Yes. But also he says he has looked into her eyes and seen . . .' she checked her notes, '. . . aggrieved and tormented soul.'

'Really?' said Jo, suddenly worried. Aggrieved and tormented souls were probably the most trouble. But then who was to say Claude was right? It did occur to her, as she glugged back delicious water, that if he stopped ogling people's rears and peering into their souls, the house might get finished a whole lot sooner.

Marcus had given up trying to keep Freddie from potentially live electrical wires and other tragedies waiting to happen, and was walking him into the village when they met Hannah on her way back to the house.

147

'We thought we'd try out the Sports Bar,' he told her. 'Fancy?'

'Are you sure women are allowed in?' she asked with a chuckle.

How lovely it was to hear Hannah laugh again. Her fair complexion had already managed to catch the sun, and she radiated a kind of contentment Marcus hadn't seen in her for years.

'Shall we go and find out?' he asked, and she immediately hooked an arm through his, then took hold of Freddie's hand, and the three of them sauntered down the road and into the square, like a perfectly perfect little family unit. Which Marcus had to keep reminding himself they weren't. So far, no mention had been made of Robin and how he felt about them coming to France. Marcus decided he'd bring it up, though, and when they were all seated beneath a screen showing football, digging into their *Croque Monsieur* – served by the elderly proprietress – he did just that.

'He was fine about it in the end,' said Hannah with a wave of a hand.

'Yeah? Well, that was good of him.'

'Mm. Freddie, eat up there's a good boy.'

'He didn't want to come with you then?' asked Marcus.

'Look, ham and cheese. Your favourites. If you eat this, Fred, we'll get you something nice in the shop.'

'Can I get a lectric drill like Claude's?'

'No, I meant an ice-lolly or something.'

'I'd rather have a lectric drill.'

'I know you would.'

'So what's he doing?' asked Marcus.

Hannah was busily cutting up Freddie's food. 'Who?'

'Robin.'

'Oh, he's gone to see his son in Edinburgh. Having a great time, I expect. Theo will have him out clubbing.'

Marcus laughed. 'Hard to imagine.'

'Yes. Good boy, Fred. There, it's yummy, isn't it?'

'And you're leaving Tuesday, did you say?'

Hannah began brushing invisible crumbs off the table, then she straightened out the plastic checked cloth and brushed at nothing again. 'That was the original plan but I'd love us to stay longer.' She looked up at him. 'I'm sure we could change our flights. If that would be OK with you?'

'And Robin?'

'Of course.' Her eyes flickered, just slightly. 'I'll give him a call.'

'Great,' Marcus said, managing a smile.

Something about it wasn't great, he knew that. Hannah had gone from calm to tense in a matter of minutes, and Marcus felt a growing sense of unease. As much as he adored them, he wished he hadn't suggested Hannah and Freddie came out to France. How could Robin – so furious at first, according to Hannah – have had such a change of heart? Perhaps he hadn't, and in that case the gods were bound to make them pay for this in some way. He suddenly saw Freddie falling from the hole in the first-floor bathroom . . . through that gap in the stairs . . . 'Oh God,' he whispered at the thought, and Hannah asked him what was wrong. 'Are you absolutely certain you want to stay?' he said. 'It's such a dangerous place for Freddie. And surely Robin—'

'*What?*'

'I only meant—'

'Come on, Fred,' she said. Her eyes had grown wild and unfriendly, her cheeks went from lightly tanned to crimson. 'No, leave that. Come on, we're going.'

'To the shop to buy a drill?' said the ever-hopeful Fred as he was lifted from his chair.

'Hannah?' Marcus called out to their backs. 'Hannah?'

He would have run after them but he needed to pay, and the man in a tight vest, propped on folded arms behind the bar and glued to the football, didn't look the understanding type. Marcus went over to him with bill in hand but then thought better of leaving, and with a resigned sigh said, '*Une bière, s'il vous plaît.*'

The man cranked himself to attention, took a bottle from a cold cabinet and knocked the cap off below the bar. '*Les femmes,*' he said to Marcus with a nod towards the door, then a shake of the head and a shrug of his hairy shoulders, 'enigmateek, *oui?*'

'*Oui,*' said Marcus, surprised to hear the guy could speak English.

He took his beer outside and sat with a couple of men of indeterminate age at an old metal table that could have done with a Claude paint job. They nodded, he nodded, and then they all watched a tiny old lady, possibly dressed in mourning, work her way steadily down the incline towards the village shop. After five minutes or so, she emerged from the doorway and Marcus and the others followed her progress back up the road and into her house with her bag of groceries.

Two vehicles in a row passed through the village, but after that there wasn't much excitement for a while and Marcus sat sipping his rather good beer until a vision of sweatiness appeared round the corner of the Sports Bar.

It spotted him, climbed the three steps to the terrace and said, 'Get me one of those beers, will you, Marcus? I'm completely shagged out. Do you want one, Keiko?'

Could Marcus have made it clearer he didn't want us here? Now he's concerned about Robin's feelings. Why didn't he think of that before rolling up in Oxford, let alone inviting us to France? Jesus, what a mess. What to do, what to do . . .

moules, crêpes Suzettes, escargots à la bourguignonne . . .

*Really wished I hadn't stormed out of the café like that –
Freddie was upset, I could tell. And, actually, now I've popped
a pill, Marcus's words don't seem quite so hurtful. Anyone in
their right mind would be worried about Freddie's safety in
this place. He's currently watching Claude assemble flat-pack
dining chairs, following him around in total awe. So sweet.
I'm sure he'd love to add Claude to his list of daddies.*

*How to play it, though. That's the thing. Marcus hasn't
returned, so is probably licking his wounds. I can't believe he's
lost all feelings for me. Can't believe the Jo thing isn't just a
one-sided crush. I should stay and see how things pan out.
Definitely. How ghastly and defeated I'd feel if Fred and I
went back home early. And besides, I'd like to get Freddie
practising the French I've tried hard to instil in him over the
past three years, with little success so far.*

*There's Jo walking up the path and past the window now.
There's the top of Keiko's head and there's Marcus. He and Jo
are chatting and laughing. Shit. Could it be I'm wrong about
them? That Marcus lied?*

*OK, fix smile to face, say a cheerful 'hello' to everyone, act
as though the café business didn't happen, then go and hide
notebook under upstairs floorboards.*

'*Je soupçonne le Colonel Moutarde d'avoir commis le crime dans
la Salle de Billard avec le Poignard,*' announced Hannah.

Marcus said, 'Pardon?'

Keiko and Freddie just stared.

'She means "Colonel Mustard in the Billiard Room with the
Dagger",' said Jo.

Hannah feigned embarrassment. 'Sorry. I just assumed we'd
all want to practise our French?'

'Ah yes, what a good idea!' said Marcus, who was being ultra-sycophantic with Hannah, for some reason Jo couldn't make out. Insisting on taking over the cooking of dinner from her while she lazed in the hammock in the last of the day's sun. He'd bring her a G & T, he said, and apologised for there being no ice yet.

Marcus cooking had been an unsettling sight and involved a lot of fumbling, swearing and head scratching. In the end, Jo couldn't hold back any longer and went to help. After dinner, he'd suggested Hannah choose an evening activity for them all. It was to be Cluedo, she announced after giving it some thought, as Freddie might find it fun. How much fun the three year old would find an entirely French Cluedo was questionable. Already he was fidgeting on his chair and shooting at *Mademoiselle Rose* – alias Keiko – with the tiny revolver he'd taken a liking to.

Jo revealed her *Colonel Moutarde* to Hannah, making sure none of the others saw, then Marcus showed Hannah a card and the game continued, in French and quite painfully.

When Marcus, finding himself in the *Salle à Manger*, decided to accuse *Madame Leblanc avec la Clef Anglaise*, Hannah straight-away pounced on him for pronouncing it 'cleff' instead of 'cleh'.

'Sorry,' he said with a big apologetic smile, when really, Jo thought, he must have wanted to stretch across the table and slap the woman. She certainly did. And poor confused-looking Keiko might have been induced to join in.

'Hey!' shouted Freddie, suddenly spotting the potential murder weapon and grabbing it. The revolver was dropped from his other hand. 'A monkey wrench like Claude's got!'

'It *is* a monkey wrench in English – well done,' said Hannah, still in annoying schoolmarm mode. 'But while we're playing this game it's a *Clef Anglaise*. Can you say that, Fred? *Clef Anglaise.*'

'It's *not* a clay onglez,' Freddie insisted. 'Claude calls it a monkey wrench and he knows everything about tools.'

'Well, Claude likes to practise his English but we want to practise our French.' Hannah looked up at the others. 'Don't we, everybody?'

Jo watched a muscle tensing in Marcus's beautiful jaw. His blue, blue eyes met hers and were saying something; she had no idea what, but it was making her feel funny. She picked up her glass of wine and drank half of it in three gulps. Then she finished it off, excused herself and went through to the kitchen and topped up. Deep breaths, she told herself. Deep breaths. She drank half the glass, filled up again and wandered back to the game, which they seemed to have abandoned.

'We're going round the table saying whole French sentences,' Teacher informed her. 'Your turn, Keiko.'

Keiko put a hand over her mouth. 'Ohh,' she said. 'My French is very bad, but I learn from whistle-shop tour how to say, "*Est-ce que vous avez la taille en-dessous?*" It means: Do you have it in a smaller size? Very important phrase for Japanese persons.'

Hannah applauded and sang, '*Très bon travail!*' while Jo took another swig of wine and quietly vowed to thrash her at table football later.

'Your turn, Fred,' said Marcus, that muscle still twitching.

Jo wanted to lean over and caress his cheek and calm him down. No, kiss his cheek and calm him down. Kiss his cheek, calm him down, undo his buttons and somehow pin him to the back of the chair with the shoulders of his shirt. Would that be possible? She took another swig while Marcus's attention was on Freddie, and tried to work out the logistics.

'*Pipi,*' said Freddie with a giggle. 'It means wee.'

'Very good,' said Marcus.

Hannah didn't look so impressed. 'That's not really a sentence, is it, Fred?' She turned to Jo and smiled stiffly. 'Your turn.'

'Oh,' Jo said, caught on the hop. She'd just been securing Marcus to the chair with his leather belt. 'Sorry. Um. Not prepared. Er . . .' Oh hell, why couldn't she think of anything? She could speak French. Was it just too much wine? 'Um . . .'

'The first French sentence that comes into your head?' suggested Marcus, making unsettling eye contact again.

Jo thought she'd forget the chair and the shirt and the belt, and just drag him up to that bedroom bathed in orange light. '*Voulez-vous coucher avec moi?*' she heard herself say, and in the quiet that followed, Freddie asked his mum what it meant. Hannah didn't answer, but calmly told Jo she should really have used the familiar *veux-tu*.

'Yes,' said Marcus, either answering Jo's question or agreeing with Hannah.

THURSDAY

Robin had chosen to cut his stay short for a number of reasons, the main one being that he hadn't heard a word from Hannah since the message about her damaged mobile. He wasn't panicking, but felt on edge and basically wanted to get home, look up Ruth and Vic's number and be reassured everything was OK. Separation anxiety, he told himself. Perfectly natural in a parent. Hannah no doubt thought he had her parents' number with him and was probably wondering why he hadn't called *them*. He tittered to himself at the silliness of it all and got on, as best he could, with the cryptic crossword in a packed train that was going to take for ever to reach Birmingham, where he'd then have to change for Oxford.

He'd also pretty much exhausted Edinburgh's tourist attractions, and as Theo was back at work again – God willing – Robin didn't see the point of hanging around and expanding his waistline with those full English – or perhaps Scottish? – breakfasts he could never resist. His new clothes would stop fitting him for a start. He filled in 4 Across, picked a couple of hairs off his jacket and wondered how Freddie would react to his new-look daddy. Hannah, too. Would it bring a spark back to the relationship, or was it simply the Robin inside Robin that Hannah didn't find very exciting? It had often occurred to him that he might not have what it took to be exciting.

He filled in 12 Across and told himself he surely wasn't terminally dull. Something had attracted Hannah to him in the first place. However, yesterday evening, with Theo's boss, Phoebe, he had sensed he might have gone on a little too long about what an absolutely ace character his son was. It was just that he wanted to supply her with enough examples of Theo's trustworthiness and conscientiousness – even as a child – to convince her she should keep him on.

Eventually, she'd said – snapped? – '*Look*, I wouldn't have sacked him anyway. He's such a charmer with the customers, and has that wonderfully upper-class voice and air of authority. Do you know what I mean?'

Robin knew exactly what she meant about the voice, but had no idea where his son got it from. He himself had deliberately toned down his accent when first becoming a poly lecturer, and had continued to keep it that way. As for the air of authority, well, Theo had obviously got that from his mother.

'Believe me,' Phoebe continued, 'it's rare to find that kind of class and style in part-time staff.'

'I can imagine,' he said, then after fetching them two more drinks from the bar, steered the conversation to the plight of the Highlanders in the eighteenth and nineteenth centuries, a topic he felt a lot more comfortable with, and one he was sure would interest the very Scottish Phoebe. He'd been mistaken. While he gave not just his views, but also actual shocking figures on the abominable Highland clearances, her eyes began skipping around the room. 'So what are your interests?' he'd asked at this point, sensing it was time to drop the subject.

'Shopping mostly,' she'd said, looking at her watch, 'Listen, I'm going to have to dash. Sorry. Early start tomorrow. Stock-taking. It's been great chatting with you, though.'

'Yes,' he'd replied limply. 'With you too.'

Robin had sat and finished his beer, feeling a little foolish. No, not so much foolish as deceptive. In the shop, earlier, Phoebe had obviously seen what she assumed to be an urbane, slave-to-style type of guy, only to discover over drinks that she'd got . . . well, Robin. Still, it hadn't been a date – not to Robin's mind, anyway. He wouldn't do that to Hannah. 'Pathologically faithful' was what a particularly debauched colleague had once called him. He'd only gone for a drink with Phoebe to make up for his gaffe, and because he thought it might be nice to have a conversation with someone over twenty.

Afterwards, he'd caught up with Theo and his friends in a stark, metal-and-white restaurant, where everyone ordered extravagantly, then Robin ended up paying. Still, it had been nice to spend a few days with son number one, but now it was time to get home and find out how the other one was.

When, at Birmingham, he changed trains and found himself opposite an attractive woman of around forty, who half-smiled each time their eyes met, he tried not to encourage her and decided he really ought to attach a 'Beware – Sheep in Wolf's Clothing!' badge to his new gear.

Something unnerving was happening to Marcus. Something to do with Jo. There. It happened again when she passed close by on her way to the garden. A *frisson*, he'd call it, since he was in France.

He pondered on it as he helped Claude with the tiling. The first time was at the Sports Bar when she'd appeared so suddenly, shattering the tranquillity – or tedium – and shaking him from the gloom Hannah had left him with by chattering on about the disastrous walk she and Keiko had just attempted. Laughing about it, with what was a bit of dirt or squashed bug endearingly stuck to her damp forehead, until he'd reached across and wiped it away. Then wiped again, unnecessarily. He'd just really wanted to touch her.

Marcus handed Claude another tile.

He'd always found her attractive, of course, but you could be attracted to someone and not always find yourself having *frissons*. It was all very odd and surprising. Three times now he and Jo had ended up in or on a bed together, and although at those times he'd felt certain things – drunk, horny, knackered – he'd never felt particularly romantic.

'It's something of a metamorphosis, isn't it?' said Claude.

'Sorry?'

'The floor. Don't you think the tiles are transfiguring the room?'

'Oh, right. Yeah. Definitely.' Marcus wasn't sure 'transfiguring' was the right word but didn't feel confident enough to challenge Claude's English. The tiles were large and a warm orangey brown, and were exactly right for the living/dining area; a place that was out of bounds for the duration of the screeding and laying. The kitchen was next on the list but that was going to be harder not to use. They'd probably all have to go and impose on Madame Bouziges's cassoulets for a couple of days. 'Quite a transformation,' he told Claude, passing him another tile for his fifteen euros an hour.

Marcus briefly wondered if he was being overpaid, but then his thoughts went back to Jo and how, quite unexpectedly during Cluedo, he'd found himself getting all churned up over her. What had triggered it off, Marcus didn't know. It was a cumulation of things, maybe. The way she'd pronounced '*bureau*' without making that throat-clearing noise Hannah went in for whenever she came across the French 'r'. The way she'd occasionally gazed his way during the game with a faraway look in her eye. The way she asked him if he wanted to sleep with her . . .

'You seem a little distracted today,' Claude was saying. He made sure the tile lay absolutely straight then took another from Marcus. 'Please tell me to mind my own business, if you wish, but I'm most intrigued by this harem of yours.'

Marcus laughed. 'It's not quite that.'

'Hannah introduced herself to me as Mrs Currie, but I was under the assumption you were single.'

'She and I are married but separated. Divorce proceedings are in progress. Hannah now lives with Robin, who is Freddie's father.'

'Ah, so you have been apart a considerable time?'

'No. Just nine, ten months.'

Claude looked puzzled, so Marcus checked everyone was in the garden, took a deep breath and explained the paternity business, the house-sitting in Oxford and how he'd rashly invited Hannah and Freddie to France but Robin hadn't been at all keen on the idea.

'You know,' said Claude, 'people outside the Cévennes lead such interesting lives.'

'More like complicated and hellish. I wouldn't recommend it.'

'And Robin?' asked Claude, lowering his voice. 'He finally acquiesced to this holiday?'

'I'm not sure he did.'

'Oh,' said Claude, eyes widening.

'Quite.'

'And Jo?'

Marcus shivered. There it was again, at the mere mention of her name. 'What about her?'

'Well . . . once more, pardon my inquisitiveness, but is it a *ménage à trois* we have here?'

Marcus sniggered. 'To be honest, it's pretty much a *ménage à un* at the moment.'

'Hard to believe!' Claude cried, then said, 'Ah, but I forget, you *are* English.'

'Scottish, actually.'

'Even worse. The further from the equator a man is born, the less romance he has in his soul.'

'Rubbish!'

'What's rubbish?' came Jo's voice from behind, making Marcus start. She was close. He could smell her sunscreen. He turned round and smiled dumbly. Claude repeated his preposterous notion to her and she laughed a little too loud and a little too long – almost as though experience had taught her the very same thing – and wandered away again.

'Actually, do you mind if I clock off soon?' Marcus asked his boss. 'It's just that we've planned a picnic by the river. That spot you told us about. For Freddie, really.'

'No, no,' said Claude. 'You go and have fun. I do believe you deserve it after the tribulations and utter wretchedness of your recent life.'

'Yes,' agreed Marcus.

'Were you planning to swim?'

'If it stays this warm.'

'Keiko too? She's brought a bikini with her?'

'Er . . . presumably.'

'You know,' said Claude, eyes twinkling in the direction of the garden, 'the ladies are not required to wear the top halves of their swimwear. Do tell them. And perhaps I may join you later?'

'Sure.'

*   *   *

160

The tribulations and wretchedness of the past couple of years was not something Marcus liked to dwell on. But as he lay in the bath soaking off the smell of tile glue, he flashed back to when he first began to wonder where Freddie got his looks from. The way Hannah would casually laugh it off whenever he brought up the subject. The growing unease he'd felt, mental and physical. At last, when they'd been walking up Lochnagar, he'd said to Hannah, 'Is Freddie mine?' and she'd broken down, confessed to her affair with a lecturer in Oxford and begged his forgiveness.

He felt it all over again, lying there in the bath. The sickness in the stomach, combined with a kind of relief at knowing for sure. He'd carried on alone, made it to the very top of the mountain and looked down on the loch, exhausted but, after a great deal of thought about the situation, resigned to a business-as-usual approach. For Freddie's sake.

Marcus felt tears sting his eyes and put it down to the shampoo trickling from his hair. He filled a big plastic jug from the taps and rinsed the suds off, then lay back and took in the spectacular view through the missing wall. But business as usual hadn't been that easy. No doubt he should have just forgiven and forgotten and carried on loving Hannah the way he had before. Nobody's infallible, after all.

His feelings for Freddie underwent a slight shift, though. That was what he couldn't forgive her for. He still adored him and intended to do everything to protect his little boy and give him a great life, but something of the invisible bond had gone. Once again the tears pricked, so Marcus shook away the memories and turned his thoughts to the forthcoming picnic. It was just what they all needed, he decided, pulling the plug out, then standing up as the water drained away noisily.

He was reaching for a towel from the nearby rail when he spotted a small colourful movement by a tree towards the end of the garden, part-way up a slope. An exotic bird? No, not in this area. A peacock, maybe? He stood still, hand resting on the towel rail, waiting for it to reappear. But when nothing happened he shrugged and got on with the business of drying himself.

Shit, had he seen her? Jo stood quite rigid behind the tree, watching him through the cleft in the trunk. She should have been more careful. Not moved at all and worn tree-trunk brown instead of pink and blue. She pushed her glasses back up her nose for better vision and carried on staring.

Yesterday, when Marcus had been bathing, she'd accidentally caught sight of him standing in the bath towelling himself. She'd been searching for dropped pegs in the grass around the washing line and happened to look up at the house. Today, though, she had to admit it was deliberate – no matter how much she told herself they were still short of pegs.

'Lovely,' she sighed when he finally stepped out of the bath and out of sight. She meandered back to the house with a smile and had installed herself next to Keiko, filling baguettes, by the time Marcus walked in and asked if he could help.

'Here,' said Hannah, handing him a bag. 'Take this to the car. And Fred's going to need his bucket and spade if you can find them in the garden.'

'Right.'

Hannah then turned to Jo and Keiko. 'You couldn't go easier on the cucumber, could you? It tends not to agree with me.'

'Ahh,' said Keiko. 'So sorry.'

Marcus reappeared. 'Anything else for the car, Hannah?'

'Yes, here's our swimwear. Has everyone else got theirs?'

Yes, miss.

Marcus nodded. 'You know, you can go topless there, according to Claude.'

'It's pretty much the norm in France,' said Hannah, as though telling them something they didn't know. 'However, I've only brought a one-piece with me.'

'I have two-piece,' Keiko whispered to Jo. 'But Japanese girls don't like sun on body much. We prefer skin light as possible. Like supermodel skin.'

'What about Naomi Campbell?' asked Jo, slipping extra cucumber into each and every one of the sandwiches. 'She's black.'

'True. But anyway, if I go back to Japan more darker than my friends, I will be odd one out. Not good.'

'Are we almost ready, then?' asked Hannah. 'We'll miss the best of the sunshine if we dawdle much longer.'

'Yep,' said Jo, mustering a smile. Just a one-piece, eh? She wrapped the last of the chunks of baguette in foil, put it in with the others, wiped the work surface and rinsed her hands.

Everyone then gathered the last of the things and filed out the door, shouting, 'See you later,' to Claude.

'Indubitably!' he called back.

Before reaching Hannah's car – the only one with a child seat – Jo said, 'Oh! Forgot something. Sorry.' She dashed back to the house and up the stairs to the bathroom, where she inhaled the remains of Marcus's steam and popped her contact lenses in. Topless, but still wearing glasses, wouldn't have been a good look.

'Uh-oh,' said Lucy. She'd nipped back to Jubilee Street with some dried food for Maidstone, his having run out way ahead of schedule. Either Marcus had resorted to eating the stuff himself, or he'd horribly overfed the cat. Through the living-room window, she carried on watching Bram delve into pockets and bag for his keys. He finally found them and let himself into Jo's house.

Interesting.

According to Pippa, Jo didn't want Bram to know where she'd gone. Also according to Pippa, Jo was 'hot' for Marcus. This, combined with the fact that Pippa was 'hot' for any man but her husband and was for the time being staying in Jo's house, could mean nothing but trouble ahead. Lucy couldn't wait to tell Dom.

She pottered about for a while, suddenly not that anxious to go and do some work on the top floor. She took clothes out of the washer/dryer, watered the plants, checked Jo's house for signs of activity. It all looked pretty quiet. Pippa was probably at the salon. When the phone rang, she hurried to answer it before the machine did. Maybe it was Dom calling from the office.

'Hello?' she said.

'Hi,' said a slightly warbly Hannah. 'We've found a spot with a mobile signal so I thought I'd give you a call.'

'Great. How are you? How's the house coming on? Did Claude go and buy the things you needed?'

'Yes, thank God. We can all sit down now.'

'Look, I'm really sorry. We weren't expecting—'

'That's OK. Anyway, this is just a quick call to say Freddie and I might stay on a while, if that's OK with you?'

'Yes, of course.'

'Look, um, Robin's going to be back from Edinburgh on Saturday and he thinks we're at my parents'.'

'Oh?'

'He didn't want us to come to France.'

'I see.'

'He may have contacted Mum and Dad and found out we're not there, and . . . anyway, I'm sure he'll be fine about it.'

'Really?'

'It's just that I thought I ought to warn you.'

'Warn us?'

'I've just left him a phone message at home, telling him where we are and for how long. He, er, may well come round and see you, and it occurred to me he might think you colluded.'

'Ah.'

'So let him know you didn't, won't you?'

Too right they would. What the hell was Hannah doing? 'When will you be back?' Lucy asked, all of a sudden feeling she *was* colluding. Other people's stormy lives were fascinating, but she didn't want Dom and herself to be part of them.

'End of next week. Ish. I haven't changed our flight yet.'

This wasn't sounding good. Was Hannah not coming back at all? 'Right,' Lucy said. 'Well, I'm not sure what you want us to do with Robin. And, to be honest, Hannah, I'm a bit pissed off that you've got us implicated in all this, or at least involved. I mean, how's Robin going to react? We'll be here dealing with the fallout, no doubt, while you're swanning around . . . hello? Are you still there? Hannah?'

Cut off. Oh well, maybe for the best. She was probably being a bit hard on her. Lucy replaced the phone and checked Jo's house again. Yes! Pippa's car was outside and the bedroom curtains were at that very moment closing! She grabbed the phone again and settled herself into the armchair with the best view. Work could wait, she decided, as she tapped out Dom's number.

'Hi, it's me,' she said, and told him about Hannah, then about Bram turning up and the curtains and everything.

'She might just be giving him a massage,' said Dom. Almost, but not quite, spoiling her fun.

What is it with cucumber? I thought I'd fished it all out but must have missed a bit, for am now in indigestion hell. Will lie down in a bit. That always seems to help.

How amazing Keiko's being with Freddie. She's playing with him now, with the ball he can't fail to catch because it's so big. She's praising him every time, then pretending to miss it when he throws. I told her she's a natural nanny and offered her part-time work when we get back to Oxford. Totally illegal, of course. She seemed keen but said she has lots of work to do on her English next term as she wants to find a job in the Japanese hospitality industry, which sounded quite dodgy till she said 'like hotel receptionist'.

We were very lucky to find this small beach-like bit of bank, and to have it all to ourselves. Slut Jo is lying on her front, sunbathing in unnaturally tiny shorts and an undone top. Obvious, or what? I want to kill her. However, Marcus is taking absolutely no notice of her, and is some distance away to our rear, deep in a book.

I'm quite concerned about Lucy's sudden onslaught over the phone, and am wondering what she went on to say after I switched off. I knew she'd take Robin's side. Knew it. She just has no idea what it's been like for me, living with a man I have few feelings for. Trapped. A bit like this wind. Ouch. Must lie down.

Marcus was having an out-of-body experience, caused by what, he didn't know. Perhaps it was because the sun was hot and he wasn't wearing a hat. He looked down on himself reading. There in front of him, some way to the left, was a pretty woman in a deep-blue swimsuit, tucking a red notebook under her bottom for some reason. She then lay flat on her back with a small groan. Hannah. Marcus watched Marcus's eyes go back to the page, then stray again to another woman with shiny reddish-brown hair spread around her head on the towel beneath her. She was to Marcus's right and closer to the river. Jo. Jo was sunning herself on her front, her top unhooked at the back.

Marcus could see that although Marcus was giving the appearance of reading, he was in fact taking in the sleekness of Jo's back and the enticing bulge of her right breast, squashed beneath her. *Turn over!* his out-of-body head was willing her, and at last she did. Marcus then saw himself raise his book in order not to be caught ogling while she slid the straps down each arm and flung the top to one side. He swallowed hard, re-entered his body and shifted himself back a couple of feet, until his head was in the shade of a tree. *Calm down*, he told himself. *Read your Flaubert. They're just breasts.*

Jo rolled back on to her front and caught Marcus's eyes darting back to his book. She smiled to herself, propped her chin on her hands and took him in while he read. For such a fair-haired man he was actually quite brown, in that kind of nice even Scandinavian way. He certainly didn't look like someone who'd burn easily. He just looked good. Firm chest and squared-off, rather than sloping shoulders. She liked that in a man.

Jo sighed and wondered how things would have been if Hannah hadn't turned up. She was just about certain Marcus and Hannah weren't having sex. First, Freddie was sleeping in with them, and secondly, Jo had lain as still as a corpse two nights in a row in the bedroom next to theirs, listening out for tell-tale noises. None. Only the odd whisper. This morning, she'd overheard Hannah tell Marcus they ought to get hold of a single mattress for Freddie. 'Is it really worth it?' he'd said. 'Just for a few more days?' His response was met with silence, while Jo punched the air and carried on past their bedroom.

Ah well, she thought, her gaze now fixed on his solid, nicely shaped thighs. No point in dwelling on what might have been.

But then his eyes rose over the top of *Madame Bovary* again and fell upon her. She smiled and he lowered the book and smiled back, then lifted a hand and started doing something with his fingers. A gesture of some sort. Definitely aimed at her, since Hannah was flat out and the other two were busy building a mud castle. Now he was beckoning her with his head. His fingers, she realised, were suggesting a walk.

She nodded and pulled on her T-shirt. As quietly as she could, she stood up and crept past Hannah in her flip-flops until she reached the grassy bank where Marcus held out a hand to her and lifted her up to the riverside path. They walked along fairly slowly for a while in a companionable silence, very gradually speeding up. Then, after looking over his shoulder, Marcus grabbed Jo's hand again and almost broke into a run as he led her to a small wooded area, away from the riverbank. Once there, they ducked behind the first substantial tree they came to and kissed hungrily, despite being out of breath.

So sudden, Jo thought, stopping to gasp at air. But so nice.

'I don't know what's going on,' Marcus panted.

'What do you mean?'

They kissed again.

'I don't know if it's the sun or France, but I can't stop thinking about you.'

'Probably the sun.'

'Yeah.'

His hands roamed inside her T-shirt then down her back and over her bottom. It felt good, and so did he. She slid fingers inside the back of his shorts. So smooth, so firm . . .

'I love your body,' he told her, hands circling her buttocks.

'Really?'

'Mm.'

'Would you call it handsome?' she asked, nibbling his ear and tasting Summer Fruits shampoo.

'Definitely not.'

'I'm glad.' They kissed some more, then she said, 'We shouldn't be too long.'

'No.' He rubbed his cheek against hers. 'Don't leave on Monday. It's Easter Monday. There won't be any flights, any trains. Don't go.'

She kissed his neck. 'Yes, there are. Anyway, I have to go back.'

'Why?'

'Work to do, mortgage to pay.'

'I'll pay it.'

'Ah, there you are!' they heard Claude call out, and they turned to stone. 'I was beginning to despair of locating you! Hello, Freddie.' His voice was becoming slightly more distant. 'What's that you're building? . . . Oh really? . . . Ah, such a wondrous day for April . . . Are you OK, Hannah? . . . Sorry? . . . No . . . No, I didn't see them anywhere. Perhaps they're exploring. Here, Keiko, let me help you with that.'

They both breathed out and Marcus continued his exploring. 'I really want you to stay,' he said.

'Yeah?' she replied, then his lips were locked on hers again and she was sliding down the tree and leading him with her, until they tumbled sideways on to the mossy twiggy ground. She pulled back. 'So much that you'd pay my mortgage?'

'And your council tax.'

'God, that's so romantic,' she said, the palm of her hand on the front of his shorts, while he was unzipping hers.

'Your water rates . . .'

'Mmmm, tell me more. I love it.'

Marcus pecked her on the nose as he tugged at her clothing. 'So much for Claude's equator theory, eh?'

FRIDAY

It was three in the morning and Robin was listening to Hannah's message for the umpteenth time.

'Hi, Robin. You'll probably have discovered by now that Freddie and I didn't go to my parents' after all.'

He took another sip of whisky. Yes, now that she'd told him, he'd discovered it. He'd been picking up messages every day, but she'd left this one only yesterday.

'Sorry for not ringing your mobile and telling you, but I didn't know your number. It was in my mobile but I left that behind as it was broken.'

He'd searched the house and not found the phone. He did, however, discover her diary and had snapped the lock apart with the secateurs.

'What happened was, Jo and Keiko and Freddie and I all thought we'd come out to Lucy and Dom's place. Keep an eye on the building work for them.'

How Hannah loved to insult his intelligence.

'Freddie's having a ball with all the tools and equipment. You

170

can imagine . . .' forced laughter . . . '*We should be back some time next week.*'

Should?

'*Listen, give all the plants a thorough soaking, would you, Robin? They'll be parched by Saturday. Anyway, hope you had a good time in Edinburgh. Better go now and check on Fred.*'

If he came to any harm, he'd kill her.

'*Lots of love.*'

Yeah, right.

Robin put the receiver down. When he'd first listened to the message at 10.30, he'd tried calling her mobile but with no luck. Perhaps it was broken after all. She'd left no contact number. Deliberately, of course. But he'd go and see Lucy and Dom in the morning, find out where the hell his son was and how he could get to talk to him.

The whisky was helping, but on the whole, Robin was feeling hurt and livid and a thoroughly bad judge of character. Not to mention cuckolded. Of course, if Hannah could sleep with *him* when she was about to marry someone else, she clearly didn't take any of her partnerships that seriously. Which would be bearable – they could just drift apart like zillions of other couples – if it weren't for Freddie. Dear, sweet little Freddie. How he'd been looking forward to seeing him.

Draining his glass, Robin got out of the chair he'd been in for hours, picked up the empty bottle, swayed a bit, then meandered to the kitchen, slamming a photo of Hannah face down along the way. Time for bed and sleep. He needed a respite from his thoughts, if only for a few hours. God, how empty he was feeling. Should he force himself to eat something? Have a comforting nightcap? *If he offers to make us both a nice hot milky drink, I swear I'll scream.* No. No more Ovaltine. Ever. Instead, he downed two tumblers of water to prevent a hangover, then plonked up the stairs on leaden legs, aimed for the smallest bedroom and got under a duvet with dinosaurs on it.

'Oh, hi,' said Marcus. 'How are you?'

'I'm fine, but it'd be much better if you rang *me*, son. That lady who picks up the phone doesn't seem to speak English.'

'That's because she's French, Mum. Anyway, how's things? Restaurant OK?'

'Busy. Easter holidays now, you know. Did I tell you we've gone Slovenian?'

'Yes, you did.'

'Vinko's been a godsend.'

'Good.'

'And such a lovely man too.'

'Great.'

'Charming, good-looking and terribly romantic.'

'Romantic?'

'Your brothers call him my toyboy,' she said with a quiet chortle. 'He's fifty-six, you see.'

Marcus laughed. She was obviously charmed by this character. 'How's the weather up there?'

'Oh,' she said, 'fair to middling. By the way, we've taken down those blinds you had up in the living room. I don't know, I always think a window's not a window without curtains. Vinko agrees.'

'But I really liked—'

'Picked up a lovely set in Edinburgh, that Vinko was particularly fond of. Deep red with a gold thread. Reminded him of home, he said.'

'Well, so long as you haven't thrown the blinds out. When did you go to Edinburgh?'

'Vinko and I went for the weekend. I showed him all the sights and we had a whale of a time. He's terribly romantic.'

'So you said.'

'Oh, aye, and we've made a few changes to the bedroom. Vinko and I found we couldn't look at that Kandinsky without feeling giddy.'

Marcus frowned and drummed fingers on the receiver. What was with all this Vinko and I? 'Mum,' he said, half tittering, 'are you, er, trying to tell me something?'

'Well, yes,' she said. 'I suppose I am.'

'Not that you and this chef are . . . ?'

'Aye,' she said with a giggle. 'It's been what you might call a whirlwind romance.' He heard her glug at something. Dutch courage? No, his mother only drank at weddings and funerals. 'And, well, now we're a bit of an item, as they say.'

Marcus slumped into one of Madame Bouziges's armchairs. True, his mother had been widowed seven years now, but this was truly outlandish. 'What do you mean, a *bit* of an item?' he asked.

'We're keeping it casual for now. No point in rushing into marriage, we thought, so we're having a little trial.'

'In my flat?'

'Yes. Sorry about that, son. Only it didn't seem right for him to move in with me. Not with all the memories of your father around.'

'No, of course not.' What was he saying? His mother had a boyfriend. Unbelievable. 'But you've always been so . . . so Presbyterian, Mum.'

'Yes. Talking of which, your Aunt Janine hasn't spoken a word to me for a week. Not since I told her I'd most likely be converting.'

Marcus threw his head back and stared at bunches of dried

things dangling from a ceiling beam, expecting to wake up any minute next to a wriggling Freddie. Converting? What religion were they in Slovenia? And where the hell was it? 'To Islam?' he asked nervously.

'Oochh, don't be so daft. Catholicism. Anyway, are you keeping warm in those mountains? How's the sweater?'

'Er . . . it's fine, yeah. And anyway, it's very warm here. Look, Mum, are you sure you know what—'

'Not too lonely there in the middle of nowhere?'

'No, no. Not at all. Actually, Hannah and Freddie are here.' A silence followed while he waited for a response. 'Just for a week or so.' More silence. 'Mum?'

'Can't talk for much longer,' she said. 'Vinko and I are off to the cash-and-carry.' She sometimes did this with things she didn't want to hear. A coping mechanism. Either that, or she hadn't been listening again.

'OK,' sighed Marcus. 'Well, don't work too hard. Get those lazy brothers of mine to help.'

'Aye, will do. Mind you, Vinko has the stamina of ten men.'

Marcus wasn't sure he wanted to hear this. 'Well, thanks for ringing,' he said. 'I'll call you back in a couple of days.' If he hadn't flown home to confront the gigolo. Marcus didn't want to cast doubts on his mother's attractiveness – she was a lively blonde who'd just turned a mere sixty-two – but it could be the guy was just after a free lunch and a stake in their business.

'You're not back together, are you?' she was asking.

'Sorry?'

'You and her?' It was always hard for his mother to say Hannah's name. 'After all you went through? *We* went through.'

'No, we're not,' he said, wishing someone would tell Hannah. She'd just changed her flight to Thursday. 'Don't worry.'

'And don't you worry, either. He's a good man, Vinko.'

'I'm sure he is.'

After hanging up, Marcus asked Madame Bouziges, very nicely and with the aid of gestures, if he could make a very quick overseas call that he'd pay for. She took the wad of euros he proffered and he dialled his oldest brother, Andrew, who told him he'd never seen their mother so alive and happy.

'So what's this guy like?' asked Marcus. 'He's not a gold digger, is he?'

'Well, he'd be digging in the wrong place if he were,' laughed Andrew. 'Actually, he seems pretty loaded. Talking about extending the restaurant and their upstairs accommodation.'

'*My* upstairs accommodation.'

'What? Oh yeah, of course. You wouldn't recognise it now, though.'

'But I've only been away—'

'Beautiful Slovenian crockery. Vinko had it sent over. And these amazing rugs.'

'How nice. But where exactly am I supposed to live when I get back?'

'Ah. Yes. I'm not sure Mum's thought that through, what with all the excitement of it all.' Andrew laughed. 'There's always her house, of course.'

'I thought you might say that.' Marcus saw the heavy sideboard, ageing Regency-stripe wallpaper, Dralon three-piece suite with wings, and that swirly carpet that made you feel hungover even when you weren't. The brown patterned kitchen tiles . . .

'Anyway,' Andrew said, 'it's a good excuse for a tart-up.'

'But she's attractive as she is,' said Marcus dreamily, his mind on the turquoise bathroom suite.

'The house, thicko. Get it all done up. Modernised. You know she's been thinking of it for ages.'

'Oh, right.'

Madame Bouziges had begun hovering by the door, looking as though she might like a few more euros for the call. Marcus gave her a won't-be-long nod and wound down his conversation.

'Gotta go,' he told his brother. 'Things to do. You know, looking for a home and stuff.'

'Well, have fun.'

'Thanks.'

'Everything OK?' Jo asked a dazed-looking Marcus as he passed her in the kitchen.

He said, 'Yeah,' and stopped. 'I mean, no, not really.'

She looked over both shoulders then slid an arm around his waist and rubbed at his back inside his T-shirt. 'Have you had bad news?'

He nodded miserably. 'My mother's living in sin with a Slovenian she's known a fortnight.'

Of course she laughed.

'And what's more, they've appropriated my flat.'

'Ah.' Should she get in quick and offer him a home? No, no, no. 'Does that mean your mother's house is empty?'

'Yep.'

'So you could always house-sit her place?'

'I could,' he said, throwing his arms up. 'It's a lovely old place. Big and rambling. But it's not really me. I mean, my mother's not very old, but the house just has an elderly person's feel. And that kind of . . . aroma. Do you know what I mean?'

'Cabbage and Germolene?'

'No, that was my grandparents' house.'

'Mine too.'

'More Sunday roast and lavender polish.'

'Sounds OK to me.' Should she jump in with an offer now? What if her house had an aroma he didn't like?

Marcus said, 'Jesus, you can see how people lose their homes and are living in doorways before they know it. Could so easily happen to me.'

'Mm, scary.' Jo kissed his chin, he kissed her brow, then they gently rubbed cheeks. Come and stay with me! she wanted to urge him. Please, oh please. I'll turf a student out and you can have your own room. But instead she said, 'Don't worry. I'd bring you bottles of meths and fresh cardboard and stuff.'

'Thanks.' He embraced her and kissed her full-on, but Jo began to feel tense. Hannah could appear any moment and kill them both with a frying pan. 'You're too good to me,' he added, his hand roaming upwards. 'But, more importantly, you've got great tits.'

Jo giggled and slowly pulled away. 'This is no place to talk dirty.'

'Fancy a walk?' he asked, bobbing eyebrows.

'Uh-uh. You've got to help Claude, remember?'

As though hearing his cue, Claude then rumbled up the drive in his van and gave Marcus two honks to come and help him unload the tiles.

'Just think,' said Marcus. 'If we get the living room finished today we could be playing French Cluedo again tonight. How good would that be?'

'Don't like Cluedo,' came a small voice from somewhere. Under the sink? Jo and Marcus blinked at each other, jumped apart, then slowly bent down to look. 'It's boring,' said Freddie as he continued to work at something with a screwdriver in the space where a cupboard should be. The thing he was screwing – or unscrewing – looked like it might be holding the sink up. 'My best game is Simon Says.'

'*There* you are,' cried Hannah, flying through the door. 'I've been looking everywhere for you, Fred.' She rushed past Marcus and Jo and scooped him up in her arms. 'Madame Bouziges is going to take us to her favourite town to do some shopping and visit the caves. Keiko's coming too. Doesn't that sound like fun, sweetie?'

Jo's heart skipped a beat. She'd have Marcus all to herself! If she didn't count Claude. She could see from the look he was giving her that Marcus was having a similar thought.

Freddie dropped the screwdriver on the floor in a resigned way as he and his mother headed towards the door. But before she got there, Hannah halted and turned. 'Coming, Jo?' she said. Her piercing gaze seemed to say, 'Don't even think about staying behind.'

'Er, yeah, why not?'

Robin had obviously got Dom's mobile number from their answerphone message. He'd called Dom at work, and then Dom and Lucy had tossed a coin to see who would go home and deal with things. Robin had said he'd be at their house in thirty minutes for the *exact* location of their French place and a contact number. Dom won – or rather, lost – the toss, but Lucy had nevertheless volunteered to go, believing she was less likely to be pinned against the wall and punched under the ribs. Well, that was what she told Dom. The truth was, she'd hoped Robin would feel free to open up and bare his soul, and she wanted to be there to catch it all. Any juicy bits of information would have vacated Dom's head the moment he heard them. Or, more likely, he'd hand over the Laroche-les-Bois details and the two of them would straight away move on to interest rates.

'Robin?' she was saying now to the man on her doorstep. He wore a very nice blue/grey jacket, a dark blue shirt with a loosely knotted blue-and-green tie, and his hands were tucked in the pockets of beautifully cut trousers the colour of a tropical beach.

'Robin?' she asked again. She wasn't going to believe it till he said something.

'Ah yes, sorry. My son talked me into a haircut.' He tried to laugh but Lucy could see it was an effort.

'Come in,' she said, and he did, wafting something delicious her way as he passed. She took a deep breath.

'Lacoste eau-de-Cologne,' he informed her. 'Something else Theo foisted upon me.'

'It's very nice.'

'Thank you.'

'Coffee?'

'Love one. Strong would be good.'

She led him through to a kitchen chair where he sat and quietly stared into space while she busied herself. But the silence began to unnerve her. 'What a surprise Hannah's note was,' she said.

It seemed to bring him round. 'You mean you didn't know she and Freddie were—'

'No. We didn't know Jo and Keiko were going either.'

'They've gone there too? God, you must be a bit pissed off with them all?'

'Not really. We just feel sorry for them. Honestly, you should see the state of the place. Nowhere near finished and, well, totally hazardous, really.'

Robin sprang from his chair just as Lucy realised what she was saying. 'No, no,' she said, grabbing his arm as he passed her – presumably on his way to Laroche-les-Bois. 'Don't worry. Our wonderful French builder has taken control in the past few days. I'm sure Freddie's perfectly safe.'

Robin sat himself down again, heavily. 'Do you know when they're coming back? Or even if?'

'Well, I just called Hannah on her mobile. Miraculously it

worked, as they were in a built-up area. Shopping, apparently. Anyway, she . . . Robin, you're not crying, are you?'

'Hay fever,' he said unconvincingly.

'She told me they'd be back at the end of next week, unless . . .'

'Unless what?' he sniffed.

'Unless they . . . weren't, I think she said.'

Lucy poured a cup of very strong coffee for Robin and a watered-down one for herself. 'Milk?'

'Please.'

She handed him the jug. While he stared at his mug and tipped so much milk in that coffee overflowed on to the table without his seeming to notice, Lucy went for a cloth and wondered if she wasn't making a complete balls-up of this. Dom's approach might have been better after all. She rinsed the cloth, squeezed it and bounced back to the table.

'Bad news about that latest interest-rate rise,' she said, lifting his mug and dabbing away. 'A quarter of a per cent makes a *huge* difference when you've got a mortgage the size of Carfax Tower.' She laughed, hoping he'd join in. He didn't.

'Freddie loved Carfax Tower,' he said, 'when I took him up that time. He thought if he waved hard enough, his mum would see him from our attic window. I secretly phoned her and told her, and she said, "Freddie, that was a lovely big wave you gave me!" the moment we got back.' Robin looked up at Lucy with his wet eyes. 'She's a good mother, you know. Just a lying and deceiving partner.'

'In what way?' Lucy asked tentatively.

'Huh. Where would I begin? You see, I've only just . . . do you know, I feel quite sorry for Marcus now. I'm ashamed to say I've never given his feelings too much thought. I was just so thrilled to discover I had a fantastic little son.'

'That's understandable,' Lucy said. While Robin gulped his

very milky coffee, she leaned over and wiped the bottom of his mug. Those new clothes were much too nice to dribble on. What a makeover he'd undergone. She didn't know Robin that well, but couldn't recall seeing him in anything that might have been made this century.

'I must have some rights,' he croaked. He sniffed and blinked away tears. 'Being Freddie's father?'

'I'm sure you do,' Lucy said, although she wouldn't have held out too much hope. 'But listen, Robin, it's just a little holiday they're taking. I bet you they'll be back on Thursday or Friday. I mean, Hannah does have to teach the following week. Although, obviously, that wouldn't be her only reason for coming back. I'm sure . . .' She stopped, aware that Robin's so-called hay fever was getting worse. Tears now filled his reddening eyes. How vulnerable he looked. And tired. Kind of attractive, though. 'You know,' she began, certain that Hannah would kill her for what she was about to say, 'you're very welcome to go and join them.'

Robin raised his eyebrows at her in a questioning, hope-filled way.

She nodded. 'But I'd take a sleeping bag.'

'I'll think about it,' he said, sniffing again and taking something from the inside pocket of his nicely lined jacket. A packet of pills, by the look of it. He took two out, popped them in his mouth and washed them down with coffee, then held the box up. 'Antihistamines,' he told her with a wipe of his eyes. 'Bloody tree pollen.'

'Between you, me and the gatepost . . .' said Claude.

Marcus laughed.

'Sorry? This is not a commonly used colloquialism?'

'Yes, yes, it's fine. What?'

'Well . . .' Claude said, lowering his voice, 'I've been a little economical with the truth with regards to my three weeks' leave.'

'Oh?'

'Mm. Not long after I started the course, I began to suspect I might find a career in air-traffic control a trifle unfulfilling.'

'Really?'

'Not to say laden with mind-boggling responsibility.'

'I can imagine.'

'So I packed my bags and left.'

Marcus passed Claude a tile and stared at him. 'I'd call that being *very* economical with the truth.'

'I know.' Claude shook his head. 'Only my aunt would be vexed. Will be. When I tell her. There were costs involved, which the family rallied round for.'

'I see. So what are you going to do now?'

'Well,' said Claude grinning, 'my immediate plan, once this tiling is finished, is to repair the missing stair. I promised Keiko it would be fixed before she returns today. Apart from that, I have no idea. I'm looking for a position, so if you hear of anything . . .'

'You could always come and teach English to the British?'

'Ho ho, I think not.'

Marcus handed over another tile. They'd almost reached the door, thank God, then the room would be usable again. It looked fantastic. Very welcoming. Very Mediterranean, too. All it needed was some comfortable seating to add to the dining table and chairs. Marcus thought he might call Lucy and Dom and get permission to go and buy a sofa after lunch. And a bookcase. One or two small tables. He could look for some lamps and nice prints for the walls. Anything to keep his mind off his flat, his mother, his mother's lover, and how careful they were being with his hi-fi.

* * *

After Claude had put down the very last tile and taken his cigarette break, he said, 'I thought I'd utilise those old boards in the smallest bedroom to repair the stairs. That room's going to need a new floor eventually. Just as a temporary measure, you understand. Could you assist?'

'Sure.'

The two of them headed for the bedroom with saws and planes and hammers and nails – Marcus thinking how Freddie would have been in his element – and before long they were pulling up the loosest of the floorboards in a room that was nowhere near fit for habitation.

'Here,' said Claude. 'You hold that end steady whilst I measure and saw.'

'OK,' Marcus said, his eye caught by a red notebook lying in the gap where the floorboard had been. Was it the one Hannah was always scribbling away in? Lesson plans, she'd told him when he asked. It looked just like it. He leaned across and picked it up, flicked it open with one hand – yes, Hannah's writing – and tucked it in his back pocket to give to her later.

'I've been feeling quite drawn to catering lately,' said Claude. 'As a business venture.'

'Can you cook?' asked Marcus, wondering why Hannah would hide her lesson plans under the floorboards.

'No, but my aunt can.'

Marcus held the board with one hand and tugged the notebook from his jeans pocket. 'What do you mean?' he said, peering down at an open page where he instantly spotted the word 'Jo'. *Slut Jo is lying on her front, sunbathing in unnaturally tiny shorts and an undone top. Obvious, or what? I want to kill her . . .*

'Have you noticed the *A Vendre* sign on the Sports Bar?' asked Claude.

'Uh-huh.'

'It's been for sale for a while now. Madame Durand, the owner, is eighty-one and feels she may have produced enough *Croque Monsieur* for one lifetime.'

'Really.' Marcus flicked back . . . *best method . . . Jo . . . poison, strangulation, or a knife in the middle of the night?* 'So what . . . you and your aunt are thinking of buying it?'

'Well, first I have to mention it to her. You couldn't hold the board a little more steadily, could you?'

Marcus apologised and put the notebook down, a nasty dread filling his insides. 'Is it going for a reasonable price?'

'Fairly. My aunt might not be compelled to sell her house even.'

When Claude finished sawing, Marcus put the board down. With the hope that Hannah had been making notes on some classic French novel or play that just happened to have a 'Jo' in it, he picked the book up again and his fingers and eyes began darting hither and thither. *Jo and Keiko are walking in the hills – here's hoping they get terminally lost . . .*

'I think I'd like to take the café upmarket,' Claude was saying.

'Well, you couldn't really take it down,' Marcus managed to quip as he read on. *Hard to push someone like that over one of the steep inclines round here.* The book fell from his hand. He squeezed his eyes shut and pictured them all wherever they might be just then . . . underground somewhere. Jo 'accident-ally' wandering down the wrong tunnel and suffering a myster-ious but fatal blow to the head. *Mrs Currie, in the Cave, with the Large Rock.* His heart began pounding and he felt sure he'd never set eyes on Jo again.

'Completely refurbish the place,' continued Claude as he rubbed at the newly cut piece of wood with sandpaper. 'Then find a superlative chef.'

Marcus nodded thoughtfully. 'You wouldn't like a Slovenian one, would you?'

SATURDAY

No more Mr Nice Guy, Robin had decided, but already he'd apologised to two people who'd carelessly crashed into his super-market trolley. Just a bit of training, that was all that was needed. Learning how to glower, for example. Or to pause, stony-faced, for a little too long before answering a person. Small gestures that managed to unsettle or undermine people, and so gain their respect.

'Sorry!' he said again to a hulk of a man who'd suddenly pulled away from the beer shelves and smashed into him. 'I mean . . .' The man gave him a watch-where-you're-going-you-cretin look and moved off.

Robin stood amid the heaving mass of shoppers and yearned for that golden age of retail when all shops shut at the stroke of one on Saturdays. Why was he here anyway? Just because tomorrow was Easter Sunday? With only himself to feed and no appetite, there really was no need to endure this hell. He abandoned his half-full trolley and was almost out of the building when someone said, 'Robin? Christ, wouldn't have recognised you! What have you done, gone on one of those makeover programmes?'

It was Paul, long-time law lecturer and great talker.

'It's a bit mad here today, isn't it?' he went on. 'No doubt they think they'll starve to death because some of the supermarkets aren't open tomorrow. Mind you, we're doing the same. Seemed to have lost Brenda in the mêlée. How are you, anyway? Enjoying the break? How's the family?'

Robin stared at his law-teaching friend. 'What do you know about fathers' rights?' he asked.

Paul said, 'Beg pardon?' and Robin ushered him to a quiet area beside the cookery books and sagas.

'Unmarried fathers' rights. You're a lawyer. Sort of. I need to find out about them. If I have any, for a start.'

'Well, is your name on the birth certificate? Were you present at the birth?'

'Uh . . . no, and no.'

'Ah. In that case have you and Hannah set up a Parental Responsibility Agreement?'

'Doesn't sound familiar.'

'Hmm. Is she about to leave you? Or making decisions about Freddie you don't approve of?'

'Something like that.'

'Right. We'd better go and grab a coffee then.'

They queued in the café, got their drinks and sat as close to the store as they could, so that Brenda would spot Paul, or vice versa. 'I like the new image, by the way,' Paul said. 'You look a bit like what's his name. Robert De Niro.'

'So I've been told. Anyway, these parental agreements. Fill me in.'

Paul took a deep breath and did. It appeared that without a PRA – why had no one told him about them? – Robin had no say in where Freddie lived, couldn't sign a medical consent form for him, and had no automatic right to look after him if Hannah died. Which, if Robin didn't watch himself, might be fairly soon. In addition, he would find it very hard to take Freddie abroad unaccompanied, and was entitled to no say in his schooling.

'OK, where do I get one of these things?' he asked eagerly.

'You can download the form from the Internet. Easy.'

'Great. I'll do it when I get home.'

'Unfortunately, you both have to sign it. You and Hannah. And signatures have to be witnessed by a court official.'

'Oh.' Robin stirred at the coffee he didn't really fancy. 'Damn.' Although she might have been willing to sign something like that six months ago, Hannah was altogether more deranged now and, as he'd learned from her diary, had nothing but contempt for him. If she was planning a move back to Braemar, the last thing she'd want would be for Robin to assert his right to have Freddie living within ten miles of him. 'Stupid sodding law,' he said quietly.

Paul agreed. 'So where is she?' he asked.

'France.'

'With your son, I take it?'

'Mm.'

'On their own, or with another—'

'Man? Yes.' Robin gave Paul a potted history, having always been pretty circumspect about the situation with his university colleagues. 'I tried calling last night and she couldn't, or wouldn't, come to the phone. Sent a message saying she'd ring back, but then didn't.'

Paul let out a long, 'Hmm . . .' which Robin didn't like the sound of. 'Is she staying, or is it just a holiday?'

Robin shrugged. 'God knows.'

Paul gave him a sympathetic look. 'I'd recommend a good lawyer but, to be honest Robin, without this agreement . . . hey, there's Brenda.' He promptly stood up and waved his wife over. She was an average-looking woman, whom Robin had met several times over the years and always found very friendly. Make-upless, pleasantly plump, and didn't bother too much with her short mousy hair. She spotted them, wheeled her over-laden trolley into the café and when she arrived at their table, she and Paul did something very surprising. They kissed on the lips. In the supermarket. After only seeing each other ten minutes or so ago. How Robin suddenly wanted what Paul had.

He bade the happy couple farewell, left his undrunk coffee and got to his car just as someone was bashing it with her driver's door.

'Watch it!' shouted the reformed Robin, only to be ticked off by the young woman for parking 'much too fucking close'. 'Oh dear,' he said. 'So I did. How thoughtless of me. Sorry.'

Marcus is being very attentive. Following me around every-where. Barely leaving my side, in fact. As I prepared lunch today, he was extremely helpful and terribly interested in the ingredients and so on. So that's definitely salt you're putting in the soup? he asked. Yes, I said, laughing. He insisted on making the salad dressing himself. All rather encouraging, particularly after I'd begun to suspect he and Jo of having something going.

During this afternoon's walk, which we all went on – it being such a lovely day and Claude wanting to screed the kitchen floor ready for tiling – Marcus was, almost embar-rassingly, right beside me the entire way. Once, I slipped an arm around his waist but he had to dart off to show Freddie something interesting. However, he was soon back, matching his steps with mine again.

We kept getting the evil eye from Jo, not surprisingly. She must be feeling a complete loser and looking forward to going home now. I know I'm looking forward to her going home. Monday. Can't wait. Freddie can be moved on to the spare mattress and Marcus and I can make love at last. I'll have him to myself for four whole days. More perhaps, if he talks me into staying longer. My teaching job can go to hell, and I'm sure Freddie would love to spend the rest of his life watching Claude at work.

Although the days are gloriously warm, the evenings cool quickly and I'm now feeling quite chilly. I suppose I should go in – especially as Marcus has just popped out for the fourth or fifth time to check on me, as he put it. But first must think of another place to hide this diary, as it seems Claude is pulling up floorboards willy-nilly. Wonder what they're all doing in there. Perhaps I'll suggest another game of Cluedo. I think they thoroughly enjoyed it last time.

EASTER SUNDAY

Marcus woke with an arm still stretched firmly across Hannah's body – psychologically, if not actually, pinning her to the bed. He wasn't sure he'd be able to keep this up for another day, but he knew he had to. One more day and one more night, then Jo would be off in the safety of her hire car.

Why he felt unable to confront Hannah, Marcus wasn't sure. He could only think that when his mother found and read his diary when he was fourteen, it had been *the* most embarrassing experience. He squirmed again, recalling her saying she'd never have believed such filth could exist under her roof. Mostly, he'd been guessing at some of his classmates' bra sizes, but to a strict Presbyterian, now clearly lapsed, it was obviously shocking stuff. Anyway, telling Hannah he'd found her little diary was somehow beyond Marcus. He'd read it all eventually, and was left with the impression she probably wasn't homicidal. Still, he thought, lifting his arm off her, no point in taking risks.

'Morning, sweetie,' she said, rolling over and kissing his cheek.

'Morning,' he replied.

'Morning,' said Freddie from beyond Hannah.

190

'Morning,' they both sang back.

Hannah stretched herself with an, 'Mmmm . . . I think I'll take a bath before breakfast.'

'Really?' asked Marcus. Hannah always had a bath *after* breakfasting. What was she up to? Keiko would have risen early, as usual, and left Jo a sitting duck – or rather a horizontal, possibly snoring duck – for anyone wanting to place a feather pillow over her face. 'Sounds good,' he said. 'Maybe I'll join you.'

'And me too,' said Freddie, suddenly on top of Marcus and bouncing a lot.

'Oh, I don't think all three of us will fit in the bath,' laughed Hannah.

'Yes we will,' insisted Marcus.

'Happy Easter!' said Lucy.

Pippa, head-to-toe in Lycra and glistening with perspiration, said, 'Happy Easter to you too,' with a big smile, but didn't look as though she was going to invite her in.

'We were just wondering if you've heard from Jo recently,' Lucy said. She heard Bram singing along to loud music, then caught sight of him flitting across the kitchen. 'About when she's coming back?' She knew really, but was just dying to discover what was going on over the road.

Pippa glanced wistfully over her shoulder, then back at Lucy. 'Tomorrow, apparently. Unfortunately, Bram's off then too. His trip got postponed, but now he has to go. Shame. It's been lovely having him. I've had *the* best week.'

'Yeah?'

'Mmm. Back home tomorrow, if I haven't topped myself at the prospect.' She rolled her eyes and laughed.

'Well, better be off,' Lucy said. 'Things to do.'

'Are you sure you wouldn't like to come in for a drink?'

Lucy was halfway to the kitchen saying, 'OK,' before Pippa had shut the front door.

'Hi,' Bram said, turning down the radio. 'Haven't seen you for ages.'

'Something smells good,' Lucy said.

'Pan-fried organic, free-range chicken. My favourite. Unfortunately, Pippa won't touch anything fried. But then, that's how she keeps her amazing figure.'

Pippa went up to him and dangled a hand over his shoulder. 'But maybe Lucy would like some, darling?'

Did Pippa call everyone darling? Lucy couldn't remember. 'Well . . .' she said. She'd left Dom sweating over spreadsheets in the attic. He wouldn't emerge for hours. 'Why not?'

Pippa went back to her workout while Lucy sat at Jo's kitchen table and watched Bram chopping and flinging and stirring and tasting – all in his body-hugging T-shirt. It wasn't an unpleasant experience. 'Jo knows you're here?' she asked eventually. He'd brought her a glass of organic wine.

'Yeah,' he said. 'We've spoken on the phone a few times. Why?'

'Just wondered.'

'Shame we missed each other. She's visiting some friend, apparently.'

Pippa swanned back into the room covered in perspiration. She came over to Bram and ran a hand up and down his back. 'You've hardly been lonely, though. Have you, lover?'

Did Pippa call everyone 'lover'? Lucy couldn't remember.

'I have date tonight,' whispered Keiko. They were in the garden, Jo on a sunbed and Keiko in the shaded hammock, fully clothed and holding a brolly.

'No!' said Jo. 'With Claude?'

'Yes,' giggled Keiko.

'That's great.' And far more than Jo could expect. Marcus had gone distant on her over the past forty-eight hours. Strangely so. Yesterday, he'd steered her into the bathroom and said, 'I'll explain later,' then kissed her passionately but briefly, before hurrying off and gluing himself to Hannah again.

'We will have dinner in gourmet restaurant after church,' said Keiko.

'Sorry?'

'Today is big church day in village for Easter. Claude must go this evening and I go with him. He says service is very beautiful with big famous choir who has recording contract.'

'Wow. Maybe we should all come along?'

'Ah yes. That would be very wonderful. Why don't you ask Hannah and Marcus?'

'Tell you what,' said Jo. She rolled herself on to her front and caught Marcus rubbing sunblock on Hannah's skinny back. He didn't look happy, which was some consolation. 'Why don't *you* ask them?'

'OK.' Keiko tipped herself out of the hammock, then smoothed extra cream on her face for the trip across the lawn. When she returned she said, 'They think good idea. Especially Marcus.'

Jo looked across at the two of them and Marcus gave her a secret thumbs-up. What for she wasn't sure but, since she was beginning to feel grateful for any scraps of attention he threw her way, it did cheer her up a bit.

'I am very exciting,' said Keiko, diving back into the shade.

Jo smiled. 'I think you mean excited.'

'Ooohh, my English is—'

'No it's not, Keiko. It's excellent.'

'I like Claude very much. He is so kind.'

'Yes.'

'And handsome.'

'Yes.'

'And I learn much English from him.'

'We all do.'

Keiko sighed, like someone in love. Jo sighed too, like someone in love.

'I am very exciting,' said Keiko.

'Good,' said Jo, giving up and going back to her whodunit. Two of Giles Donne's lovers had died after dining with him, and Chief Inspector Grenville was confounded. Meanwhile, Betsy the cook, who loved Giles in an unrequited way, was off on her bicycle to purchase more poison for those pesky rats . . .

Can't recall when I was last this happy. When Marcus and I first got together? I really, really don't want to leave here. Ever. Would Lucy and Dom sell this place to me, I wonder. To us? If not, Claude might be able to find us a property. Freddie would go to the village school – become a little French boy. I could teach English. Conversation classes. Or do translation. Marcus would find an occupation. He's a bit short of skills – failed lawyer, mediocre restaurateur – so something like a little market gardening maybe. Growing courgettes and things. I keep dropping hints about settling in France and he says Yeah, great idea. I'm certain he'd like us to stay. He's constantly asking when Fred and I are going home. Friday, I tell him each time, and he says, Oh right, so you haven't changed it then? – obviously hoping I'll postpone our departure again. Sweet.

Just tonight to get through, then slut Jo – who seems incapable of fastening that bikini top – will be gone. An early afternoon flight, apparently, so they'll have to leave around 9.00, 9.30. We're all off to some tedious church service this

*evening – bound to be in Latin and a bore for poor Freddie
– but we'll go because Marcus was surprisingly keen.*

*3.30. Might get Keiko to play with Freddie while I go and
have a nap. Sexual frustration and a rather cramped bed are
definitely not conducive to a good night's sleep. But hey ho,
one more day to go.*

While Jo sunbathed and Freddie was passing on to Keiko all he'd
learned from Claude about pivots and fulcrums, Marcus crept
upstairs with a dining chair and positioned himself on the landing,
just along from the bedroom door. If Hannah suddenly awoke
and came out, he planned to jump on the chair and pretend to
be changing a lightbulb. Ridiculous behaviour, he knew, but
Hannah having been in a fantastically good mood for days didn't
mean she wouldn't slip a black widow spider in Jo's bed.

He stretched out his legs and opened *Madame Bovary* in his
lap, but couldn't concentrate too well on the words, his eyes
growing heavy in that four-in-the-afternoon way. He yawned,
closed the book and was placing it on the floor beside his chair
when, in the room opposite, he caught sight of a speck of bright
red under the battered old chest of drawers Claude sometimes
used as a workbench. Marcus knew immediately what it was,
but wasn't sure if he was feeling strong enough to examine it
again. He took a deep breath, shook off his fatigue and tiptoed
into the room, slowly closing the door behind him.

'What?' he kept whispering as he read Hannah's latest entries.
'*What?*' This was far worse than he'd imagined was going on in
her head. Courgettes? Turning Freddie French? He finished
reading, vowed he'd give Robin a call, and slid the book back
under the chest of drawers – or 'chiffonier' as Hannah insisted
they call it.

*   *   *

'Oh dear, should we be dressed formally?' Jo asked Claude, who was smarter than she'd ever seen him, in a beige suit and no workmen's boots.

'Just a touch more demurely than usual,' he replied. 'Ah, here comes Keiko, perfectly attired.'

Keiko slowly descended the stairs looking truly glamorous in red dress, red lipstick, black jacket, black shoes and one or two bits of gold jewellery. She was followed by Hannah in pastels: a chic calf-length dress and scarf. Behind her was Marcus in nice jacket, tie. Jo felt giddy at the sight of him.

'Look,' she said, conscious of her jeans and sandals, but aware she hadn't brought anything dressy with her either. How come they'd all packed church-going clothes? 'I'm a bit behind,' she explained. She passed the others on the stairs as she went up two at a time. 'Haven't changed yet. Sorry! You lot go ahead and I'll catch up.'

'Demure, demure, demure,' she said as she rummaged through her things in the bedroom. Perhaps Keiko had something? She went over to where her roommate had cleverly converted the deep-set window and its curtain rail into a wardrobe, having wisely thought to bring hangers with her. Everything was small, of course, and after several attempts at squeezing herself into tops, skirts and, on her, half-mast trousers, she almost gave up on the idea of going to the abbey. But then she went back and tugged some creased black linen trousers from her case, gave them a shake and decided no one would be looking at her anyway. Not with a famous choir and a dazzling Japanese woman in the building.

When she guessed she looked presentable – white top, a dark grey suit jacket of Marcus's she'd nicked from his room, and some of Keiko's expensive earrings – she set off for the village centre with a kind of end-of-holiday malaise hanging over her. In two days' time she'd have to face not only life without Marcus but, worse still, Sergei's next chapter.

Robin was in the Sports Bar, wired up after driving all night and all day, then consuming three welcome but awfully strong cups of *café au lait*. He was seated by the window overlooking the square, aware of how to get to the house but, owing to not quite feeling himself, determined to leave that till tomorrow. The charming old lady who'd served him had given him the name of a small guesthouse in the next village, which was sure to have vacancies, and he'd thanked her profusely in his best French.

All around him were empty tables and chairs, so with nothing else to distract him and no mental strength to rehearse his opening lines to Hannah any more, Robin watched the football on a large screen near the ceiling. Until, that was, a burly man in a tight-fitting suit came and switched it off apologetically. The café was about to close, he explained. He and his mother had a church service to attend. He pointed through the window at a large, cathedral-like building.

'Ah,' said Robin, who'd wondered why so many cars were pouring into such a small village. He drained his cup, chucked euros on the table and went out on to the small terrace, wondering if he was feeling better or worse than when he'd arrived. Just different perhaps.

He breathed in the cooling evening air and checked that he'd put the address of the guesthouse in his shirt pocket. Out of the village and turn first right, she'd said, then second left. Or the other way round. Oh well, he'd find out. He swayed slightly with fatigue, slipped an arm in his jacket, then caught sight of Hannah, Marcus and Freddie walking down a narrow road towards the square. They were behind Jo's Japanese student, who was on the arm of a swarthy young man not much taller than herself. Robin's knees buckled and, as luck would have it, his bottom landed on the seat of a metal chair.

Freddie – dear Freddie – was skipping in an ungainly way, holding his mother's hand on his right, and Marcus's on his left. Every few steps they swung his little boy up in the air and down again, and from across the square, Robin could hear him giggle. It was a sound and a sight that cut to his very core. In all his years with Judith, dealing with her dalliances, he'd never felt the kind of jealousy he was experiencing now. As he watched Hannah, Freddie and Marcus follow the other two into the church, his head and heart felt close to exploding. Why was Hannah going to church? She didn't do that. Must be Marcus's influence. This was terrible. He could be influencing her and Freddie in all sorts of ways.

Robin sat for a while feeling a strange combination of powerless and galvanised before leaping from his seat. '*Papier?*' he demanded, charging back into the café. '*Je voudrais le papier, s'il vous plait.*'

The barman held up a pad.

'*Non, non. Plus grand!*' cried Robin, stretching his arms wide. '*Comme ça.*'

The man shrugged a couple of times, murmured something under his breath then disappeared and returned with what looked like a roll of wallpaper.

'Perfect,' said Robin. '*Et une plume? Une* felt tip, *peut-être? Ah, merci.*'

He left the café again, apologising in English because he couldn't think of the French, and sat himself on the terrace while the barman shook his head and very swiftly and firmly locked up.

*   *   *

Contact lenses, thought Jo. Definitely. She turned around and went back to the house, unlocked the front door, ran up the stairs and exchanged glasses for lenses. That was better. She hated getting all dressed up to go out, then ruining the whole look with the same old specs she wore day after day. It was a bit like always wearing the same necklace, or hat or something. When she became rich, she'd have a different pair of glasses for every day of the week. Better still, laser correction. She locked up again and walked as fast as she could, almost trotted, so that she wouldn't have a thousand heads turn as she arrived late through a huge creaky, squeaky wooden door.

But there it was when she got there, the big wooden door. Shut. Through it, she could hear the vague muffled sound of a priest chanting in that Johnny-one-note way. Damn. Should she go in now, get the humiliation over and done with? Or wait for a few more stragglers to arrive and slip in with them? She looked around and saw not a soul. A couple of dogs barked and whined in a lonely-sounding way, as though the only inhabitants of Laroche-les-Bois' houses at that very moment were its pets. What a field day a burglar could be having. Suddenly, the choir struck up, ethereally but loudly, providing a better opportunity for her to steal in unnoticed.

Here goes, she told herself and was lifting the door's enormous iron latch, when something fluttered down from the heavens and landed noisily at her feet, frightening the life out of her. It was a large sheet of paper – five or six feet long – now half-curled up on the ground and with something written on it. She let go of the latch and approached the ghostly thing with apprehension. 'FATHERS' she read, gradually untangling it, 'HAVE FEELINGS!'

What fathers? She looked up at the sky. Not *the* Father, surely? But then it was Easter Sunday, and didn't Jesus ascend to his dad on that day? Things were getting spooky, but maybe this was some kind of sign, sent especially for her. One of those incredible religious moments that change people's lives for ever. Crikey, she thought. All she needed was to understand it.

'Yes?' she called out hopefully, when something else fell at her feet. A small box. She bent down and examined it. Hay fever tablets. What could this all mean?

'Fathers have feelings!' came a distant voice, and Jo swallowed hard and stepped back from the church to get a better view of heaven.

'Pardon?'

'Fathers have feelings!' she heard again and there in the bell tower – or half on it, half in it – was a figure. It was a man who sounded a lot like Robin, and looked like him too. Only better groomed. Short hair, smart jacket.

'Who are you?' she shouted, just as the big door opened and a man in a gown came out. He must have heard her fiddling with the latch.

'It's me!' yelled the guy above, and the priest or whatever ran to her side and stared upwards with her. 'Tell Hannah I want my son back!'

More people were coming through the door to investigate and the priestly chap tried ushering them back in, unsuccessfully.

'Don't do anything stupid!' Jo shouted through cupped hands as a crowd gathered round. 'I'll go and get her!'

Robin hadn't intended to draw attention to himself, only his message. Scaffolding along one side of the building had eased his passage to the top, but what he'd not thought of in his haste and haziness was something to attach his message to the church tower. He'd managed to wedge one end into a gap in the stonework, but then, when steadying himself for a moment, the whole thing had come adrift and fallen from his grasp. When he looked down and spotted Jo, his plan underwent a slight change and he'd voiced his message instead.

Now more and more faces were staring up at him, though not the one he wanted to see. But then, he wondered, ought Freddie to be subjected to the sight of his daddy clinging precariously to a bell tower? If his son were older, he'd understand that Robin was doing it out of love and desperation, but this could simply scar the little boy for life. Oh, well, too late now. In for a penny, he decided, and again shouted, 'Fathers have feelings!' to the congregation below. 'Give us all PRAs! Give us our due rights!'

Someone began yelling at him in French. A man. He had no idea what the chap was trying to tell him, but he was shaking his fist in a very French way. Robin shook his fist back. 'Fathers have feelings!' he called out. If he hadn't been so fuzzy-headed he'd have tried to translate it. *Les pères ont . . .*

'Daddy!' he suddenly heard to a background sound of an angelic choir.

He peered over the edge but couldn't see Freddie anywhere. '*Fred?*' he pleaded. 'Where are you?'

'Dadd*eeee*!' he heard again. The voice was echo-like and near.

Robin manoeuvred himself right back inside the surprisingly spacious bell tower to see a little face appear on the internal stone staircase that led up to it.

'I want to get to the top,' Freddie puffed. 'Like in Carfax Tower.' He heaved himself up the last step and stood proudly and breathlessly just inches from Robin. Behind him was Marcus, looking understandably concerned.

'Well, you're at the top now,' Robin said, a lump forming in his throat. He picked his son up and the two of them took in the view through a large hole in the round tower. There below, with hands on her hips and, Robin imagined, an appalled expression, was Hannah. He kissed his son's deliciously chubby face and said, 'Why don't you give Mummy a nice big wave?'

MONDAY

At 1 a.m. they decided Keiko might not be coming back to share their mattress, and began to get passionate under the duvet.

'So are you going to explain now?' asked Jo, stopping mid-kiss.

'What?'

'Why you've slavishly followed Hannah around and snubbed me for days.'

'Oh, that.'

Marcus tried kissing her again but she wasn't having it. 'Well?'

'Look, I thought she might try and kill you.'

Jo laughed, much too loudly but she couldn't help it.

'Shhh,' Marcus said, pulling the bedding over her head. 'I honestly did.'

Jo bit hard on the duvet until she calmed down. 'What on earth made you think that?'

'I can't say.'

'What do you mean, you can't say? Did she tell you she wanted to kill me?'

'Does it matter?'

'Yes, it does rather.'

'Anyway,' he said, 'it turned out I was mistaken. So let's just forget it, huh?'

'I want to know.'

'It really isn't important.'

'It is to me.'

Marcus sighed. 'Tell you what,' he said. He ran a hand up her leg and kissed her. 'If you put that jacket of mine on again, I'll let you know why I didn't trust her.'

'Really?'

'You looked so great in it.'

'Well, OK then. Pass it over. It's on the floor, by you.'

'My best suit!'

'Sorry.' She took the jacket from him, sat up and slid it on over her nakedness, trying to think of something she'd like Marcus to dress up in. Nothing came to mind. How strange men were. 'Anything else?' she asked.

'Definitely not.'

Jo was still awake at 2.30, promising herself that if she and Marcus one day got together properly she'd *never ever* keep a diary. She rolled on to her side and tried once again to get to sleep. Eyes shut tightly, focusing on her breathing. But it was impossible, and so annoying as she knew she had to be up early to do the packing she hadn't got round to. The more she dwelled on how awful it would be not to sleep at all, the more she seemed to be making that happen.

Maybe a milky drink would help. She slipped out of bed – well, off the mattress – and crept through the room to the landing where moonlight through a window lit her way and where she heard the sound of someone crying, or at least snif-fling. She stood still for a moment and listened to what was almost certainly a very upset Hannah. Sniff. Sniff, sniff.

Robin had come to reclaim her and Freddie, and was now lying beside them both, no doubt completely out of it after his long journey. Jo couldn't pretend not to be relieved at this development, while at the same time feeling pity for screwed-up and possibly dangerous-to-know Hannah. She was just thinking that Robin might be able to knock some sense into the poor woman, when he loomed out of the darkness, making her yelp.

'Aaat*chooo*,' he went loudly before seeing her and jumping himself. 'Aaat*choo*!'

'Bless you.'

He sniffed, thanked her and plodded down the landing, saying, 'God knows what I've done with my antihistamines.'

'Is that them?' she whispered.

'I think it's a stone,' sniffed Robin. 'But let me check. Yes, just a white pebble.'

The church forecourt-cum-car park was part paving, part gravel, and despite the light of an almost full moon, in ten minutes they'd spotted only false alarms.

Jo said, 'Shame the torch conked out.'

'Yes.'

'I expect Lucy and Dom had to use it a lot when they had no electricity.'

'Hey, look,' Robin said, charging away from her and bending over. 'Is this . . . ? Yes!' He stood up, kissed the box in his hand, then took a couple of tablets out. 'They're a bit squashed, but well done, Jo.'

'I should have picked them up when you first dropped them, but in all the excitement . . .'

'Oh God, don't remind me. What on earth was I doing?'

'Apart from scaring the life out of us?'

Robin sneezed, then said, 'It won't get into the papers, will it? You know, the *Oxford Times* and so on.'

'Don't be silly.' She pointed at the tablets. 'How long do they take to work?'

'About fifteen minutes.'

'Let's sit on that bench while they kick in.'

'Are you sure? I mean, this is very good of you.'

She shrugged and they sat in their coats, side by side in the deadly quiet but very chilly village and talked in hushed voices, mostly about Robin's tenuous position. 'Well, Marcus is clearly determined to get them back,' he said eventually.

'I think he may have come to Oxford with that fantasy in mind,' said Jo. 'But the thing is . . . and he's talked a bit to me about this, he . . . well, this sounds terrible, but he seems to have gone off the idea. Kind of slowly.'

Robin sniffed and his face lit up. 'Has he?'

'I think it dawned on him, once and for all, that Freddie wasn't his son. Sort of emotionally.'

'Oh?'

'And on top of that, he and I are, you know . . .'

'You and Marcus are . . . ?'

She nodded.

'That's wonderful.'

'Yes. Yes, it is.'

'But Hannah must be gutted?'

'We're not sure she's aware. Marcus has been putting on a remarkably good act for her.'

'Oh, right.'

'To be honest, I think you've saved his bacon turning up like this, just as I'm about to leave.'

'When are you going?'

Jo looked over at the church clock. 'In about five hours.'

206

'What? Oh God, I'm sorry. Keeping you up like this.'

'Don't worry. With a bit of luck I'll sleep on the plane. I hate flying.'

'Maybe Hannah would give you one of her magic pills. I talked her into taking three of the things, to completely knock her out.'

'Sounds severe.'

He smiled and looked very attractive with his new hair and clothes. His eyes had stopped watering at last. 'Maybe,' he said. 'But you don't think I'd be here having a nice chat with you if there was a chance she might be conscious, do you?'

Jo laughed. 'No, I suppose not. She could have been packing Freddie into his car seat, or anything.'

Robin turned to her goggle-eyed. 'Let's get back, shall we?'

'Yeah, OK. Hey, wait for me . . .'

Robin didn't wake until almost midday, and the first sound to hit him was that of Freddie, singing an unfamiliar song. It wafted up from the garden, through the window as Robin slowly emerged from sleep. Such a sweet little voice. He wondered if they should do something about it. Get him in a choir? He pictured Fred in the dear little uniform of Christ Church Cathedral School, down in the heart of Oxford, becoming a chorister by age seven, eight. But then, when he came round properly, Robin remembered he was an athiest and ardent socialist. He got up and stuck his head out the window.

'What's that you're singing?' he called down.

Freddie stopped and looked up. '"*Il était une bergère*",' he said. 'It's my best song.'

'Oh, yes?'

'Claude learned me it.'

Taught, Freddie, *taught*. 'That's nice. Where's Mummy?'

'Asleep.'

'Oh. So who's looking after you?'

'Marcus and Claude,' Freddie told him. 'We're airplaning the shelves 'cos they don't fit. Look.' He pointed to a plank of wood as long and wide as himself. In his other hand was a small plane from his kit. 'And my second best song is "Fairy Sharker".'

'Uh-huh?'

While Freddie went through the first verse of '*Frère Jacques*', Robin's head remained outside the window. It might have been rude to disappear. 'Lovely,' he said when he'd finished. Which it had been.

'It's French.'

'Yes, I know. Where's Mummy sleeping?'

'In the car,' Freddie said matter-of-factly.

'Really?'

Robin went and checked. Hannah was upright and dead to the world in the passenger seat of her hired car. He hoped it was because she hadn't wanted to disturb him, not because she couldn't bear to come and doze beside him in the bed. After checking Freddie was still happy, he had a quick shower, then headed for the kitchen where he found Marcus gathering Freddie's things together.

'I'm assuming you'll want to all leave today?' Marcus said.

'Er, yeah. I suppose so,' said Robin. 'Hadn't thought that far ahead, actually. Listen, are you OK with all this? I mean, I can't be sure what Hannah's told you, but I was adamant I didn't want her to bring Fred here.'

'I guessed as much,' said Marcus. 'Dreaded it, should I say.' He held up a pot. 'Coffee?'

'Please. You know, I'm determined not to lose Freddie. Not now I've discovered him, as it were. I know it's been tough on you, the estrangement and everything . . .'

'Oh, don't worry about me,' Marcus said as he filled a large cup. 'Yeah, it was hard at first, but not so much now. Take them home. They belong with you. Freddie especially.'

Robin took the coffee cup from Marcus just in time, for a streak of something human flew into the kitchen and slapped Marcus's face, causing him to take two unsteady steps back. 'I'm sure I deserved that,' Marcus told a retreating Hannah, while Robin found himself thinking, just fleetingly, that it might be quite nice if Hannah disappeared from both their lives.

'I'll go and help her pack,' he told Marcus.

'Cheers.'

THURSDAY

Marcus and Claude were sitting at the dining table. Claude was chain-smoking and Marcus was drumming his fingers. With Lucy and Dom calling a halt to the repairs and refurbishment, there really wasn't much else for them to do. They'd pretty much exhausted table football, Marcus having thrashed Claude over and over, as he always did. He may have been a mediocre restaurateur but he knew how to smash that ball into the goal. It was the only thing he'd ever seen Claude truly annoyed by. They couldn't even go out and walk or fish or canoe or anything, since the weather had decided to be typical for April again: squally showers all over the region; sky the colour of slate most of the time.

'It's just that the building society have rejected our top-up application,' Dom had told Marcus over the phone. 'And the bank won't increase our loan. So we can't pay Claude any more. Apologise to him, would you?'

'Sure.'

'You can stay on as long as you like, though.'

'Thanks,' Marcus said, not sure he wanted to.

It was all pretty miserable really. The high drama of the previous week had left him feeling first horribly guilty – poor old Robin, and poor Hannah, so cross she'd actually hit him – then plain empty. The house certainly felt empty, especially at night. And he missed Jo badly.

'We could play a word game,' suggested Claude.

'Mm?'

'There's this one that's terrific fun. You see, I say a letter. The first letter of a word I've thought of. Then you say the second letter, with a word in mind. You always have to have a word in mind, and the longer you make it the better. The loser is the one who completes the word.'

'I'd rather not,' said Marcus. Play Claude at a word game? He'd be mad to. 'Do you mind?'

Claude took out another Gauloise. 'No, of course not. I just thought it might distract you from your erroneous affiliations.'

'You mean crap relationships?'

'Yes.'

'I am feeling bereft,' said Marcus. 'That's for sure.'

'Me too.'

'Bummer, eh?'

'Mm, most dispiriting.'

'What's more, neither of us seems to have a job or any prospects.'

'No. Not since my aunt pooh-poohed my Sports Bar idea.'

'And I haven't even got a home.'

'No?'

Marcus explained about his mother and the gold-digger.

'How awful,' said Claude. 'But perhaps you could go and live in—'

'Her house? Yes, it's been mooted. The place needs a lot of work, though. General updating. New kitchen. Things she's

211

been talking about doing for ages but didn't want the disruption and, anyway, couldn't afford. Mind you . . .' Marcus stopped swinging back on his chair and the front two legs thumped to the ground, 'she was telling me one of her insurance policies has just matured . . . plus, easier to have the work done while she's not living in the house.'

'That's true.'

'And better if she had a couple of blokes she could totally rely on doing it, not bottom-of-the-barrel builders who have six jobs on the go and don't finish any of them.'

Tut tut tut, went Claude. He took a drag of his cigarette and exhaled. 'How can people be so dishonourable?'

Marcus smiled to himself. Should he remind Claude he'd left Bertrand in charge of things? 'There are loads of cowboys around, that's for sure.'

'Well, you must ensure your mother doesn't use any of these dubious characters.'

'You mean, find her someone more like you?'

'Why, thank you. But yes, that is what I'd recommend. Someone . . .'

'Punctilious?'

'Exactly.'

'Got a passport?'

'Of course.'

Ernst, bless him, was trying his best to cheer them up. Telling jokes about Bavarians, making Jo and Keiko a late-afternoon snack neither of them could eat. Not because it was inedible, they just couldn't eat.

'And did you hear about the Bavarian on the train?' he asked.

'No,' said Jo, and she didn't want to. As long as she lived she wouldn't get his humour.

'The sign on the train it said, "Do not lean out of the window." But the Bavarian leaned out of the window and his head was knocked off by an electricity pilot.'

'Pylon.'

'Sorry. Pylon.' He laughed while Jo waited for the rest of the joke. 'It's very funny, yes?'

'Mm. Have you got homework tonight, Ernst?'

'Unfortunately, I have. I must write an essay called "What I did in the holiday".'

Original, thought Jo. Would teaching EFL be a doddle compared to copy-editing? She'd spent most of the day close to tears with one of Sergei's chapters. But then it might have been Marcus rather than convoluted English upsetting her.

'Ah yes, I have remembered another excellent one,' Ernst was saying. 'A Bavarian man he walked into a bar . . .'

'How about you, Keiko? Any homework?'

'Yes,' she said heavily. 'But my heart isn't on it. My heart is on Claude.'

'. . . and he asked for a beer. The barman said, "I'm sorry, we cannot serve people who are wearing lederhosen."'

'Maybe the homework would take your mind off him, Keiko?'

'Do you think so?'

'"That is OK," the Bavarian said, and in the middle of the bar he took off his lederhosen and was only in his shirt and knickers.'

'Underpants,' said Jo. This one was sounding almost promising.

'Sorry, underpants. "*Now* I would like a beer," said the Bavarian. Ha ha. Actually, maybe not so funny as the train joke.'

'No, just as funny.' After a quiet moment Jo said, 'So what *did* you do in the holidays, Ernst?'

She tried to listen but found it hard, lost in thoughts of France and Marcus and their sad farewell. She and Keiko had

had to leave early. Robin wasn't even up and Hannah was ambling around like someone who'd taken three sleeping pills. She'd said a cursory goodbye to the two of them then, oddly, gone to sleep in her car. Jo too had been groggy after just a few hours' sleep, which was good because it numbed her a bit when it came to parting with a very huggy Marcus. 'Call me in a couple of days?' he'd said, looking forlorn. 'Tomorrow, even?' Claude turned up to see Keiko off, and they'd cuddled a lot too. Keiko was shedding tears that didn't stop until she fell asleep on take-off. So now, they were here and the men were there and Ernst was embarking on another joke.

Jo jumped in with one of her own. 'What's the difference between an onion and an accordion?' she asked.

'Ha,' said Ernst, 'I think there are a lot of differences between an onion and an accordion. For one, an onion does not have all those small buttons.'

'Ernst, you're just supposed to say, "I don't know. What *is* the difference between an onion and an accordion?"'

'Oh. Sorry. What *is* the—'

'Yeah, OK. Keiko?'

'I don't know. I'm so sorry.'

'Well,' said Jo, puffing herself up for the punchline, 'nobody cries when you cut up an accordion!'

Ernst rubbed his chin. 'But wouldn't it be difficult to cut up an accordion? I think they are very strong.'

Jo groaned and went back to staring at the phone. Should she call Marcus again? It would be the fourth time in two days. Would Madame Bouziges get pissed off? This morning, he'd said he'd buy a card to use in phone boxes. It was a nice cheap way of calling and he'd be able to talk to her without Madame Bouziges listening in. 'I'm sure she understands more than she lets on,' he'd added in a whisper.

'But maybe a Bavarian would try to cut up an accordion!' said Ernst, finally laughing.

The phone continued to do nothing. Had Marcus got hold of a card? He said he thought they sold them in the Sports Bar. If he had, he'd be bound to call this evening. But then, he and Claude had no doubt been busy working on the house all day, or driven miles to get supplies. He could be knackered. The place was going to be great when it was finished, though. Fabulous, even. Perhaps she and Marcus would holiday there again. Often. She looked around her and sighed. It was nice coming home to a house where everything worked and there weren't holes and things, but her little Victorian terrace definitely lacked something. Probably Marcus.

'Excuse me,' said Keiko, holding up her retractable pencil, notebook open. 'But please explain, who is Anna Cordion?'

He called around 5.30. She pictured him in the phone box in the square; the shape of him, what he might be wearing. 'How's it going?' she asked.

Not so well, he told her. The weather had turned filthy, and Lucy and Dom had been forced to let Claude go, due to lack of money.

Jo said, 'Well, he'll be going back to air-traffic school soon, so I don't suppose he's too bothered.'

'Actually, he quit that.'

'Oh dear. Anyway, what about you?' she asked, crossing fingers. 'Any plans?' *Come to Oxford, come to Oxford.*

'Well, Claude and I had this crazy idea of doing my mother's house up for her. I just rang her, and she's well into the idea.'

'Really?' said Jo, trying not to feel miffed that he'd called his mother before calling her. 'What a good idea.' But then if he hadn't called his mother first he wouldn't have been able to tell

Jo his news. Bad news, as it turned out. Back to Scotland?

'Claude's thrilled because he'll be much closer to Keiko. You'll both have to come up.'

'Yes,' said Jo miserably. It was hardly a day trip and there was Ernst to take care of. 'Tricky, though.'

'Hey.'

'What?'

'Cheer up. We'll work something out.'

'Yeah, yeah.' Another long-distance relationship? She wasn't sure. 'Look,' she said. She was close to tears but didn't want to go girly on him. 'I was just on my way out. Call again tomorrow?'

'Jo, are you al—'

'Bye. Must dash. Sorry. Bye.' She put the receiver down with a 'Shit', and went and made herself a calming herb tea, then sat back at the kitchen table, wiping her eyes. There were some people, she decided, who were destined never to experience a live-together relationship. Strange thing was, up to that point she'd never wanted one. Of course, it might have helped if she'd told Marcus the future she had in mind for them.

'Guess what,' she said to Keiko, who'd wandered in with her long face and what looked like a homework query in her hand.

Keiko shrugged and sat down. 'I don't know.'

'Claude is coming to work in Britain.'

Keiko breathed in sharply. 'In Oxford?'

'Well, no. Scotland.'

'Ohh, I want very much to see Scotland. Adam, my teacher, said it is very beautiful.'

'Yes, it is.'

Keiko jumped up and beamed. 'I will get map.'

Jo said, 'Good idea,' feeling mildly cheered up by her lodger's exuberance.

When Keiko came back with the British road atlas, Jo pointed out Braemar and Edinburgh, and Loch Ness and Aberdeen. 'Does Scotland have airport?' she was asked.

'Several,' said Jo, laughing for the first time in days.

Keiko clapped. 'Then it is easy. I go Heathrow then Scotland?'

'Well, yes . . .'

'For a big weekend.'

Jo said, 'I think you mean long weekend.' Or maybe she did mean big.

'Ohh, my English is very—'

'No it's not.'

'I am so exciting!' Keiko said, just as the phone rang again.

Jo reached over and picked it up. 'Hello?'

'I thought you were going out?'

'I lied. I was upset.'

'I know,' he said, then they talked and talked on his cheap-rate phone card. He didn't feel it was right to be in Oxford, he told her. 'Not right now.' He was hoping Hannah and Robin would patch things up. Repair all the damage he, Marcus, had done. 'I kick myself every day over it.'

Jo tried to say all the right things. She understood. She didn't think he had anything to blame himself for. Look at what Hannah had done to him, for goodness' sake. Yes, she'd come to Scotland to see him. Yes, she'd wear his suit jacket again . . .

'Oh, and one more thing,' he said, 'before the card runs out.'

'Mm?'

'Well . . . Bram. I was hoping you wouldn't—'

'I wouldn't.'

They were playing a fun game. Robin was diving underwater, swimming around for a bit, then surfacing next to Freddie and giving him a fright. Freddie, floating in his armbands, never knew where his dad would come up and say, 'Boo!' or

'Raarrrghh!' and was finding it hilarious. Each time Robin tried to stop the game for fear he'd give his son a lifelong water phobia, Fred would say, 'One more time, Daddy. Pl*eeeze.*'

'OK, this is absolutely the last time,' Robin said, needing a rest and meaning it. 'Down I go!' He arched his body and dived under, thinking this time he'd play a different trick. He swam around counting to ten then slowly ascended and, grabbing Freddie's foot, had a little nibble on it, before bursting through the surface right beside a blond-haired, blue-eyed boy with a terrified expression. 'Oh, I'm sorry,' Robin said. 'I'm *really* sorry. No, don't cry.'

'Feo's a cry baby,' sang Freddie, leaping on Robin's shoulders.

'Who?'

'This is my friend Feo, from nursery.'

'Are you all right, Theo?' asked a woman swimming over. Robin recognised her as a nursery mum.

'I think I gave him a bit of a fright,' he said. 'Sorry. Thought he was Freddie.'

'Hello, Freddie,' said the woman. She stopped swimming, stood up and turned to Robin. 'He seems fine now. Don't worry.'

'Yes,' he said, trying not to stare at her lovely shape in her pale green swimsuit. Blonde – naturally, he thought – and blue-eyed like her son. Great teeth when she smiled, which was what she was doing now, watching the boys. Freddie and Theo were having a race but not getting very far in their armbands, just splashing a lot and looking ridiculous.

'I've booked Theo in for lessons,' the woman said. 'Is Freddie going to take them . . . um, I'm sorry, I don't know your name.'

'Robin.' How come he'd never noticed how attractive she was?

'I'm Sadie. Hi.'

'Hi,' he said, the Beatles' 'Sexy Sadie' coming to mind. They shook hands, which felt like an odd thing to be doing in a toddler pool. 'I don't know about the lessons. Sounds like a good idea, though.'

'Yes. The earlier they learn the better, they say.' She sank down into the warm water and floated on her back for a while. 'You know they get on like a house on fire, those two.'

'So I see.'

'Freddie should come round some time. For tea.'

'I'm sure he'd love that.'

Sadie gave him her toothy smile again. 'They're back at nursery on Monday, so how about then?'

'Yes, OK. One of us usually collects Fred around four, four thirty . . .'

'I'll give you our address and phone number,' she said, swimming breast stroke towards the boys, 'before we leave here.'

'Great.'

'The thing is, Adrian, I honestly don't think these sessions are doing a bloody thing for me. If anything, I've got worse and am having to take more antidepressants. Floating round in this half-awake state all the time. I mean . . . What did you say? . . . Oh sorry, I thought you said something. Chance'd be a fine thing, eh?

'Anyway, I *was* feeling thoroughly betrayed by Marcus. Tricked. Stupid. "Take them home," he said to Robin on Monday. He didn't know I was listening outside the back door. "They should be with you. Freddie especially." How utterly cowardly, I thought. Do you know what I did? I went into the room and slapped his face. Quite hard. He went out somewhere – just like him – and I didn't really get to see him again before we left.

'Robin's been typically Robin. Very understanding. But, God, you should have seen him on the top of that bloody church. I couldn't believe it was him at first. Not just because risk-taking isn't his thing, but because he looked so different. For the better, that is. His son talked him into a change of style. I even noticed heads turning in Paris. We stayed there overnight, Monday. Robin turning Parisian women's heads!

'He's a great partner, that's for sure. He's kind and loyal and involved, and, as I discovered in France, he can be extremely passionate when roused. I'm not talking sex, I mean over Fred. Yes, a wonderful loyal partner . . . but not for me, Adrian. Not for me. You see . . . I realised, after giving it thought on the way home, that it wasn't cowardice on Marcus's part, but altruism. He was willing to give away the two people he treasures most in life, for well . . . our sakes, and Robin's sake. An amazing gesture, but a mistake.

'No, there's only one man for me, Adrian. And he and I both know it. Adrian, are you still there? Oh, right. Anyway . . .'

So this is how it happens, thought Robin while he dried first Freddie, then himself. A chance encounter – or a chance nibbling of the wrong child's foot – a slight dizziness at the sight of the person . . . and then *pow*, you're suddenly considering infidelity for the first time in your life. She hadn't been wearing a wedding ring. He'd checked. Beautiful hands with long tapering fingers. Piano fingers.

'So tell me about Theo's daddy,' he said to Freddie.

'What.'

'Well, does he come to nursery and collect him sometimes? Does Theo talk about his daddy at all?'

'I don't know. Can we come swimming tomorrow?'

'I expect so.'

'And the day after, and the day after, and the—'

'No, Fred. Not every day.' Was this going to be his new obsession? Could be a lot more exhausting than DIY, though maybe easier on the ears. 'But we might see if we can get you into beginners' swimming lessons.'

'Aaww,' groaned Freddie. 'I don't like lessons. At nursery, Millie pretends she's a teacher and we're her children and she tells us off all the time. Specially me.'

'Well, maybe if you didn't pinch her? Anyway, they won't be anything like Millie's lessons, and Theo's going to be coming to them.'

'Feo my bruvver?'

'No,' said Robin patiently. 'The other one.' How strange – or indeed fateful and significant – that he and Sadie had sons with the same name 'Here, can you put your trousers and socks on by yourself? We need to be quick because we're going to meet Theo and his mummy by the door. You're going to go and have tea at his house next week.'

'Hooray,' said Freddie.

And Robin thought *Hooray* too, but didn't know why he was getting so excited. Sadie was far too young for him, and now that he and Hannah were settling back into what they had before, this would hardly be the time to begin living dangerously. However, there was this unfamiliar fluttering going on in his tummy and his head felt light and carefree. Even if it was for only one afternoon, he'd enjoy it while it lasted.

FRIDAY

They decided to drive. Well, Claude did.

'My tools are of inestimable value to me,' he told Marcus. 'And, knowing what I know about the aviation business, I'm disinclined to hand them over to baggage handlers. What do you say we take my van? It'll hardly be first-class travel, but there's a CD player and I've got a great collection of French pop music.'

Marcus would have to pick his car up from Stansted. French pop all that way? It could be less painful to walk and swim to Essex. He said, 'Let me have a think about it.'

But Claude pulled a face. An apologetic one. 'I believe my aunt has already booked us on to a weekend ferry.'

'Oh?'

'Midday Sunday.'

'Jesus. So we'd need to set off . . . ?'

'Tomorrow, yes. Spend the night in Le Havre.'

'Will that be fun?'

'I think not. Anyway, my aunt has also booked us into some very reasonably priced accommodation. One star. But one star in France is equivalent to three or four in Britain. No offence meant.'

Marcus couldn't believe so much had been organised before he'd had his first cup of coffee. 'None taken,' he said, and as he tried to wake up properly, he began to question if he really wanted to go and do this huge exhausting job for his mother. Particularly as the sun had reappeared. Why didn't he just stay in France and write a brilliant novel? No, even harder work. His least favourite things at school had been composition and cross-country running. He'd never seen the usefulness of either. 'I'd better pack then,' he said. 'Can we fit the table football in?'

'No,' said Claude emphatically.

Pippa was on the doorstep in masses of make-up and with an enormous wheelie suitcase. For a moment Jo panicked. Did she want to move back in?

'I'm off to, er, Italy for a week or maybe a bit longer,' Pippa said, 'with . . . a girlfriend. Jane. Yes, Jane. But anyway, just thought I'd let you know I've had an email from Bram. Several, in fact.'

'Have you?' Jo hadn't had any.

'His boat's been delayed, so he's got a couple of weeks to kill.'

'Uh-huh.'

'Says to give you his love.'

'Right.'

'Could be away a couple of months this time.'

'OK. Would you like to come in? I found a couple of things of yours you left behind.'

'Oh, keep them,' said Pippa with a wave of her bejewelled hand and wrist.

'Well,' Jo said, 'have a great time with your . . . girlfriend.'

'Oh, I'm sure we'll have a ball. Jill's never been to Spain before, so . . . oh, there's the taxi.' Pippa waved at the driver, crawling along the street as he checked house numbers. He stopped and pulled in, then sat with the engine idling, looking up Pippa's short skirt as she leaned forward to kiss Jo goodbye.

'See you when you get back,' said Jo. 'In fact, when will you—'

'Bye!' Pippa said, rushing at the taxi. 'Bye!'

Jo closed the door and went straight to her email. No new messages. She decided to write one herself. 'Hi Bram,' she typed. 'When Pippa arrives, could you tell her thanks anyway, but I probably won't have any need for two second-hand thongs and *Great Breasts After Forty*. Love, Jo.'

She sent the message then wondered if she might, in fact, hang on to the book. She stared at the screen, deep in Marcus thoughts. He'd be on his way back to the UK now. How tempting it was to jump in her car and drive to Stansted for a quick kiss and cuddle before he set off for Scotland. But maybe not. He'd said why didn't she and Keiko come up next weekend, so she'd just have to wait. And anyway, she was snowed under with proofreading, as was often the case in the summer term. No, she'd go at it all week, then fly up to Aberdeen with Keiko on Friday.

It'd be great. Maybe.

She was slightly worried that things wouldn't be quite so passionate and romantic in the cooler temperatures of mid-Scotland, and without Hannah's presence to make it all deliciously illicit. But still, no point in speculating when there was a dissertation on the South American feral parakeet to get going on, and two students to feed. Keiko's appetite had increased alarmingly, which was good. Would her lodger like Scottish food? Jo was remembering her stay in the Highlands and wonderful red-deer stews, when her screen told her she had mail. She opened the new message.

'Will do!' it said. 'Love, Bram.'

SUNDAY

I absolutely don't understand it. I'm so certain I put my diary in the bottom of the wardrobe, under that unused fondue set Marcus insisted I take with me. A long-ago Christmas present from my parents. I'm positive that's where I left it, but who knows? I was in quite a euphoric state when I set off for France. Perhaps I put it there, then moved it somewhere less accessible? Mind you, I've scoured the place for a week now. Robin said he hasn't seen it, and Robin tends not to lie. So very strange.

I went back to the same shop and got another one. I need to plan, that's why. Writing helps crystallise my thoughts, in a way that talking to Adrian doesn't. You always feel he's being judgemental. Silently, of course.

OK. My plan. My plan is . . . no idea. But I'm sure inspiration will come. I believe Marcus will come too. Just now I rang Madame Bouziges, who told me he and Claude were crossing the English Channel this very minute! Claude was desperate to see his new Japanese girlfriend, she said.

Marcus, on his way to Oxford – yes!

It all must have been so hard for him, poor thing. We'll have a little talk when he gets here – where will they stay? Lucy and Dom's? Yes, we'll have a talk. Work something out. With Robin. Some kind of Freddie-share arrangement. As we'll probably live in Scotland – Oxford's way too expensive to buy or rent in – it'll most likely be a case of Fred spending one weekend every couple of months with Robin. Maybe a bit more in the holidays. Yes, I'm sure we can come to some arrangement like that. Amicably. Behave like sensible, rational adults. None of this scaling church towers nonsense. Honestly, what was he thinking?

They were at the pool for the fourth day in a row.

'Daddy, can we play the diving game?' asked Freddie. '*Can* we?'

Robin was fed up to the back teeth with the diving game, and couldn't understand why his son wasn't. Robin simply wanted a quiet time, lying on his back watching the entrance to the women's changing rooms, waiting for Sexy Sadie to appear. He hadn't seen her since their first encounter on Thursday, but he lived in hope. Even if she didn't turn up today, there was always tomorrow teatime at her house. It wouldn't be *quite* the same, though. She wouldn't be wearing her swimming costume – presumably – and there might well be a partner in residence.

'Aren't any of your friends from nursery here?' he asked Freddie.

'Only Jasper, but he smells. Please dive, Daddy.'

'No, Freddie. Which one's Jasper?'

'There,' said Freddie, pointing.

'He looks nice, and I'm sure he doesn't smell in the water. Let's go and see him, shall we?'

'No.'

227

'Come on. It'll be someone for you to play with, instead of wearing your poor old dad out.'

'But Jasper's smelly.'

'He won't be smelly in the water, I promise you.'

Freddie said, 'Oh, all right, then,' and followed his father across the pool.

'Hello, Jasper,' said Robin. Jasper looked puzzled. 'Freddie's come to play with you.'

The little boy's face lit up and he said, 'Goodie,' and the two of them began splashing around and leaping on each other in the way boys do; Freddie clearly forgetting all about the personal hygiene thing.

Robin relaxed at last and lay on the top of the water, locking his eyes on the women's changing rooms again, just as Sadie walked out with her son. Yes! Robin manoeuvred himself on to his front and swam a few yards. 'Hey, Freddie,' he said. 'Look who's here. Theo. Come on, let's go and say hello.'

'No, don't want to,' said Freddie, giggling. He and Jasper were giggling a lot, bashing each other with their big armbands.

'Please?' said Robin, taking hold of Freddie's hand and attempting to guide him to the far side of the pool, where Sadie and Theo had slipped into the water.

'No!' shouted Freddie. 'Jasper's my best friend now and I *don't want* to go to tea with Feo after nursery tomorrow. Feo's a cry baby.'

'Yes you do, and no he's not. Come on.'

'No!' screeched Freddie, yanking his hand away.

Behind them a voice said, 'Everything OK?' and Robin spun round. 'Hello, again,' Sadie said, and catching sight of her pretty smiling face, Robin couldn't think of a single thing to say. Instead, he grinned at her and hurriedly ducked under the water to hide the smattering of grey hairs on his chest, telling himself he was being ridiculous. How old was she? Thirtyish? Crazy. And what's more, he was a happily partnered man. Hannah was behaving normally again, and certainly being nicer to him since the whole France escapade. Partly due to remorse, he suspected, but he'd also wondered if his new look had anything to do with it. Whatever it was, things were much calmer at home and Robin was feeling relatively safe, especially after that little chat with Jo. So, he told himself, *behave*. Be *good*. Stop looking at Sadie's golden legs, flapping gently while she treads water. Think, instead, of something tedious. Marking essays . . .

But it was hard, because Sadie was staring long and hard at him with a definite glint in her eye. 'I was hoping you'd be here,' she said, before swimming in a circle all the way round him.

If he hadn't already been crouching, Robin felt sure his knees would have given way.

MONDAY

Marcus woke to the aroma of old Sunday roasts and lavender polish and a worrying hissing noise. No light was coming into the room, owing to the dark and heavy mock-patchwork curtains, plus their linings and the net curtains beneath. He stretched out an arm for a switch, and the tasselled bedside lamp was soon illuminating two pictures of his father: one when he was young and dashing, and one when he was older and dashing. More than ever, Marcus could see how much he resembled him. On the other side of the double bed, his mother's ancient tea-maker was doing its business. She'd always believed in starting the day as she meant to go on – drinking tea.

His mother also believed in blankets, and Marcus was weighed down by three of the things, in addition to a candlewick spread in faded lemon. He was hot, he realised. Very hot. He threw sheet, blankets and everything else aside and got out of bed. When he reached the window he prayed hard, then quickly tugged at the curtains to discover his prayer had been answered. It was a beautiful day. And a beautiful day in Scotland was hard to rival. He opened one of the larger windows and breathed in the clear air. Home again, he thought. Fantastic.

The contraption beside the bed began gurgling and burbling excitedly, then filled its little teapot and alerted Marcus of its accomplishment with a high-pitched alarm. 'Yeah, OK,' he said, rushing over to press the off button. 'Very clever.' He poured tea into a mug, added milk and got back into bed to admire the view of the Cairngorms, wondering what Claude would make of them.

They'd arrived in the dark last night, following a journey that had been painfully slow after Stansted, what with having to stick together in the inside lane most of the time, so Claude wouldn't get lost. The winding and weaving mountain roads had been tricky too. Several times, Marcus had stopped to check they were still Claude's headlights behind him. They'd arrived around midnight to a warm welcome from both his mother and a handsome, late-middle-aged man with fairly Slavic features, an incredible head of grey hair and a thick accent. 'Sossor about yr flet,' he said to Marcus.

'Pardon?'

His mother helped out. 'He says he's so sorry about your flat.' She kept looking at Vinko adoringly, touching his arm territorially.

'Oh, don't worry,' said Marcus.

'Pliss leave in flet's sparoom?'

'Sorry?'

His mother smiled. 'He says, "Please live in our flat's spare room".'

Freddie's old room? The one that took a cot and a chest of drawers, but only just. 'No, no, we'll be fine here,' Marcus told them both before hinting that he'd rather like to turn in for the night.

Claude had collapsed in the second-largest bedroom soon

231

after they'd arrived. 'Please excuse me,' he'd said to the three of them. 'I'm feeling enervated from the rather protracted journey.' After he'd gone, Marcus's mother commented on what a beautifully spoken young man he was, but then she had spent almost a month listening to Vinko.

As he enjoyed his tea on the bed, gazing out at the majestic hills and mountains, Marcus pondered on the strange twists and turns of recent weeks. He'd left Scotland with one definite aim in mind: spending time with Freddie; and one small dream that he hadn't been that optimistic about: getting Hannah and Freddie back. He'd had no idea, setting off on that long drive to Oxford, that he'd end up in France and in love with someone else. Nor that it wouldn't be Hannah and Freddie he'd be returning to Scotland with, but a Frenchman with better English than the Queen.

It had been an eventful time, to say the least, but this probably wasn't the way someone fast approaching forty should be living. If only he'd stuck at his Articles, he'd have been a lawyer by now. A solicitor of some sort. He was just wondering why 'lawyer' sounded so much sexier than 'solicitor', when Claude put his head round the bedroom door and said, 'I'm sorry to disturb you, but I can't find the fresh coffee.'

'You'll be lucky,' laughed Marcus. 'Here, have some tea.'

Claude looked as though he'd been offered a nice cup of hemlock. 'I think I would rather die of thirst. Or at least drive to the nearest café.'

'Again, you'll be lucky. I've got an idea, though.'

It was dark and thick and kind of Turkish tasting, with lots of grainy bits in the bottom, and Marcus was guessing from the expression on Claude's face that he was wishing he'd gone for the tea.

'It's very . . .' began Claude.

'Slovenia has bescoffee in wirld,' said Vinko, pouring more sludge into everyone's tiny cups.

'Mmm,' said Marcus, who quite liked it. 'So where's all my stuff?' he asked, turning to his mother. It certainly wasn't in their flat. His flat. How weird it felt, sitting surrounded by these alien items, with his mother and her *new boyfriend*. Surreal. Not that the past couple of weeks had been unsurreal.

'It's all safe and sound, don't worry. Your Aunt Janine offered to take care of it all, now we've kissed and made up.'

'Have you? That's good.'

'But, as you know, her house never sees a duster, so your brothers put all your stuff in my loft.'

'Oh, great. Half the roof tiles have slipped.'

'I'm sorry, son,' she said, taking her hand from Vinko's knee and placing it on Marcus's. 'But be happy for me, won't you? Eh?'

Marcus nodded and smiled and tried not to think about his six-hundred-pound stereo. His mother pinched his cheek playfully before returning her hand to Vinko.

They were here not only to get Claude a cup of coffee, but also to discuss with his mother what she wanted done to the house. Claude had already got the ball rolling and had pen and paper out to write down instructions.

'I thought nice sliding glass doors between the lounge and the dining room,' she was saying.

'But, Mrs Currie,' said Claude, 'don't you feel—'

'Ooch, call me Moira.'

'Moira. You don't think sliding glass doors are a little, how shall we say . . . *passé*?'

'And one of those wall-length, teak-effect units Janine and Bob had put in. You know the one, Marcus?'

'Yes,' he said with a shudder.

'With compartments for your television and video and whatnots. They're grand, they are. Do you have them in France yet?'

'I don't believe so,' said Claude. 'And what about the floors, Moira? A good durable hardwood, perhaps?'

'Janine and Bob have a wee slot for their phone directories too. Very handy.'

Marcus could see Claude was writing it all down, but in a slow, reluctant hand, as though not quite believing what he was hearing.

'And Vinko would like a bit of a bar to make cocktails on his evenings off. Nothing too showy.'

'Well, if you're sure . . .' said Claude. He scribbled something and surreptitiously passed the sheet of paper to Marcus. 'What time's the next ferry home?' it said, and Marcus chuckled while his mother talked about some nice kitchen wallpaper she'd seen in a house makeover programme.

'A lovely wee pattern it had on it. Winter vegetables and kitchen utensils.' She shook her head. 'Heaven knows why they were ripping it off.'

'I have to say,' said Claude, as Marcus drove them both back to the house, 'as stunning as the scenery is, I do find your Scottish mountains a little denuded.'

'Huh!' replied Marcus, insulted. But of course Claude was right. Deforestation and intensive grazing had left them nowhere near as lush and tree-covered as those of the Cévennes. Marcus explained, then said, 'Luckily, there's quite a bit of reforestation going on these days,' but Claude didn't seem to be listening. He was examining the notes he'd taken earlier and shaking his head.

'Here, give that to me,' Marcus said. He took the piece of

paper and tore it in two while he steered with his arms. He then crumpled the two halves into balls and chucked them to the back of the car. 'I think we can ignore all that. She'll never remember what she said, anyway.'

When they pulled up outside the charming old former farmhouse that Marcus had called home since the age of seven, they sat and took it in for a while, engine off.

'White walls and sanded floors?' asked Marcus.

'I think so.'

'Stainless steel and wood kitchen?'

'Absolutely.'

'Swirly carpet the first thing to go?'

'You're reading my mind.'

Ernst had cycled back in the school's lunch hour to eat with Jo. He occasionally did this and she found it touching, especially when lunch was on him. Exotically filled rolls from town, or fish and chips from just round the corner. Today, though, she'd made a salad, stopping work at 12.15 to do so, knowing he'd charge through the front door at around twenty to one. Which was just what he'd done a minute or so ago, breathlessly and carrying fresh orange juice.

'Today, I had some bad news,' he said, settling himself at the kitchen table.

'Oh dear.'

'Our teacher, Sue, has said that we must prepare a presentation for next week about our impressions of a part of this country, but not Oxford. Somewhere we have visited. But me, I haven't visited anywhere. Only Heathrow airport, twice. I don't like to go on the school's weekend trips to Brighton and Stratford and places, because some of the other students are . . . is there another word for "arseholes"?'

'Not really.'

'This means I must go to London at the weekend, but I have heard that it is dangerous and expensive. Ahmed has had his phone stolen in London.'

Jo helped herself to salad. 'Honestly, Ernst, London's not that scary. And, besides, didn't you go to Manchester on an exchange?'

'Yes, but it rained so much and all the time we were in a little house with only a small concrete garden. To speak for fifteen minutes on Manchester would be impossible for me.'

'Here,' said Jo, handing over the salad spoons. 'Help yourself.'

'Thank you.'

'It's a shame you're not coming to Scotland with Keiko and me.'

'Ah!' he cried. 'What an excellent idea!'

'But . . .' she said. Was this what he'd been fishing for all along? She and Keiko had been talking about their trip all weekend. Poor Ernst must have felt left out.

He took scoop after scoop of salad and suddenly seemed much happier. 'I will look on the Internet for my own accommodation, then I won't be playing . . . oh, what is the word? When you are alone but the others they are a couple. I think it is a berry.'

'Goose?'

'No. I don't think it is playing goose. Not a bird.'

'I meant gooseberry. Playing gooseberry. And anyway, you wouldn't be.' Much. 'Let me check it out with Marcus, yeah? Wangle you an invitation.'

'I like this word "wangle". What does it mean?'

'Oh, to be a bit devious to get something. Manipulative, even. Someone who wangles is a wangler.'

He looked puzzled and a little shocked. 'Is not a wangler someone who is very annoying and stupid?'

'Different word, Ernst.'

'I don't suppose Marcus is here?' asked Hannah.

At the sound of the doorbell, Lucy had charged down from the top floor where she'd been working on a brochure. She was still out of breath and, without thinking, said, 'Shouldn't you be at school?'

'I've taken a sickie. Terrible thing to do on the first day of term, but there you are. Well . . . is he?'

'No. Why?' Lucy toyed with the idea of inviting Hannah in, but there was the brochure to get on with. Mind you, she had wanted to ask if she'd feed Maidstone over the coming weekend. 'I thought he and Claude were going straight to Scotland.'

'What?'

'So Jo said.'

Hannah coloured up. '*What?*' she asked again, before doing an about-turn and crossing the road towards number 15.

Lucy didn't shut her door; just stood glued to the bristly mat beneath her bare feet, thinking maybe the brochure could wait.

'Is she in?' Jo heard. It sounded like Hannah, but it couldn't be. Not on a school day.

'Yes,' Ernst said, and then the front door closed and Hannah followed Ernst into the kitchen. 'It's your friend,' he told Jo.

'Hi,' she said. 'We're just having lunch. Would you like—'

'Where's Marcus?'

Jo went cold inside, but not as cold as Hannah's eyes. 'I'm not sure,' she said. It was true. She had no idea where he was at that precise moment.

'Isn't he coming to Oxford? With Claude? Claude's aunt said he desperately wanted to see Keiko.'

Hannah was wringing her hands and Jo imagined her neck inside them. If only Marcus hadn't told her about the murder plan. Jo wanted to alert Ernst to her current danger, but he'd ploughed back into his lunch and was quietly humming as he munched.

'I don't understand,' Hannah went on. 'Why aren't they here? Claude's aunt said he desperately wanted to see Keiko.'

Wringing her hands *and* repeating herself. This wasn't good. 'Why don't you sit down, Hannah?' Harder to kill someone when you're sitting down. 'I'll put the kettle on.'

'Fuck the kettle.'

At this, Ernst stopped humming and looked up at the two women.

'Or . . . there's this really nice orange juice?' Jo murmured.

'How *come*,' said Hannah, her voice growing louder with each utterance, her face redder, 'nobody *ever* tells me what the *fuck's* going on?'

'Ah,' said Ernst, piercing a bread roll with his knife, then smiling Hannah's way. 'It's easy. Marcus and Claude have gone to Scotland, and me and Jo and Keiko will go to visit with them at the weekend. Simple. Unfortunately, I am going to be playing gooseberry, ha ha.'

Jo jumped behind Ernst and his chair for protection. Now *her* hands were itching to get wringing, being so close to Ernst's neck.

Hannah said, 'Eeaarrghh,' or something similar, thumped a fist on the table, and before Jo could plunge a hand in Ernst's shirt pocket for his mobile, two doors had been slammed and Hannah was gone.

For a while, Jo stayed where she was and the two of them stared at the closed kitchen door.

'Perhaps,' said Ernst, 'you could wangle for your friend to come to Scotland, too? I think maybe she needs a holiday.'

It was incredible what you could get done in only a few hours, thought Marcus, when there were two of you and you both hated the carpet. They were burning it now, in the garden, protecting themselves from noxious fumes with Claude's masks. Luckily, there weren't any other houses for miles; something Marcus resented as a child, but loved now. It really was a picturesque spot, even with bits of burned, swirly patterned carpet raining all over it.

'You see the top of those buildings over there?' he asked Claude, lifting his mask. 'Buried in the valley?'

Claude brushed smoke aside, lifted his mask too and said, 'Yes, I think I see them.'

'That's Balmoral Castle. The Queen's Scottish home.'

'Huh,' said Claude, clearly unimpressed. 'And how many homes does she have?'

'I don't know. Quite a few.'

'Why?'

'Because she does, I suppose.'

'You don't ever question the ethicalness of such an arrangement?'

Was ethicalness a word? He'd check later.

Claude was staring at him. 'You don't consider your royal family greedy and lacking any social conscience? Surely, such spacious and sumptuous homes could be made available to, say, the impoverished children of single parents, or battered women or asylum seekers, on occasion? What delightful short breaks they could take there.'

'Hm,' said Marcus. 'Nice idea, but I'm not sure the tabloids would go along with that.'

239

Claude rolled his eyes as if despairing of Great Britain, then handed Marcus the stick he'd been prodding the fire with and said, 'I'm just going to phone Keiko, if that's all right?'

'Again?'

'I'll reimburse you for the calls.'

'Oh, don't worry about that,' said Marcus, laughing. 'You're putting me to shame, that's all. I've only called Jo once today.'

'I'm sure the ladies don't compare notes,' Claude said, but Marcus wasn't so sure.

He watched Claude walk back to the house, through the old vegetable patch that no one had kept up since his father died, over the vast overgrown lawn and past the flowerbeds his mother had always attended to lovingly, but not these days, it seemed. Marcus had always assumed that he and his brothers would inherit all this – large farmhouse, large garden, large barn ripe for conversion – but now, of course, it could all go to Vinko, should his mother recklessly throw herself into marriage. Maybe he and Andrew and Fraser should have a word with her. Or, better still, a word with Vinko. At night. In a quiet alley somewhere.

When Claude traipsed back ten minutes later, he told Marcus there was a 'jocular' answerphone message from Jo for him.

'Oh, yeah?'

'I listened only superficially,' Claude said, 'not wanting to feel like an eavesdropper, but I did catch the words "Hannah", "homicidal" and "help".' He tittered, poised to put his mask back on. 'British humour can be very dark, I've found.'

Robin had lectured, seen a couple of students one to one, and was now hurrying from the building before anyone else accosted him. He walked briskly towards the staff car park, head down to avoid eye contact. It was twenty past four and, although he'd hoped to go home first and freshen up a bit, he realised he ought now to go straight to the nursery. Anyway, he knew he looked OK because so many people had told him so today. 'Robin, great outfit.' 'Love the hair, Robin. Knocks years off you.' He'd had his leg pulled too. 'Who is she?' Bill had asked with a smirk. Robin had been tempted to tell him.

'Sadie, Sadie, Sadie,' he said to himself as he pulled out on to the main road. *Whatever you do, don't call her Sexy Sadie.* He put the car radio on, tuned it into Radio 2 and listened to some blasts from the past, requested by Pete from Rochdale. Pete from Rochdale was obviously of a similar age, since Robin was able to sing most of the lyrics to all three songs, though they wouldn't have been his choice. When was the last time he sang in the car? Not counting 'Wheels on the Bus'. Decades ago, that was when. Wow, he thought, how great it was to be alive sometimes. Even Headington's London Road shops looked good today, plate-glass windows shimmering in the late-afternoon sunlight.

Robin parked as close to the nursery as he could, being in a bit of a hurry. He checked himself in his rear-view mirror, just in case Sexy Sadie was also collecting her son – *don't call her that* – then got out and dashed into the building.

Right, where was he? Fred, Fred, Fred, he said under his breath, scanning the room of twenty or so children: some busy, some dozing, two having a small battle over an item. Fred, Fred, Fred . . . Perhaps he was in the toilet, Robin thought, and was on his way to check when Mrs Jessup looked up from where she was helping with a jigsaw and said, 'Freddie's mum collected him earlier.'

'Sorry?'

'During quiet time.'

No, this couldn't be right. 'Isn't quiet time straight after lunch?' Hannah would have been teaching.

'That's right. One thirty till two thirty. As I expect you know, we prefer not to have mummies and daddies calling in then. Perhaps you could remind your wife.'

'Are you sure it was her?' Robin asked. A chill ran through him at the thought of a mentally ill child-snatcher picking Freddie up. 'Not some stranger?'

Mrs Jessup gave Robin a withering as-if-I'd-let-that-happen look and went back to her chunky puzzle.

He got home in record time, ignoring all speed cameras. Hannah's car wasn't there. Where could they be – the swimming pool, the supermarket? He rushed into the house, didn't find a note, so picked up the phone and dialled her mobile. It was switched off. He took the stairs two at a time and, once in Freddie's room, opened drawers and cupboards. Had things been taken? It was hard to tell. Fred had so many clothes.

Perhaps he was overreacting, Robin kept telling himself. But no, Hannah would have called him at work to tell him she was collecting Freddie, if she hadn't been up to something. Up to what, though?

He went to their bedroom and more or less ransacked it, hunting for her new diary. Next he searched the kitchen, but with no luck. Then the living room. It was there, casually slotted into the newspaper rack. 'Ha!' he said, and went out to the shed for the secateurs that had quickly done the job last time.

Once again, Robin felt his world fall apart as he sat on the brick floor of the shed, not caring if his expensive new trousers got oil or whatever on them. One weekend every couple of months? Was that the morsel he'd be thrown as a so-called 'absentee' father? Unbelievable.

It appeared from Hannah's jottings that Marcus was going to be in Oxford again. Perhaps he'd arrived and they'd gone to see him. Perhaps they were having this 'little talk' she mentioned. Perhaps, perhaps, perhaps . . . *Lucy*, thought Robin. They were all at Lucy and Dom's house having tea. Tea . . . Oh, *Christ*. Sadie. He checked his watch: 5.15. She'd be wondering where they were.

He found her number and dialled, and after he'd apologised and explained that there'd been a mix-up, she asked, 'Are you all right, Robin?' in such a very tender way. 'You sound a bit low.'

'Well,' he said, and then he was off, pouring it out. All of it. Marcus coming to Oxford, France, even the embarrassing church business.

'Oh, how awful for you,' she kept saying, sounding so kind and as though she really cared. Then, when he'd finished, she said, 'You know, you couldn't be more different from my ex-husband.'

Ex? The day was looking up. 'In what way?'

'He doesn't have much time for Theo, unfortunately. Bit of a drifter. He's in Ireland now. The benefits are better there, he says.'

'So . . .' began Robin, thinking of how to word things without sounding predatory, 'you're available, then?' No, not right.

She laughed quietly down the phone. 'Not for just any old body, I'm not.'

Robin wasn't sure how to take that, or indeed how to respond to it.

'Why don't you come round?' Sadie said. 'And we'll talk over what we should do about Hannah.'

We?

'OK, see you soon,' Robin said abruptly, aware he was getting all choked up. He put the phone down, blinked tears from his eyes – hayfever, still? – then climbed the stairs to have a shower.

Quickly, before she changed her mind. When he got to the bathroom he received a jolt. Freddie's little toothbrush and special toothpaste weren't there.

'Hi, Adrian, it's Hannah. I'm afraid I'm not going to make it to tomorrow's session. Thought I'd better leave you a message, even though you're bound to charge me anyway.

'I'm on the M6, you see, on my way to Scotland. No, I know I shouldn't be using my mobile phone while driving, but how often do you see police cars on a motorway these days? Freddie's asleep in his seat, luckily. He won't last the whole journey to Braemar, so I'm planning on stopping overnight somewhere. We'll take pot luck. Cumbria, maybe.

'The thing is, I'm having to do what Marcus wasn't able to. He being a good person and me being . . . well, me. Honestly, you should have seen how close we were before Robin showed up in France. Marcus couldn't stay away from me. I hope you believe that. It was almost like a second courtship, only without all the rampant sex we had first time round. Owing to Fred sleeping in with us, you understand. Anyway, I expect I've told you all this.

'Once Freddie and I left France, Marcus left too. What does that say? Mm? Claude has come over with him. According to his aunt, it's to see his Japanese girlfriend. You know, Jo's lodger. I told you about her. But the odd thing is, they went up to Scotland instead of coming to Oxford, and I think that must have been Marcus's idea. I think he's avoiding Jo. She's not getting the hint, though, and has already got a trip to Braemar organised. Would you believe it?

'Do you know, talking to you like this – leaving you a message – doesn't really feel any different from one of our sessions. You're being just as responsive. Think, Adrian, of all the time you could save yourself if your clients would only phone in their troubles! Not only would you not have to say anything, you wouldn't have to listen either, if you didn't feel like it. Fuck, cop car looming in wing mirror. Gotta go. I'll call again in a minute.'

TUESDAY

Robin woke to an empty house and a sense of impending doom. Then he remembered Sadie, and the whole ghastly situation didn't seem quite so terrifying and impenetrable. Sadie, Robin had been relieved to discover, was quite a bit older than she looked. And, as luck would have it, was a part-time social worker. Exactly what Robin was in need of. She was caring, a good listener and had a practical, organised approach to life. If the gods had made him fall for a sculptor or accountant or something, he not might have been feeling quite so hopeful this morning.

Sadie had made a short list. He reached for it now; it had been the last thing he'd read before going to sleep. Number one was *Stay calm*. Easy to say, hard to do, when your son was God knows where. On his way to Scotland, presumably. This fact Robin had discovered on returning from Sadie's last night, when he'd gone to his study – the one room he hadn't searched for Hannah's diary – and found a note resting on his keyboard. She and Marcus *had* to be together, apparently. This contradicted what Jo had told him, or Marcus had told him, but God knows who'd got the right or wrong end of the stick. Alternatively,

Marcus could have been stringing them all along. The note had been scribbled hurriedly by the look of it, and talked of lawyers and sorting out access. She'd call once she got to Braemar, she promised, but Robin thought he wouldn't put money on it.

Secondly, *Get a good family lawyer*. Yes, he'd do that this morning. There were fathers' organisations that must be able to recommend a local solicitor.

Third on the list was, *Keep up the contact with Freddie*. It was all too easy, Sadie had told Robin, to become distanced from your child just by not being involved on a day-to-day basis. Robin protested, saying, 'No way. Not me.' But Sadie, apparently, had seen it happen time and time again.

Finally was, *Don't stop going to work*. The last thing he needed, according to Sadie, was to lose his job, however all-absorbing the fight for reasonable access was. 'Reasonable access?' he'd cried. 'It's custody I'm after, not reasonable access.' Sadie had pulled a dubious face and told him the mother would have to be off her rocker and a drug addict not to be named primary carer in this country. In that case, Robin said, he thought he stood a good chance.

He read through again. *Stay calm*. Yes, he felt reasonably calm compared to last time. Hannah running off with his son was almost becoming a way of life. *Don't stop going to work*. OK. He wouldn't do that. Today, he had a late-morning lecture on Mosley – something he could now do backwards should anyone request it – and two afternoon seminars. There was also that paper on Britain's embryonic, pre-1914 welfare state to be working on but, considering the current crisis, perhaps that could wait.

Robin got up and made coffee, then went to his study. *Get a good family lawyer*. He switched his computer on, picked up one or two emails from students, impressed himself by replying to them immediately, then started searching for a website that would point him in the right direction. He found one, jotted down a couple of phone numbers, switched off the computer, picked up the phone and mentally thanked Sadie. Sensible Sadie. What a lifesaver she was. Just look at how rational and together and methodical he was being. He tapped out the first number and a youngish-sounding man answered. Another dispossessed father?

'Ah, hello,' Robin said, when his eyes fell upon the rectangular wooden clock on the bookcase. It was the one Freddie made. The one with the very uneven, funny-shaped hands that always said twenty past six, because that was the time when he'd made it.

'Hello . . . ?'

Freddie had written the numbers all the way round the edge with a black marker pen that Robin told him to be very careful with. But he hadn't quite got the spacing right, and so at the top, where a 12 should be, was the number 9.

'Hello?' the man repeated. 'Can I help you?'

'Yes, sorry. I . . .' Robin's heart was thumping, his eyes still on the clock. He felt something sear through him. Anger, panic, a horrible sense of bereavement. 'I'm sorry, I . . . wrong number,' he said, putting the phone down. Bloody, bloody Hannah. How *dare* she?

Before he knew it, Robin was grabbing his keys, double locking his front door, and in the car. He checked he had a road atlas, started the engine and headed north.

Marcus had left Claude to the floor sanding and was helping his mother lay tables for lunch. Vinko was singing something Slovenian in the kitchen, in a really-not-bad voice.

'He's pretty good,' said Marcus.

His mother smiled proudly. 'Aye, beautiful voice. Friday night is music night now. Vinko on vocals and your Aunt Janine on keyboard.'

'*Here?*'

'Over there in the corner. We have to move a few tables, but I can tell you it gets packed. And everyone leaves in great spirits.'

'I'm not surprised,' said Marcus, who'd been checking out a menu. *Young Goat in Wine, Carp in Wine, Wine Cake.* 'They're probably completely pickled.'

'It's not all Slovenian music. He does a lovely "My Way".'

'Ah.' Just when Marcus was thinking they'd come along on Friday.

Better to leave it till Saturday, perhaps. The four of them could come. No, five. He kept forgetting Ernst. It should be fun, he decided, and a lot more relaxed than things had been in France, now everything was sorted. Sort of sorted. Yesterday, Jo had seemed worried about Hannah, but he'd reassured her that it was *him* she was livid with. He told her about the face slap in France, but that didn't seem to help. 'I just want to get up to Scotland this weekend and feel safe,' she said, and Marcus had understood what she meant. Since arriving north of the border, he'd felt much safer.

'And a wonderful "Jumpin' Jack Flash",' his mother was saying, as she did things with napkins Marcus wouldn't master in two lifetimes. 'Does all the actions. One customer swore she wouldn't be able to tell Vinko and Mick Jagger apart.'

'Is that right?' said Marcus, laughing. Perhaps they would come along on Friday. He'd give the Young Goat a miss, though. Was that even legal?

Jo was trying very hard to concentrate on feral parakeets, but every now and then she'd lean forward and peer round the curtain, just to make sure Hannah wasn't coming up her front path. And occasionally, she'd look at the time and see that she was an hour or maybe half an hour closer to Friday morning, when they were all going to skip the day's work and fly to Aberdeen.

A domestic flight!

Jo pictured the small aircraft. A tiny cramped fuselage, over-loaded with people and their luggage. Rickety wings and an under-the-weather-sounding engine. Ernst and Keiko might have to knock her unconscious and carry her on, but how great it was going to be to reach Marcus and his waiting car in just a few hours. It would take an entire day to drive up there. Who'd be mad enough to do that?

When the phone rang she hoped it was Marcus, but it was Lucy calling from her office to ask if she'd feed Maidstone over the weekend.

'Can't, I'm afraid,' Jo said. 'I'm going away.'

'How about one of your students?'

'They're coming with me.'

'Damn.'

'What about Hannah?' asked Jo. 'Doesn't she usually feed him?'

'Yes, but I think she must have gone somewhere. I've been trying to get hold of her at home and at her school. They say she hasn't been in at all. And she's not answering her mobile. Did she say anything to you yesterday?'

'No, she didn't.' Nothing repeatable. 'How about Robin?'

'He's not home either. Or at work.'

Jo frowned. Could the two of them have gone off somewhere to patch things up? It was a best-case scenario, and way too much to hope for. She put it to Lucy.

'You could be right.'

'Pippa's away too,' Jo said, 'but you could ask Ray to feed the cat.'

'Yeah, right. The walk would kill him. Listen, don't worry, I'll find someone. Where are you off to, by the way?'

'Braemar. To see Marcus.'

'Oh, he's back already, is he?'

'Mm.'

'So . . . let me get this right. Marcus is in Scotland, and Hannah has disappeared?'

Jo put her head in her hands and took a few deep breaths. 'I'd better phone him, hadn't I?'

'Hi, Adrian. Me again. Just felt the need to speak to an adult. We're in our bed-and-breakfast place, killing time till the pills I took to sleep last night wear off. Two when we arrived, two when I went to bed, and two when I woke up feeling anxious at four o'clock.

'We were supposed to be out of our room by eleven a.m. What's that, forty minutes ago? But the landlord's being understanding. I told him I had a bad headache.

'Freddie's moaning a lot, which doesn't help. Keeps saying he wants to be at nursery because he's got a new best friend, Jasper. And Theo might steal Jasper, or something. What I need is a good strong, decent cup of coffee. Of course, there's nothing resembling that in this establishment. Will make a cup of something with these sad little sachets they put in your room. Why are these places so hopeless? Freddie asked for apple juice at breakfast and they didn't even have that. Anyway, will love you and leave you. Thanks for listening. If you have.'

'Oh *hell*,' said Marcus. Hannah on the loose again? 'She wouldn't come here, would she?'

'I don't know. As I told you, she was pretty angry yesterday.'

'Well, no sign of her yet. But you say Robin's disappeared too?'

'According to Lucy. I just called his department and he hasn't turned up for a lecture this morning.'

'They could have just gone away somewhere. The three of them.'

'That's what Lucy and I hoped.'

'Yes, of course,' said Marcus, breathing out again. 'That's what they've done, I'm sure. Gone off to do a bit of bonding.'

'Probably.'

'How are you, anyway?' Marcus asked. 'You must be excited at the prospect of seeing me?'

'Uncontrollably. But not excited at the prospect of flying.'

'Oh, you'll be all right. Take one of your beta-thingies. And remember, more American airline pilots die from chainsaw accidents than in plane crashes.'

'Actually, I'm not sure I find that very reassuring. I mean, if they couldn't control a saw, what were they doing flying planes?'

Marcus laughed. He was so looking forward to seeing her. '*If* you make it, I'll be at the airport to meet you,' he said. 'I'll be the tall, blond, healthy-looking, handsome one.'

'Yeah, and I'll be the one with the Munch *Scream* expression still in place.'

'Can't wait.'

'Me neither.'

'Hi, Adrian. Just to let you know I'm feeling a lot better. Fred and I took a stroll around the village. Such wonderfully fresh air up here in Cumbria. Beautiful views. Well, it's cleared my head and lifted my spirits, so now we can get back on the road.

Just a couple of hours and we'll be in Braemar. Home again. Might call you en route.

'Over and out.'

Jo was half dozing over parakeet distribution charts. It was almost always a mistake to proofread in the comfort of her favourite armchair. She put the work to one side, heaved herself up and went over to the computer screen to check the time: 16.12. She picked up the phone and dialled Marcus's number.

'No sign of her?' she asked.

'Nope. I think I'm probably safe.'

'Good. How's the work going?'

'Very well. Not that I'm doing much. Just watching Claude sand floors. I had a go at it, but the machine ran away with me.'

'Call yourself a man?' she said. 'Anyway, better get back to the parakeets. Let me know if . . .'

'Don't worry.'

'Hi, Adrian. I'd like to think you're listening to all my messages, but hey, what the hell . . . it works for me. We're fast approaching Scotland. Just passing Carlisle. Freddie's chatting away in his seat, glad to be back on the road again. It's a fabulous day, and I am *so* looking forward to seeing Marcus. The very first thing I'll do is apologise for slapping, oh, *shit* . . . what the . . . ?'

Ten hours after leaving Oxford, Robin was settling himself in the corner of a restaurant with the unfortunate name of MacDonald's. He guessed, looking around him, that this one had been here long before the Mc variety arrived. He was in a large high-ceilinged room with a tiled floor and cream walls. There were a dozen or so tables – four occupied – all nicely adorned with fresh flowers and starched, artistically arranged napkins. The tablecloths were a very white white and the chunky silver cutlery gleamed under modern, twisted-metal chandelier affairs.

He'd asked for the table in the far corner, in order to keep an eye on the door. If they came in that way, he wanted to see them before they saw him. He presumed, however, that there was a back way in from the flat upstairs, which was where the three of them probably were. Their flat. The one Freddie had spent his babyhood in. For some reason, Robin pictured it still full of his early photos and tiny Babygros and teething rings.

The small blonde woman who'd accompanied him to the table came over and asked if he'd like a drink while he perused the menu. Since he was in Scotland, he asked for a whisky.

Leaning back in his chair, he studied the menu without really seeing it. It had been a long day. He'd stopped three times on the way, twice for nourishment and a pee, and the third time for a nap in a service station car park. On arriving in Braemar, he'd booked himself into a large hotel in the centre and made enquiries with an old-timer as to the whereabouts of the Currie family, only to be told there were dozens of Curries in the area. 'They've got a restaurant,' he said, and the chap's face lit up with recognition.

Robin's eyes began to take in what he was reading. Slovenian, it boasted at the top. He looked up at the pictures and posters surrounding him. They all seemed to be views of, or advertisements for, Slovenia. It all looked rather lovely. He and Judith had once been on holiday to Yugoslavia, before it became 'the former' and they'd been very impressed by the country and the friendliness of the people. Perhaps he'd return one day. Take Freddie. '*Brodet,*' he read. 'A Mediterranean fish stew.' In the wilds of Scotland? Maybe not. '*Struklji . . . Belokranjsko Curtje*

. . . *Matevz* . . .' English descriptions were given, but Robin couldn't be bothered with them. He wasn't even hungry, but he knew he'd have to order food if he intended to sit watching the door for what might be a while. So, when the nice lady came back with his whisky, he pointed to the most recognisable item on the menu – Leg of Lamb – hoping it wasn't an entire one.

'I don't think you'll regret it,' she said, jotting it down. 'Have you come far?'

'Lincolnshire,' said Robin, aiming to stay incognito for as long as possible.

'Oh, aye? A lovely part of the country, I'm told.'

'Yes. A bit flatter than round here, though.'

'Most places are.'

'True.'

Robin was amazed at his ability to converse so normally, when any minute now Hannah, Freddie and the unfathomable Marcus might walk in. Had Marcus asked her to come back? He'd seemed certain in France that Hannah and Freddie belonged with Robin. Was he just two-faced and devious, or was Hannah so screwed up that she couldn't see clearly? Robin had asked himself these things for the length of the journey and was now tired of pondering on the business. He'd just have to ask the chap outright.

'Moira!' someone called out from the kitchen, and the waitress turned and said, 'Coming,' and Robin suddenly realised who she was. He'd heard a lot about Marcus's mother, Moira. Never seen a photo of her, though. She looked normal. Nice, even. Nothing like the fussy, interfering witch Hannah had described.

A man in an apron and white hat appeared from the kitchen. He was grey-haired, tallish and dignified-looking. Definitely foreign and, guessing from the menu and décor, Slovenian. He slipped an arm around Moira's waist and kissed the top of her head, and Robin thought perhaps it was another Moira after all. Lucky he hadn't said anything.

The chef handed the waitress a mobile phone, and Robin heard her say, 'Oh, aye, son, I've kept you a table, don't worry. And tell Claude the dish of the day is a nice French cassoulet, Vinko style.'

Claude?

'OK, Marcus. See you in about ten minutes.'

They were the longest ten minutes of Robin's life, even though they turned out to be just seven. Marcus walked in first, followed by Claude, and while Robin's heart raced, waiting for Hannah and Freddie to appear, the door closed itself behind them. Marcus kissed his mother's cheek, then Claude did the French three-kiss thing on her, a bit of jolly chat was entered into, and the two men were directed his way.

Robin stood up, his chair scraping back over the tiles and Marcus stopped dead when he saw him, clearly shocked. 'Robin?' he cried. 'What are you doing here? Are Hannah and Freddie with you?'

Robin was thrown. This wasn't right. Not the way the script should be going. He suddenly felt awfully tired, so lowered himself back on to his chair.

'This gentleman's come all the way from Lincolnshire,' Moira was saying. She was straightening cutlery on the table next to Robin's, removing the Reserved sign.

'Aren't they *here*?' Robin asked quietly and Marcus shook his head.

'He's ordered the Leg of Lamb, but I'm wondering if he might like Vinko's cassoulet.'

'They set off from Oxford yesterday,' said Robin. 'She left

me a note saying she was coming back to you. That you and she *had* to be together.' By the look on Marcus's face, this was news to him. 'I take it you didn't . . . ?'

'Absolutely not. I haven't heard from her since she slapped my face in France.'

'I can vouch for that,' chipped in Claude. 'Is it not possible that Hannah stopped overnight somewhere, procrastinated, then returned home?'

'Perhaps I should ring her mobile phone,' said Robin. 'Or home even.' He could feel himself beginning to shake. Fatigue and anxiety were the worst mix.

Marcus stood up. 'Use the phone under the counter,' he said, then led Robin to it.

He thought he'd try the mobile first. No luck. Then he rang home. Please answer, he willed her. Please answer, then let me speak to Freddie. Wish him good night. But Hannah didn't answer, so at the appropriate time he tapped in the pin number to pick up messages. He had four new ones, he was told. The first was received at 12.58 that afternoon.

'Robin,' said a strange voice. 'This is Adrian Lillis, Hannah's therapist. I was hoping to get you in person, but still . . . I'm concerned, you see. Hannah was driving to Scotland, and she rang me from her mobile just now, while she was driving, some-where near Carlisle, and then, gosh, I'm slightly shaken . . . well, she may have been in some kind of accident. She screamed, you see. And then there were these ghastly . . . Look, I may be completely wrong and, golly, I do hope so. Perhaps you'd give me a call and let me know she's OK?'

Adrian started to reel off his number, but by then Robin was halfway to the floor, where his fall was broken by the chef, who said, 'Efter only one whisky, yes?' and laughed.

Marcus took hold of the receiver. 'Press *one*,' Robin managed to tell him, while he was being hoisted upright. 'And it'll play the message again. Quick. Oh God, they're dead, I know they are. And it's all my fault.'

He was helped to a chair by Moira, the chef and Claude, and as Marcus listened in he turned pale.

'There's one from the police,' Marcus whispered, and Robin covered his face with his hands. This was truly the most horrible moment of his life so far, but he had a feeling there'd be worse to come. 'Oh, please, *no*,' he whispered. '*No*.'

Marcus asked his mother for a pen and she whipped one from her blouse. 'Now it's the hospital,' he said while he listened and wrote on an order pad. He pressed a button to replay the message, then scribbled more things down.

A customer came up and asked of no one in particular where their desserts had got to.

'Ooch,' Moira said. 'I'm terribly sorry. Let me fetch them now. Two Wine Cakes, wasn't it?' She hurried off, the grumpy customer returned to his table, and Marcus finally put the phone down.

'Well?' asked Robin shakily, even though he knew the absolute worst had happened.

'They're in the Cumberland Infirmary,' Marcus said. 'Carlisle. There was an accident, involving another car. Someone from the hospital rang at five thirty this evening. There's a number to call. Here.'

Robin couldn't bring himself to take it from him. 'Would you?' he asked, and Marcus nodded and picked up the receiver again.

'I see,' Marcus kept saying, when he got through to someone who seemed to know something. 'I see.'

Robin still shook, but he also began to feel icily cold inside. Even the large whisky the chef had just handed him wasn't warming him. Why had he wished Hannah out of their lives? Such a terrible thing to do. His head spun, his palms sweated, his insides got even colder. He felt as though he were in a dream, or a film. Something not real, anyway.

'Yes,' said Marcus. 'We'll be there as soon as we can.' He put the phone down. 'Freddie's absolutely fine,' he said, which was, deep down, all Robin wanted to know.

They arrived just after eleven and a young woman in ordinary clothes, who could have been a doctor, an administrator or the tea lady, took Robin to one side while Marcus was outside parking the car. 'She's going to be OK,' she told him. 'Couple of fractures and some bruising. As far as we know, there are no internal injuries, but we've got her on a starvation diet and a saline drip, just in case. We found high levels of antidepressants in her bloodstream. Very high. Could have contributed to her veering into an oncoming car.'

Robin found himself forming a fist.

'We also believe, but can't be certain, that she was talking on her mobile phone.'

Although they'd already guessed this, Robin now found himself forming a second fist. It might not be beyond him to go and pummel a defenceless woman on an intravenous drip. 'I know my son's OK, but how are the other people?' he asked, perfectly normally. 'The couple in the other car.'

'Fine,' she said. 'A few bruises. Hannah's mobile phone came off worst, completely smashed, while young Freddie, as you know, emerged unscathed, due to having a decent kiddie seat.'

Thank God they'd gone for quality, thought Robin. 'Can I take him home?' he asked her.

'Yes,' said the tea lady or doctor, and with that he was off down the corridor, checking out side wards. 'Excuse me!' she called out to him. He turned and she was beckoning. 'This way.'

When Robin caught up with her, she said, 'I take it you are her husband?' and laughed.

'No, no. He's just parking the car.'

She came to a sharp halt. 'But you called Freddie your son?'

'Long story,' he said.

She frowned but nevertheless led him to a room with a dull clanging sound coming from it. Inside was a sleeping Hannah with tubes attached, her plastered leg in traction. There were three other beds in the room, all empty, although on one sat a battered and crumpled toolbox.

'Fred?' called out Robin, and his little head appeared above the bed.

'I'm fixing the wheels,' he said, before going back to work. ''Cos they don't work, 'cos the bed won't move. Only the nurse wrapped my hammer in my pillowcase, so I don't wake Mummy.'

Robin swallowed past the lump in his throat and said, 'Uh-huh?' He ventured towards his son, hoping not to see any un-expected damage – a missing limb, or something – but he found him all in one piece and gently picked him up, then squeezed him and kissed his soft plump cheek. Freddie smelled of anti-septic and beef stew, but then the whole place did. 'I expect the nurse has put the brakes on,' Robin explained, moving the toolbox over and lowering them both on to the bed.

Freddie turned and pulled a face at him. 'Like Mummy put the brakes on when she screamed and said that word that Mrs Jessup makes Nathan go and stand in the naughty corner for?'

'Yes, Fred. Just like that.'

FRIDAY

'The food it seems very interesting,' said Ernst. He was looking though the menu and pulling a face. 'But I didn't realise garlic was so very different from German and English. It has many consonants, yes?'

'Gaelic,' said Jo.

'Yes.'

'But actually, it's Slovenian.'

Now he was looking more confused, so Jo explained about Vinko, who was at that moment hoisting himself on to a stool, next to Marcus's Aunt Janine and her keyboard.

'So . . .' said Ernst, 'I must get this right for my presentation. Vinko is a Slovenian chef who cooks Slovenian food in a Scottish restaurant called MacDonald's, but which does not have one single burger on its menu. *And* he not only cooks, also he does the cabaret. Do you think he will sing "My Bonnie Lies Ofer the Ocean"?'

'Maybe,' she said, very much hoping not. Jo thought she wouldn't add to Ernst's astonishment by filling him in on Vinko's love life.

On her left sat Marcus. He had a hand in her lap under the tablecloth, stroking her thigh through her trousers while he chatted away to Robin, directly opposite him. They were talking about salmon farming, for some reason. Jo guessed it was easier than discussing important things, such as Hannah, who was now on her way to Leicestershire with her parents for the 'couple of days' rest' suggested by the hospital. Beside Robin, propped on cushions, was Freddie, who'd opened his menu, turned it on its side and was flying a fork into it with a 'Yeeeoowww'.

Beside Freddie was Keiko, deep in a one-sided conversation with Claude. She was throwing in the odd, 'Ahh, interesting,' staring at her man lovingly, as though he were reciting Keats rather than talking EU subsidies. 'There's bound to be misappropriation,' Jo heard him say, while Keiko nodded, wide-eyed.

'So, does everyone know what they want?' asked Marcus. His mother was hovering with an order pad.

Freddie shouted, 'Chips and ketchup!'

'I'm sure we can find some of those for you,' said one of Marcus's brothers from behind the counter. The two brothers looked similar and a lot like Moira, but neither resembled Marcus much. They were quite a bit shorter and both were receding. Last night, Marcus had shown her photos of his father; a gloriously handsome man who may have just pipped his son in the looks department.

Jo quite fancied chips and ketchup but, because she was an adult, asked for the lamb. Claude said he'd like the catfish, so Keiko ordered that too. Ernst ordered chips and ketchup.

As Moira was taking Robin's order, the keyboard struck up an intro. It was vaguely familiar. Jo knew she knew it, but because of the way it was being played – each note exactly the same length – she couldn't name it. Dah, dah, dee, dee, dah . . .

After Robin had ordered the lamb from the charming Moira, who seemed to have warmed to him despite his past misdeeds, Vinko began singing 'Every Breath You Take' by the Police. All at the table cheered and gave him a round of applause, as though Vinko himself had taken the song to the top of the charts. He bowed and continued, moving on to the second verse with his idiosyncratic diction. Robin drank in the words, bringing a whole new interpretation to them. Yes, he'd be watching his son. Every move, every breath, every step . . .

'Nice voice,' said Jo, and they all agreed. 'Are you OK, Robin?' she added.

'Fine,' he said, and he managed not to lose it before the song came to an end, at which point he excused himself, went to the Gents, blew his nose and told himself off for being so soft.

Returning to the restaurant, Robin saw Freddie's chair was empty and his insides seized. Where . . . ah, there he was, on Vinko's knee. Centre stage, if you could call it a stage. Robin took his place and wondered if he'd ever feel secure enough to let Freddie out of his sight again. Even leaving him at nursery was going to be hard. Not that Hannah, with a broken arm and leg, would be able to steal Fred for a while yet. Perhaps, when she was well on the way to healing, he'd accidentally trip her up.

'Freddie had a request,' explained Jo.

Robin laughed. 'Now there's a surprise.' His son was lapping up, and now taking advantage of, all the attention he was getting from his former family. Moira, who'd been desperate to see Fred when she heard he was so close, had been spoiling him rotten for two days. The day after tomorrow, though, they'd head south again, going via Leicestershire to pick Hannah up. How Robin wished they didn't have to do that detour. How he yearned to go straight back to Oxford with Freddie, set up home with Sadie and little Theo, and never look back.

Freddie was waving and beaming at him, still perched on Vinko's knee and, by the sound of the keyboard intro, about to sing 'Wheels on the Bus'.

His Aunt Janine's version was the old politically incorrect one, and whenever she sang about mummies on the bus going yack, yack, yack, or daddies reading the newspaper, Freddie scowled at her and sang the words he'd been taught.

At last it was over, and the applause died down and Freddie was back at the table. Marcus watched his brothers flying through from the kitchen with steaming plates and bottles of ketchup and bottles of wine, and eventually, everyone had their food and Vinko moved on to his next song.

'Is very special song,' he told his audience. 'From Net King Cole, many years go. Is for very lovely lady. Moira.'

Marcus looked over at his mother, who blushed as all eyes fell on her, then did a little curtsy.

'Is called "They Try to Tell Us Wirr Too Young",' said Vinko, and the restaurant gave a communal, 'Aaaahhh.'

He sang it beautifully, and in a heart-felt way, and when he'd finished Marcus's mother wiped tears from her eyes with her waitress pinny. Vinko got off his stool and went over and gave her a hug.

'Aaaahhh,' went everyone again, and Marcus suddenly found himself feeling extremely happy for his mum and not caring a jot about his lost inheritance. In fact, he was feeling generally good about everything and everybody. He was pleased for young-and-in-love Claude, so very relieved that Freddie was still in one piece, happy for Robin and thrilled for himself at having Jo for a whole weekend. Marcus even began feeling goodwill towards poor old Hannah. Yes, she'd treated first him, then Robin, abysmally, and she'd taken risks with her son's life, but she wasn't all bad. And maybe now she'd been weaned off the antidepressants in hospital, the fog would clear and she'd see that her place was with Robin. Good old Robin, currently showing Freddie a conjuring trick with a 10p. The little boy was amazed every time the coin popped out of his father's ear, or sometimes his own. Marcus hoped that one day he'd be a dad like that, then remembered he already had been. How lucky Hannah was in her choice of men, but how unlucky in other ways. Poor old Hannah, he thought and, in an overwhelming moment of fondness, found himself standing up with his glass of wine.

'I'd like to propose a toast,' he said above the hubbub. Everyone round the table raised their glasses. 'To Hannah. May she recover quickly and be back with us soon.'

'To Hannah,' the others said, with the possible exception of Jo.

'Oh, Marcus, that's so sweet,' came a voice from behind.

He turned and saw his wife, on crutches, just inside the doorway. Next to her were her stony-faced parents.

'I am back,' she said, her eyes intensely on his.

Marcus looked at her parents for support. 'She made us turn round,' her father told him apologetically. 'Threatened to throw herself out the bloody car.'

No one spoke. They'd stopped mid-chew. Mid-sip. Even the other customers. Vinko's 'It's Not Unusual' had ground to a halt. Marcus sensed the entire room was holding its communal breath.

'You know,' said Ernst loudly, and all eyes swung round to him to save the situation. 'These are the best MacDonald's

French fries I have tasted in my life, ha ha. Ah yes, that reminds me about the Bavarian who went into a burger bar.'

'Ernst,' said Jo.

'Yes?'

'Not now.'

SUNDAY
SPRING BANK HOLIDAY

Jo was at her computer, literally propping her eyes open over Sergei's concluding chapter. Almost at the end, she told herself. Only five pages left, so try to keep going. But then she thought, hell, five whole pages. She saved the changes and checked her emails again. Another one from Pippa. Jo had the feeling her friend was being communicative out of guilt. Maybe she'd reply to this one.

'Hi, Pippa,' she typed. 'Congrats on preventing the GM maize delivery. It did rather sound as though you turned that ship around single-handedly, though I'm guessing Bram was there to help!! Hope the bone knits itself together soon. Yes, I'm sure the comfrey tea will speed up the process. Talking of broken bones, I've noticed Hannah's walking normally again now – as gracefully as before, damn her!'

For weeks she'd been hobbling past Jo's window, on her way to the playground with Freddie. At first on crutches, then with a stick, now unaided. It wasn't far to go, from Pippa's house to the swings, but it could turn into an afternoon excursion for the two of them. She'd never call in on Jo, even though they were now neighbours.

'Lucy said to tell you Hannah's taking great care of your house, even with Freddie there half the week! Oh, and that Ray came back the other day for his armchair. Said his parents' three-piece didn't do it for him.'

A major disadvantage of house-sitting, Jo realised, must be that the owners could whip bits of furniture away when they felt like it. Or come home early, as Lucy and Dom had done. But Pippa, it seemed, wasn't intending to come home early. After their GM heroics, she and Bram had gone to rest at his Amsterdam home. If they kept that up it would be good for Hannah. With no rent to pay, she could save for her own place. Hopefully not in Jubilee Street. She'd be back teaching after the half-term break, according to Lucy. Everything was according to Lucy, or occasionally Robin when Jo bumped into him.

'Anyway, not much other news here. My two students will be leaving in a couple of weeks' time, which is gutting, but on the other hand, it means I can go and spend time in Scotland with Marcus. They've just about done up Marcus's mum's house now.'

Finished by the end of June, he estimated. Keiko was hoping Claude would fly out to Japan with his earnings, but Claude talked of putting the money towards buying the Sports Bar now his aunt had had a change of heart. Marcus also thought Claude's head had been turned by Vinko's visiting niece, a Slovenian beauty. Poor Keiko. Jo had been dropping small hints by telling her how long-distance relationships were impossible to sustain, and giving her new definitions for her notebook: 'love rat' and similar.

She went back to her email. 'I can't wait to see Marcus again. Of course, he'd come here if it wasn't for a certain neighbour – but please don't feel bad about that. You needed a housesitter, she needed a home. Besides, Marcus and I have had two lovely weekends together in the Peaks.'

And a whole glorious summer ahead of them. Then what? Jo had already got Lucy and Dom's guys to make her a website, so she could pick up work should she find herself living elsewhere. She pictured herself proofreading by email in a cosy croft by a lofty mountain. Marcus throwing peat on the fire . . . or was that just an Irish thing?

'Anyway, must get on,' she typed. She signed off, sent the email and turned her thoughts to dinner. Would they notice if it was pasta again? Keiko had gone high-carb/low protein, which was proving more of a pain than Atkins, although cheaper – 'Would you like more bread with your bread, Keiko?'

OK, pasta. She'd make a separate protein-packed sauce for Ernst, who swore Keiko's new diet was giving him smaller 'muskles'. 'When I arrived I was like Popeye after his spinach, now I am Olive Oyl!' Best not to send the students home malnourished, she thought, and decided on a tuna sauce.

Robin had the Parental Responsibility Agreement in front of him again.

'Sure,' Hannah had said when he'd brought up the PRA issue. 'Seems only fair. Let's wait till I'm back at work, though, shall we? Just in case my being on sick leave and having counselling negates the agreement?'

Although he could see sense in what she was saying, Robin had been champing at the bit for weeks now, just desperate to get her signature on the damn thing. Anyway, having dumped Adrian for Belinda, a wonderful woman counsellor a few streets away, Hannah did appear to be making a lot of progress. She was always pleasant these days. Good-humoured. Almost eager to please. He couldn't foresee any problems with getting the thing sorted once and for all.

Late Friday morning was the time they'd set aside for getting it witnessed by a court official, after they'd both finished teaching. Freddie was to go to Sadie's for tea again. Safe Sadie. Port-in-a-storm Sadie. Robin looked at the photo beside his computer. They'd been at Cotswold Wildlife Park and she was kneeling with one arm round Theo, the other round Freddie. Robin had managed to get most of the llama in too. A nice day. They'd had lots of nice days out. What he and Sadie hadn't had, though, were lots of romantic and steamy nights in. None, in fact. It just hadn't happened, somehow. As much as Robin still hoped for more with Sadie, he knew he was guilty of holding back. Afraid a new entanglement would upset Hannah and set her off again? He certainly sneaked to his study every time Hannah called in, and put the photo in a drawer. It could be that he and Sadie had got past the point of starting up a physical relationship. He guessed that happened.

Meanwhile, Robin watched the real love of his life splashing around in the paddling pool with the little boy from next door but one. It was a gloriously hot Bank Holiday. Sadie and Theo had gone off to her parents on Friday but – Robin checked the time again – might actually be back by now.

He put the PRA down and called her number.

'Oh, *hi*,' she said warmly.

He invited them round and she said yes, that would be great. 'I've been thinking about you a lot,' she added, 'over the weekend. About us.'

'Oh yes?'

'Mm. I quite missed you, you know.'

'That's nice.' Why couldn't he say 'Me too'?

'Anyway, we'll be there shortly.'

'Good.'

'Um . . .' she said quietly, 'I was wondering if a sleepover would be OK?'

'Yes, of course. Freddie will love that. Bring all Theo's night things.' Robin waited for a response. 'Hello?'

'See you soon,' she said in quite a different tone, and he suddenly realised what she'd meant.

He felt terrible. But no, they couldn't. Not now. Too risky with only a couple of days to go. 'Great!' he said, far too jovially. 'I'll put the kettle on.'

Marcus was listening in to a second message from Hannah, receiver in hand, heart in his boots. He and Claude had been clearing a vast area of garden and had come in for a rest and a beer. 'Unfuckingbelievable,' he said as he took in what she was saying.

Claude frowned and reached for Marcus's mum's dictionary.

A few days before, Hannah had left a message thanking him for his get well card and apologising for not contacting him sooner. She'd wanted to get completely better first. 'Anyway,' she'd said before hanging up, 'I'll call you again. Or ring me?' She reeled off Pippa's number and said goodbye.

He hadn't tried calling her. Hadn't seen the point. But here she was again, this time saying something about a form Robin was going to force her to sign. How that meant she and Fred couldn't live more than ten miles away from Robin. How it would put paid for ever to 'you, me and Freddie being together again'. How she had to get away from Oxford a.s.a.p., and how Freddie was coming back to her tomorrow, and so that might be a good time for them to make their escape. 'What do you think?' she asked.

Marcus couldn't possibly put into words what he thought.

He pressed a button and forced himself to listen again, just in case he'd missed something vital, such as 'Only kidding!'

He wrote down Pippa's number, replaced the receiver and gulped back his beer.

'You've had some irksome news?' asked Claude.

'Yes,' said Marcus. 'I'm definitely feeling irked.'

He told Claude the latest and Claude shook his head and swore in French. 'It's like sitting through the same horror movie,' he said. 'Over and over. I believe it may be time to tell her about you and Jo. Make it clear and unambiguous. Get straight to the point. No shilly-shallying.'

'Yeah, you're right,' Marcus said. 'No more sparing Hannah's feelings for fear of what she might do.' He picked up the phone again and Claude slipped out of the room. Actually, he probably would shilly-shally a bit, out of sensitivity. Break it to her gently. Tell her how he and Jo had sort of slowly grown on each other.

'Hello?' she said.

'Hi,' said Marcus warmly.

'Oh, thank God. I was beginning to worry that—'

'Jo and I are an item,' he said, suddenly going for blunt.

'Pardon?'

'We're in love.' Marcus screwed up his face, waiting for whatever was about to be blasted his way.

'Hmm, well. I guessed as much.'

As his features gradually relaxed, Marcus said, 'Really? Then why the message?'

'Oh, I don't know. Last-ditch attempt maybe.'

Marcus couldn't believe this was going so well. Had they finally achieved closure? Hard to believe. Hard to trust Hannah, either. He needed more convincing. 'What will you do?' he asked.

'I don't know. Go back to teaching, I suppose. Find a place to live. Sign that bloody form for Robin.'

It was worrying Marcus, how resigned she was. He said, 'Are you sure you're OK about all this? No more wanting to push Jo over a precipice?'

'I never said I . . . Hang on, have you been reading my diary, Marcus?'

Whoops. 'Just had a bit of a flick-through. Once.' Or twice.

'Bastard!' She chuckled good-humouredly. 'Anyway, you must realise it was all written in the heat of the moment.'

'Of course.'

'Good. Jo didn't read it, did she?'

'No, but . . .' Marcus paused. 'Well, I did tell her I thought you had a contract out on her.'

'Really?' said Hannah, clearly amused. 'That must have made her a bit on edge?'

'Just a bit.' Marcus thought he'd get out while the going was good, and began winding down the conversation. 'Look, we must keep in touch,' he said and she agreed. 'Send me photos of Freddie?'

'Will do.' She promised to let him know when she moved, and they said their goodbyes, and then Marcus stared into space until Claude popped his head round the door.

'How was she?' he asked.

Marcus turned and blinked at him. 'Friendly, charming, totally accepting of the situation.'

'Oh,' said Claude. 'How very disquieting.'

'Yes.'

Jo was watching the pasta boil, thinking about Marcus's call just now.

Of course Hannah had to be told some time. And how great

that she'd taken it so well. Now everyone could move on. Great. She lobbed some herbs into the pasta, just to give Keiko something to taste, then grabbed the garlic and was about to pull off a clove when the doorbell went. 'Bugger,' she said, turning down the heat.

It was Hannah, on her doorstep for the first time in months and this time with large, very sharp-looking scissors in her hand. Jo's first instinct was to slam the door in the woman's face, but then she saw a bunch of white roses in her other hand, so instead took a small step back and subtly held the garlic up between them. 'Hi,' she said nervously.

Hannah smiled. 'Sorry to disturb you. I was just out the front picking roses when my door slammed behind me. Pippa said you had her spare key?'

'Oh, right. Yes. Now where did I . . . Ah, I know.'

'Phew,' said Hannah, stepping into the house. 'Lovely day, isn't it?'

'Yes.' Jo had begun walking backwards down her hall towards the kitchen, feeling her way along the walls, eyes riveted to the scissor points aimed at her heart. 'Bank holidays are so often a washout,' she added. There was a step down to her kitchen, which she thought could be her undoing if she wasn't careful.

Hannah said, 'Lovely in Scotland too, I hear.'

'Yes.' There was nothing for it but to spin round and hurry to that kitchen drawer, so she did.

Now breathing heavily, Jo rummaged through all the things she'd thrown in there over the past five years. Pippa's key was on a key ring. An Eiffel Tower, if she remembered rightly. She heard Hannah step down into the kitchen and waited for the scissors to plunge themselves into her back. She thought about the will she'd made recently, sitting on her desk waiting for two witnesses to sign it. She hadn't been able to use Ernst and Keiko because they were to be beneficiaries: Keiko the piano, and Ernst her dumbbells, so he could get his muskles back. Gestures, rather than serious bequests, although she could see Keiko having the piano shipped.

Jo's hand fell upon the distinct shape of a small tower. She could hear the pasta boiling away much too energetically. Did she have time to turn down the heat before she died? 'Here we are,' she said, pulling the key out and turning to face whatever Hannah had in mind for her.

'Oh, thank God,' said Hannah, looking relieved. 'Just think what I'd have had to pay a locksmith to come out on a bank holiday!'

'Yes,' said Jo, exhaling. 'A fortune.'

Hannah gave her another big smile. 'Thanks. Listen, we ought to get together for a cuppa or drink some time.'

'Er, yeah.'

'Or I could cook you some supper?'

Jo tried to nod. Supper she wouldn't be so keen on.

'Let me know when's good for you,' said Hannah, making her way to the door.

'Sure,' said Jo, following her, eyes still firmly on the scissors. She saw her out and dashed back to the kitchen to find the pasta – the last of it, unfortunately – had boiled itself to liquid form.

'What is for dinner?' asked Keiko, now behind her. Unlike Ernst, she could glide down those stairs without making a sound.

'Pasta, er . . . soup,' said Jo, giving the saucepan a loving stir. 'It's a traditional Whitsuntide dish.'

'Aahh.' Keiko nodded. 'Like very burned pancakes is traditional for Shrove Tuesday?'

'Yep.'

This is going to be such fun. Her face when those scissors were coming her way! Now, what was that fish Keiko was trying to tell us about at the restaurant . . . fugi? The Japanese delicacy that can cause instant death to diners if not prepared absolutely correctly. Fugu, maybe. I could buy some cod or something and pretend it's fugu. No, no, I'll say. Don't worry, Jo. I know what I'm doing.

Perhaps I'll suggest Friday evening to her. It'll give me something to look forward to after I've signed away all my parental rights. Maybe. Belinda says I should sign it. Thinks I've been presented with too many choices over the past couple of years and, having a 'planner' personality, the PRA might provide me with much-needed structure. I think she's right. Belinda's right on most things, really. Thinks I should look for a man who'll stand up to me. Answer back. Marcus would bottle things up, then explode at me, which isn't the same thing at all. Passive/aggressive, Belinda called him. Said Robin probably is too. Or that I bring that out in them, anyway. Yep, she's pretty good, Belinda. Her 'directional' therapy definitely suits me better than Adrian's lazy approach – but, my God, can the woman talk!

When the doorbell chimed, Robin's heart gave a little leap. Sadie was here. He jumped up from his office chair and made for the stairs, but then turned around, went back into the study and picked up the two letters he'd been poring over. One was from Adrian Lillis stating that Hannah had been on the phone to him at the precise time she'd crashed, and the other, signed by Mrs Newby, said she'd seen Mrs Hannah Currie talking on a mobile before she'd collided into their car. Both 'witnesses' had been induced by Robin, for Freddie's sake, not to say anything to the police. Not yet, anyway. Hopefully, never. If Friday went according to plan, he'd tear the letters up, of course. The doorbell rang again and Robin tucked everything into a file with 'PRA Insurance!' handwritten on it, then charged down the stairs to let Sexy Sadie in.

As soon as he opened the door, he stepped forward, slipped an arm around her and kissed her on the lips. Theo, meanwhile, had charged into the house. 'You know that sleepover you suggested?' he said, pulling back a little.

'Oh well, I . . .' She waved a dismissive hand and coloured up.

'Friday would be good.'

Ernst, bless him, was making out it was perfectly OK to be drinking pasta. He did, however, give the impression he was very much looking forward to German food. '*Knackwurst*,' he said with a sigh. '*Wienerschnitzel, Schinkenwurst . . .*'

Such poetic names, thought Jo.

Keiko nodded to herself. '*Miso* soup,' she said quietly. '*Onigiri . . .*'

Jo rolled her eyes. 'Look, why don't we abandon this and go and eat in town?'

'Special treat?' asked Keiko.

'Yes, special treat. It is a holiday, after all. Come on. It's such a nice day, we could walk.'

'Shall I change to walking boots?' asked Keiko, who'd only ever bussed in before; asleep, no doubt.

'Not necessary,' Jo told her. 'It's not far.'

By the time Jo had gathered bag, jumper and keys, Ernst was at the front door holding it open for her. 'Have I told you the joke about the two Bavarians who were walking along the road?' he asked.

'Don't think so.'

'Ah. Well, one Bavarian he said to the other Bavarian, "Look at that dog with one eye." So the Bavarian . . . not the first one, you know, the one he was with . . .'

'Yes, yes,' said Jo, slamming the door behind them. Had she closed the small kitchen window? Was it wide enough for Hannah to slither through?

'. . . he covered one of his eyes and said, "Where?"'

Jo, striding down her path, stopped in her tracks. 'Ernst, that's almost funny.'

'Thank you.'